Free at Last

Donna Every

Free at Last
Copyright © 2017 Donna Every. All rights reserved.

No part of this publication may be reproduced, stored in a retrieval system or transmitted in any way by any means, electronic, mechanical, photocopy, recording or otherwise without the prior permission of the author except as provided by USA copyright law.

This book is a work of fiction. Names, characters, places and incidents are either products of the author's imagination or are used fictitiously.

Cover design © 2017 by CrossMedia Designs. All rights reserved.
Cover photography by Julie Chalbaud
Model: Dominic Seale

ISBN: **1545248664**
ISBN 13: **9781545248669**

Author's Note

I know that many of you have been waiting expectantly for William's book or, more likely, the conclusion of Sarah's story. However, I feel that I should give you a caveat before you read it. You will find that this book, unlike the other two, includes more of the horrors of slavery. I have done this to give a more holistic picture so that the series does not disregard the darker side of slavery which was very real. Rest assured, however, that I do not fully describe the gory details. Many of the scenarios that I have included are not figments of my imagination (I could never dream up such things) but are based on extracts from the diaries of Thomas Thistlewood.

Thomas Thistlewood was an Englishman who moved to Jamaica and became the head overseer at a plantation called Egypt in Westmoreland from the mid to the late 1700s. Thistlewood kept diaries in which he recorded minute details of life on the plantation, including his considerable sexual exploits with the slave women. One historian states that: "Much of the historical literature on slavery in the British West Indies is seasoned with material from Thistlewood's extensive diaries, which are among the richest surviving documents for the period."

I have therefore loosely modelled William's story and his life in Jamaica on Thomas Thistlewood, even though he was from a slightly later period. However, I have not included any of the extremely horrific stories of the sheer brutality that he subjected his slaves to.

So, in spite of using him and his information about life in Jamaica as a model for William's character, rest assured that I have not fully made William into Thomas Thistlewood or completely followed his story. If I had, you would not come to like him as I hope you will by the end of the book. Many historians believe that Thistlewood's slave "wife" Phibbah, whom he was with for 30 years, civilised him. So too we will see the civilisation and redemption of William, albeit in a somewhat different way.

You will also be happy to know that Richard, Deborah, Thomas and Sarah will be reappearing in this book as I bring their stories and the series to an end. Before I give away too much more of the story I will end here and only say: Enjoy!

Donna Every

Chapter 1

The flight of panicked birds followed by the sudden eerie silence in the surrounding bushes sent a shiver of fear through William. The only sound he could now hear was the frantic beating of his own heart and the ring of the horses' shoes on the stony ground. Before he had time to voice his concern to the driver of the cart, the silence was displaced by wild shouts that chilled his blood. Moments later, the cart road was blocked by fierce looking Negroes, dressed in ragged pants and nothing else.

The muscles of their arms and chest boasted of their strength, but it was the hatred in their eyes, as they drew nearer, that terrified him. He looked around frantically for a means for them to escape, but his guide seemed to be paralyzed. His muttered exclamation, "Maroons!" was the last thing William heard before one of them roughly pulled him from his seat on the cart. He felt himself falling, falling, falling...

William jumped up and looked around the darkened room in a panic. The relief at finding himself still in the small bunk of the boat that was taking him to the town of Black River, made him fall back weakly. He laughed faintly at himself, realising that the anxiety of travelling to Westhall Plantation had spilled over into his dreams. He had been assured that he would easily find someone to take him to Westhall when they docked and that there had been no maroons seen in that area for some time. He certainly hoped so. It was bad enough that he had been banished to Jamaica by his father, but he had no desire to die at the hands of Maroons in this God-forsaken country.

❖

February 24, 1697
Westhall Plantation, Jamaica

> *I have finally reached Westhall Plantation which is a good few days travel from the nearest town, Black River, by horse and cart. My father could not have found a more fitting punishment than to banish me to this island, far away from everything and everyone I know. It is a veritable cesspit of disease and it is only by the grace of God that I did not succumb to the malaria that took hold of me the very first days of landing in Kingston. I say God, but surely it was the devil who saved me for it is said that he looks after his own.*
>
> *I was shown to my house after briefly meeting the owner, Peter Westhall, from whom the plantation derives its name. He and my father were friends in England and became reacquainted when he visited Barbados on his way here and they kept in touch. I have not met his wife yet. It is just the two of them*

as his children have returned to England. I cannot say that I blame them.

He seems to have a lot of confidence in my ability to manage this plantation so perhaps my father has exaggerated my skills. He is therefore most eager to leave me to run things and take himself off to England to join his children. How I wish I could accompany him! Who would have thought that I would long for England after being sent there by my father for two long years where I wanted nothing more than to return to Barbados? What I would not do for the cool English weather and freedom from the infernal insects and diseases that plague this country.

I hope my father has received my letter asking him to speak to Richard to see if he will allow me to come back to Barbados. It is not as if I need his permission, but he did threaten to end my life if he saw me again. Barbados is small, but I think it is still big enough for me to live there and not encounter him and Deborah. She has always been an affront to me and my mother and never will I acknowledge that we share the same blood. It is like salt rubbed in a wound that she and her mother have what I do not. They are enjoying life in Barbados, while I have been sent, like an outcast, to this hell called Jamaica.

William Edwards closed the journal and slid it into the drawer beside his bed. He had started writing in the book the day that he left Barbados as he found that pouring out his thoughts on paper helped him to pass the time on the journey. He absently rubbed his fingers along the slight ridge of the two-inch scar on his cheek that was almost healed. Another reminder of why he had cause to resent Deborah. Forever he would be marked by the knife that she wielded against him.

Glancing around the room, he could find little fault with it. It was not as grand as his room at The Acreage, but it was comfortable. The bed he sat on was soft enough and there was a desk and chair made of a dark wood, as well as a chest of drawers and a wash stand. Crossing to the wash stand, he poured the cold water into the basin to wash his face and hands. He used his wet hands to smooth back his thick hair before drying them with a small towel that was folded next to the bowl.

He dug through his trunk for a fresh shirt and jacket to wear to dinner where he would meet the mistress of the house. No doubt it was she who was urging her husband to return to England, which was quite understandable. Between the weather, the diseases and the maroons he did not know who would want to live in Jamaica. Tossing aside the travel-stained shirt and jacket, he dressed in the fresh, if somewhat wrinkled, garments, tied his cravat and made his way to the front door of his small house. At least he had his own house which would give him a measure of privacy.

The overseer, Colin Marsh, had shown him where he was to live and made no effort to hide his resentment as he indicated his own smaller house nearby. After living at The Acreage and at his uncle's house in England, the small house that William had been given was very much beneath him, but to someone like Marsh, no doubt it seemed like luxury. He had not been overly impressed with the overseer, who was surly, taciturn and obviously begrudged his appointment as manager. He could not really blame him since, in truth, he knew less about the operations of a Jamaican plantation than Marsh. Surely it could not be too different than operating one in Barbados. He would still be helping his father on his plantation if it was not for Richard.

Richard, his mother's nephew, had come to The Acreage from Carolina when he was in England so he had not been acquainted with him. He had wanted to learn how slaves were used on sugar plantations as he was planning to buy slaves to cultivate rice in Carolina. However, he had not returned to Carolina, at least not to stay. He had obviously been bewitched by Deborah and had broken his engagement with a woman in Carolina to come back to Barbados to marry Deborah.

William had been livid to discover that his father had sold Deborah to Richard, while she had been off-limits to him and had been responsible for him being shipped off to England in disgrace. The fact that his cousin had freed her and then married her was unthinkable, tarnishing the family line with a coloured woman. If they had children, they would probably look pure white, but everyone in Barbados would know that they had Negro blood in them. What a disgrace to their family!

❈

"William, come and meet my wife, Julia." Peter Westhall stood to greet him and ushered him into the dining room. The table could seat ten people but it was set for four and the overseer, Colin Marsh, was already at the table, seated to the left of the head. William was surprised to see the overseer at the same dinner table as the family as this would never have happened in Barbados. Perhaps the Jamaica society was less concerned with class than in Barbados. He supposed he would have to adapt to the Jamaican way of life if he was to survive here.

Julia Westhall sat on the right of her husband. She was a solid-looking, middle-aged woman with a pleasant face. By no stretch of the imagination could she be called beautiful but she had a reasonably attractive face and her sharp eyes assessed him as if she could read his every thought. He tried to appear undaunted by her penetrating stare. After all, she knew nothing about him, did she? He now wondered what information his father had given them when he asked for the position for him.

"It's a pleasure to meet you, ma'am," he said respectfully, taking his seat beside her.

"It is good to meet Thomas' son. We have known him for many years but you would have been a mere boy when we were in Barbados."

William smiled politely.

"Now let us eat dinner before it gets cold." With that she gestured for two slave girls to bring in the food. William deliberately kept his eyes from them, as he could feel Julia Westhall's gaze on him, probably to determine if he was one to partake of slave women. There would be plenty of time for that later.

Free at Last

"That's a fresh-looking scar you have there. How did you get it, if you don't mind me asking?"

Actually, I do mind, said William to himself. Aloud he answered, "I'm afraid I found myself on the wrong end of a knife a few months ago." He offered no further explanation. Not that it is any of your business, he added silently.

"How horrible. Not that it has ruined your looks. If anything, it gives you a dangerous look," she smiled.

William glanced at her husband who did not seem to find anything strange with his wife making such personal comments to a virtual stranger. He had forgotten how much more informal people were in the islands than they were in England. Jamaica seemed even more so than Barbados.

"We must have a small dinner party to introduce you to the planters in the area before we leave," she announced.

"Yes, yes," agreed her husband absently.

"You have to meet George Fuller and his lovely daughter, Grace." She smiled knowingly at William. "They are our closest neighbours. They have some strange ideas about dealing with their slaves, but they are good people. Grace is nineteen and unmarried. She is a lovely girl and looks after the household now that her mother has died. Poor Ruth succumbed to yellow fever a few years ago."

Her husband rolled his eyes at the information she was sharing with William. The last thing he wanted was his new manager marrying Grace and going over to run the Fuller's plantation since George had confided that he wanted to go back to England. That would leave Marsh alone at Westhall and the man knew nothing about keeping the books and records of the plantation. All he knew well was how to use a whip.

"We are glad that you finally made it, after being delayed with the malaria attack. We can now make plans to head back to England," his wife continued. "You are very lucky that you survived that awful disease. You should be much stronger going forward now, as long as it does not keep recurring."

The overseer grunted, focusing on his food. William somehow got the impression that he would not have minded if he had succumbed to the malaria and knew that he would have to be on guard with him. The last thing he needed was a disgruntled servant who knew more about running the plantation than he did. His cruel face, reddened by the sun, told William as clearly as if he had seen it for himself, that he was likely a sadistic task master and therefore the slaves would not be easy to deal with.

Although there were a few beatings at The Acreage, their plantation was not one that was known for cruelly ill-treating their slaves. Basing the management of his plantation on the Instructions of Henry Drax, his father believed that treating his slaves well and rewarding them led to their loyalty and, for the most part, he had been right. But he had heard that the slaves in Jamaica were nothing like those in Barbados. They were seemingly more aggressive and more than outnumbered the white population so perhaps they needed harsher treatments to keep them in line. He would do whatever was necessary to get the job done.

❖

A week later

William dismounted from his horse and gave the reins to a stable boy. The Westhall's plantation was easily five hundred acres of which about half was planted with cane, while the rest supported livestock and other crops. The soil was rich and fertile, unlike the Barbadian soil which the planters had been having to add fertilizer to for several years to increase the yield of sugar.

He felt rather overwhelmed at the task ahead of him, especially since he could not ask Peter Westhall for help. He had quickly realised that, unlike his father, Westhall did not get personally involved in the running of his plantation apart from doing the books, which he had shown William one night after dinner. He seemed to leave it to Marsh who, until he was hired, had full control of the slaves and the planting of crops. He knew that he would get no help from Marsh, who would instead take great pleasure in seeing him fail. For the first time in his life he was determined to succeed at something. His pride was at stake and he would not let Marsh see him defeated or let down Peter Westhall.

On his third day at the plantation, Marsh had taken unholy delight in showing him the head of a slave that had run away from another plantation. It had been sent around to all the nearby plantations as a deterrent to the other slaves. William had been unable to keep his meal down at the sight, which provided considerable mirth for Marsh, who promptly mounted it on a stick in the yard for the slaves to see.

Having failed the first test, in his own eyes, William made a vow to himself that he would learn as much as he could about the plantation and implement some of the methods that his father used to increase yields and get the most out of the slaves. He decided to start by exploring every acre on horseback over the rest of that week to see where the various crops were planted and how efficiently the slaves were working. Now every muscle in his body protested at their treatment and made it known to him as he dismounted. He had not realised how soft he had gotten in England and it did not help that he had not made a very big effort to exert himself once he returned to The Acreage. However, that would change.

He was at least thankful that the time in England had not all been wasted. While his father had sent him there in the hope that he would come back more "civilised" as he said, he was now knowledgeable about keeping the books for a plantation and recording planting schedules and crop yields. The information being kept by Peter Westhall was sorely lacking and he realised that the plantation could be a lot more profitable than it currently was by improving that alone.

He halted his stiff walk towards his house and turned around as Marsh's angry voice travelled across the yard.

"Cudjoe, how many loads of cane you cut today?" he demanded.

Cudjoe was a tall, well-built Negro with a fierce expression and scars on his cheek.

"Three," he answered sullenly.

"Three, who?" prompted Marsh.

"Three, Mister Marsh," the grudging answer came back.

"And how many you cut yesterday?"

"Five."

"So what make you think I would be happy with three today? Get your black carcass over to the whipping pole; maybe 200 lashes will make you think twice about short changing me."

William's eyes sought the slaves' in the yard, but all had their eyes cast down as if making eye contact with Marsh would earn them a similar punishment. Cudjoe's eyes narrowed and he looked as if he would kill the brutal overseer if he had the chance. William had never heard of any slave at The Acreage being ordered that many lashes, even for the great offence of stealing sugar. Could a slave survive that many lashes? And if he did, how would that affect his productivity the next day?

Westhall Plantation seemed to reflect the harsh nature of Jamaica, or was it just Marsh? Perhaps he had been foolish to think that he could apply the approach that they used at The Acreage here, not if he wanted to keep these slaves in line and certainly not if he wanted to stamp his authority. William hardened his heart against the sound of the whip connecting with the slave's back and his stifled grunts of pain as he sought to deny Marsh the satisfaction of hearing him cry out and turned once again towards his house.

Speaking of stamping his authority, he would send for one of the women tonight. It had been several weeks since he had enjoyed the prostitute in Kingston and he needed physical relief. There was a young, buxom one called Bella that had caught his eye with her firm, supple-looking body and smooth dark skin. She would do well and the fact that Marsh seemed to favour her would only add to his satisfaction. He would show the overseer who was boss and he would start by laying claim to Bella. Anticipation caused his body to stir and almost made him forgot the aches in his muscles.

Chapter 2

March 17, 1697
Westhall Plantation

The living room of the Westhall's house was crowded with their friends and neighbours. True to her word, Julia Westhall had, in a short time, arranged a dinner party to introduce him to those who owned plantations in that part of the country. William had been introduced to the Draxs, the Dorrills and the Faulkes, planters who had been in Jamaica for several years. The Barbados Draxs were friends of their family and he was pleased to meet their Jamaican cousins. He was also happy to learn some valuable lessons about Jamaica from the planters he met and was cautioned several times that the slaves there were nothing like the passive ones in Barbados.

"Sorry to tear you away, William," interrupted Mrs. Westhall, "but our dear friends and closest neighbours, the Fullers, have just arrived. I would like you to meet them."

William excused himself and followed Julia Westhall across the room to where the Fullers were talking to Peter Westhall. George Fuller was a slim man of medium height with reddish brown hair and a face that bore traces of ill health, which William assumed was from one of the diseases that was rampant in Jamaica. Grace Fuller was a tiny woman, shorter than both men with the same colour hair as her father and a wonderfully voluptuous figure.

"George, Grace, this is our new manager, William Edwards, who has recently arrived from Barbados. His father is a good friend of ours and owns one of the largest plantations in Barbados," Julia Westhall announced. She could not have been more obvious. "William, this is George Fuller and his lovely daughter Grace from Friendly Hall Plantation."

George Fuller extended his hand and gave a greeting which William returned before trailing his eyes over Grace. She barely reached to his shoulder and her rich reddish-brown hair was swept up in a simple but attractive style. Her eyes were an unusual shade of green and were framed by thick lashes. Her skin looked soft and smooth and he could just make out a smattering of pale freckles across her nose which he found very appealing. In fact, he found everything about Grace Fuller pleasing.

"Pleased to meet you, Miss Fuller," he greeted, offering his hand. The hand that Grace extended in response was swallowed in his before she extricated it from his grasp. Her eyes met his briefly and widened slightly as if in surprise at some discovery. William found that he liked the feel of her delicate hand in his and was sorry that she had removed it so soon.

"George, come and see our other guests whom you probably have not seen for a while. I'm sure you might want to discuss the price of sugar or whatever you men talk about. Peter, I heard Randolph Watkins saying that he needed to speak to you. We can leave William and Grace to get acquainted," she finished with a satisfied smile.

George Fuller did not fully approve of that suggestion, but he did not want to offend Julia Westhall who was a good friend. He would prefer to know this William Edwards better before he got too well acquainted with his daughter, no matter how big his father's plantation was.

"I will do that, Julia," he acquiesced. "But William, you must come over to dinner after Peter and Julia leave as you will be sorely lacking in company. Julia, do let us know when you plan to depart so that I can send William an invitation."

"That's a wonderful idea," Julia enthused.

"That is very kind of you, sir," William said politely. George Fuller nodded to him before joining Julia Westhall as she led him over to the other planters.

Grace looked after the retreating backs of her father and Mrs. Westhall longingly, as if she had no desire to be left in William's company. The thought concerned William for some reason. He didn't want her to feel uncomfortable in his presence. Granted, if she knew his past, she probably would want to have nothing to do with him at all.

Being the only son of a wealthy plantation owner, especially in Barbados where men were quite scarce, he was accustomed to being sought after by the daughters of other estate owners. Even in England he had been quite popular with the young ladies. However, he knew better than to trifle with them as he had no desire to marry for several years. In any case, he had found most of them rather boring and somewhat self-absorbed, like himself if he were honest. On the contrary,

Grace Fuller did not seem to be the least interested in him. That alone piqued his interest.

"Miss Fuller, have you lived in Jamaica your whole life?"

Her eyes came up to meet his. She really had beautiful eyes with those thick lashes. Come to think of it, her lips were also very appealing, pink and surprisingly full. Sensual. They hinted at a passion that belied the sweet innocent image she projected. He wondered what they tasted like. He would bet that she had never even been kissed. He wouldn't mind introducing her to that pleasure.

"We moved here ten years ago."

Grace did not like how William Edwards was looking at her, as if he was assessing her for some nefarious purpose. His green eyes, which seemed rather cold at first glance, were now focused on her lips and getting warmer and darker, making her distinctly uncomfortable.

Her gaze was pulled, almost against her will, to the scar on his cheek and she couldn't help but wonder how he got it, especially as it did not look as if it had been there for a long time. Granted, he was very handsome, even with the scar, but she was not interested in any dalliance with him so he could look elsewhere.

When she decided to marry, she would go to her husband untouched, something she was sure that he would not understand or appreciate. So, she would ignore that she liked the feeling of her small hand being engulfed in his stronger and larger one. And she would ignore how attractive he was and how his gaze on her lips made them tingle in anticipation of something unknown to her. Those things were of less importance than his

Free at Last

character, which she was yet to determine. If this was the way he looked at an unmarried lady on their first meeting, it did not bode well of his character.

"And how do you like it?"

Grace had a moment of confusion before she remembered that they were talking about Jamaica.

"It has grown on me. It's a harsh land, but it is also very beautiful, especially the mountains with their beautiful sapphire haze. However, only the strongest can survive here."

"So, you are strong?" he teased lightly.

"Yes. I am stronger than I look." That sounded like a warning to William. "My mother died of yellow fever two years ago, but I was fortunate not to catch it."

"I am sorry to hear that. I contracted malaria in the first week of being here and I would not wish it on my worst enemy."

"Yes, I know. My father suffers with it as well."

"You must be a great comfort and help to him."

"I try to be. It has not been easy for him since my mother died. I think he has lost his love for Jamaica and wants to return to England." Grace was surprised to find herself sharing such personal confidences with him.

William was surprised at the loss he felt at the thought of her leaving Jamaica.

"I would hate for you to leave before I get to know you," he flirted. Grace did not even bat an eyelid. If anything, her gaze hardened slightly.

"I doubt that we will have opportunity to get to know each other very well, as we are both busy people. You have this plantation to run and I have my father's house to look after for him."

That certainly made things clear as crystal. Mrs. Westhall was obviously under the false impression that Grace Fuller was interested in finding a husband. Not that he was interested in marriage, but he found her a challenge. Pulling his eyes away from her lips once again, he encountered her stare and he could tell that she was less than impressed with him. He smiled inwardly at the challenge she presented. She was definitely not boring. For the first time since he had arrived, Jamaica was looking promising.

"Surely you cannot be busy all the time," he persisted.

"I take Sundays off from working. We celebrate the Lord's Day. Perhaps you can join us for services one Sunday." Grace issued her invitation knowing that it would unlikely be taken up.

"Perhaps," he murmured noncommittally. He could not imagine a worse way to spend a Sunday.

"What brought your family to Jamaica?" he asked, changing the subject. He had no desire to attend Sunday services, but he wanted to prolong his conversation with her. He found her interesting despite her apparent piety.

"My father inherited the plantation from a relative. We are Quakers, so my father came here with the intention of sharing the gospel with the slaves and improving their living conditions."

Quakers? William thought with a sinking heart. That explained the Sunday services. He knew all about the Quakers. Barbados had had its share of them, but they had mostly been run out of the country. They had accused the planters of ill-treating their slaves which was bad enough, but they had a reputation of refusing to partake in civil duties such as defending the country, or paying levies to help maintain the island and often refused to give evidence in court. And Grace was a Quaker.

"But you own the slaves, do you not?" he accused.

"Yes," she admitted quietly, "but we treat them humanely and ensure that they live under the best conditions. They are well-fed, well-clothed and housed in clean, dry huts. And we plan to free them."

"How convenient. So how does all that humane treatment affect the profitability of your plantation?" William asked pointedly.

"Mr. Edwards, there are more important things than profits."

"Such as?"

"If you have to ask me that then I feel sorry for you. Please excuse me."

With that, she walked off to join a group of ladies who were chatting near the doors to the patio. William couldn't help but watch the sway of her hips as she crossed the room. He was right; her lips definitely did not fit on a Quaker, if that made any sense, and a woman of piety should not have such an alluring walk. They only served to put wicked thoughts in his head. Grace Fuller was off limits for all kinds of reasons so he had better put her out of his mind. However, his body had other ideas. He would have to call Bella tonight to give him relief after his encounter with Grace Fuller.

❦

April 14, 1697
Friendly Hall Plantation

Grace was not looking forward to dinner. As promised, when the Westhalls left, her father promptly sent an invitation for William to come to dinner. Knowing that he was from a wealthy Barbadian family, she had gone all out to make sure that the meal she set before him was the best that Jamaica had to offer. Tonight she would serve a veritable plantation feast. Not that she was trying to impress him, but neither did she want him thinking that they were backwards in Jamaica either.

She eyed the dinner table critically. It was set for just the three of them, with her father at the head, of course, and she and William facing each other across the table. The silverware and glasses gleamed in the candlelight and the flower arrangement that graced the centre of the table gave it an added touch of elegance. She was well pleased with it.

She smoothed her hair, which tonight was done a little more casually than the last time, pulled into a clasp on one side of her head and draped over her shoulder, falling nearly to her waist. Her pale-yellow dress was fancier than she would normally wear for a dinner at home but she had felt like dressing up tonight and it had nothing to do with William Edwards, she told herself. Voices from the hallway announced the arrival of their guest and she went to join her father who was greeting him.

William looked devastatingly handsome in his tan jacket and breeches and white shirt and cravat. His thick dark hair was a little longer than it had been when she met him a few weeks before and he wore it slicked back. The scar on his cheek added interest to his face and once again made her curious to know how he had gotten it. Maybe tonight she would find out. Her eyes were drawn to his as he gallantly lifted her hand to kiss the back of it in greeting. They were warm tonight and held a teasing glint as if he remembered their last meeting with amusement. The feel of his lips on the back of her hand was disconcerting and it was all she could do not to yank her hand from his grasp.

"Miss Fuller, I am delighted to see you again, despite the way we parted company last time." He would have to bring that up.

"Oh, and how was that?" asked her father interestedly.

"We were in disagreement about whether or not profit was the most important thing in running a plantation."

Her father laughed. "Don't get Grace started. She is quite passionate in expressing her opinions."

"Father –" Grace began to protest.

"Indeed?" William cut in with a smile, assessing her afresh. He liked the idea of a passionate Grace.

"Let us go in to dinner. The girls have been keeping it warm." Grace hurriedly changed the subject.

George gestured for Grace to lead and for William to follow her, leaving him to bring up the rear. William was quite happy to follow Grace for it gave him the opportunity to enjoy her walk again and he was sorry when they quickly arrived at the dining room.

"I have been terribly remiss in not complimenting you on how beautiful you look tonight, Miss Grace." William said softly near her ear as he held out her chair for her to be seated.

The warmth of his breath on her ear did strange things to her tummy. She murmured her thanks, glancing at her father to see if he had observed the exchange, but he appeared not to.

"William, what can I offer you to drink? We do not partake in spirits here, but we have a number of juices or water if you prefer."

No spirits? thought William. My God, how did they deal with the hardship of plantation life without some spirits to gladden their hearts at the end of the day? The first miracle the Lord did was turning water into wine. Even a heathen like him knew that. So what was this ridiculous notion about not drinking spirits?

"Juice of some sort would be fine," he said aloud.

Once they were seated, an older woman and a slave girl came in bearing platters of food. It all looked wonderful to William, considering the fare he had been having since the departure of the Westhalls. William was surprised to hear Grace thanking them for serving the food. Who thanked slaves for doing their work?

"Grace, would you like to say grace?" her father asked with a chuckle at his play on words.

"Certainly, Father," she agreed and said a brief prayer, asking for blessing upon the food.

"So William, tell me a little about yourself," invited George as the dishes were passed around. "Julia Westhall said that your father owns a plantation in Barbados?"

"Yes," William acknowledged, tasting his food which was delicious. He complimented Grace on the meal, although she would not have prepared it herself.

"And I assume you helped him to run it before coming here."

"Yes, for a few months."

"Didn't I hear you say at the Westhall's party that you had recently returned from England? What took you there? Business or pleasure?"

What was this, an inquisition? William wondered.

"Um, business. I was learning the theoretical aspects of running the plantation and how to keep the books. That sort of thing."

"Good, good. That is very important." George nodded approvingly. "Although I cannot say it is my favourite activity."

"How was it living in England? I can still remember the different seasons. That is what I miss the most," Grace said reminiscently.

"It was fine, but I must say I prefer Barbados."

"Then you couldn't have been happy to come here. What made you come to Jamaica?" Grace probed.

A love for my neck, William admitted to himself.

"Would you believe because my father asked me to and being a dutiful son I agreed to come?" William joked to avoid answering the question. He saw her raise an elegant eyebrow in disbelief.

"That is a good quality to have," commended her father, causing Grace to almost roll her eyes. William stifled a laugh at her expression. Dinner was certainly not boring, spirits lacking or not.

After the dishes had been cleared and they had partaken of a wonderful dessert, Grace suggested that they have coffee in the sitting room.

"I hope you will excuse me, but I have some work that cannot wait until the morning," George claimed. "William, I'm sure that I can trust you to be a gentleman with my Grace."

Grace looked at her father sharply as if the last thing she expected was for him to leave her alone with William. William hid a smug smile, knowing that he had received the seal of approval from George Fuller who, apparently, was not as discerning as his daughter.

"Of course, sir. I will also endeavour not to overstay my welcome," William assured him, shaking his hand.

"Then I should show you to the door now," Grace murmured as she led him to the sitting room while her father turned towards his office.

"Grace, I heard that! Are you saying that you do not welcome my company?" William teased.

"Mr. Edwards —"

"William," he corrected.

"William, my father might be trusting, but rest assured that I have good discernment."

"Can you discern what I am thinking right now?" William asked, lowering his voice an octave and drawing closer to her.

"It does not take a lot of discernment to see what you are thinking. I do not know what kind of women you are accustomed to keeping company with, but I am a virtuous woman," Grace informed him.

"Do you plan to keep your virtue forever?"

"That is none of your business," she rasped, stepping back and finding herself against the sofa.

"What if I want to make it my business?" William asked, following her and trapping her between his body and the arm of the sofa.

The long hair that draped almost to her waist looked soft and silky, tempting him to feel it. Picking up several strands, he rubbed them between his fingers sensuously while holding Grace's eyes with his.

"As silky as I imagined," he murmured.

Grace's startled eyes looked huge in her flushed face and her breath forced past her lips in small quick bursts. William's eyes had closed a bit but she could still see that they darkened to nearly black and had taken on an expression that she had no trouble identifying as desire.

"Mr. Edwards, I believe that you should leave now," she whispered breathlessly. "You have definitely overstayed your welcome."

"Are you sure?" he asked huskily, looking at her lips.

"Yes," she whispered, wishing she sounded more convincing.

William immediately stepped back and gave her a little bow.

"I would not like to overstay my welcome or I fear I will not be invited again. I will see myself out."

Grace was relieved when he turned and sauntered confidently from the room. She made sure that he had closed the door before she collapsed onto the sofa. The last thing she needed was for William to know how he affected her. He was dangerously attractive but, despite what her father thought, he was not to be trusted. Imagine making advances to her in her father's house. How disrespectful! She knew that he would have kissed her if she had not stopped him. And if she was honest with herself she had to admit that she was curious to know what his kiss would be like. She closed her eyes in shame.

Chapter 3

June 15, 1697

William felt disquieted in his spirit and could not sleep. After tossing and turning for an hour or more he finally lit a lantern on the table beside his bed and took his journal out of the drawer. He had not been writing very often because he was busy on the plantation during the day and worked on the books in the evening after which he would call for Bella to see to his needs. While life had settled down into a routine of sorts, he still wanted to leave Jamaica and Westhall as Marsh had become more intolerable since the owners had left. With the knowledge he now had and his newly discovered motivation, he would be happy to return to Barbados and help his father with the running of The Acreage.

> *Tonight, for some reason, I feel a restlessness in my spirit and even tiredness from the day's work and bedding Bella have not enabled me to sleep. The Westhalls have been gone for two months now and every day Marsh grows more belligerent. At first he rode around with a look of great derision on his face, knowing that I knew very little about running the*

plantation and had to rely on him for much of my learning.

Now, between the discussions I have had with the other planters and the books that Westhall left in his library, my knowledge will soon outstrip his and that is his great worry. After the humiliating incident with the head of the slave he wrongly believed that I was without backbone and could not deal with the slaves. Instead, it hardened something in me and I can now share lash for lash with him.

Yesterday I ordered 150 lashes for Sam George although I had to get Francis and Abel to finish giving them as my hands began to wear out after about 50. I caught him stealing and sucking cane when he should have been cutting it. But I could never be as bad as Marsh. I nearly lost my dinner again last week when he told me that he had cut off the ear of one of the slaves for not answering when he called him and made him eat it. I need to get out of this country. No one can tell me that God has not turned his back on Jamaica. Even the Fullers are planning to leave, from what Grace has told me.

Grace. She is a temptation to me. Every time I see her at a social event all I want to do is taste her lips and introduce her to the pleasures of the flesh. Of course she wants nothing to do with me and has made it plain. It is a good thing that I have any number of slave women here to slake my lust upon. I have had Kitty and Susie a few times, but

Bella is my favourite. She is happy to do whatever I tell her to, without question. The fact that she was Marsh's woman makes my satisfaction even greater. I have told her that she is for my exclusive use, so now Marsh hates me more than ever, but I care not.

The man is the spawn of Satan, I swear. Only a few days ago I had to pull him off Little Mimber who is nine years old! He was reeking of alcohol. Thank God Bella came to get me in time. I gave him such a beating that he is unlikely to try that again.

I am afraid this country will turn me into the basest of men, save Marsh of course. I trust my father has received my letter. Every day I hope to get one from him telling me that I may return to Barbados. If I do not hear from him soon, I will catch a boat and go to America or perhaps back to England. Although I cannot, in good conscience, leave the plantation that Westhall entrusted to me in the hands of that devil Marsh. I would have to find someone to replace me first.

Three weeks later

William's tiredness left him as soon as he spotted his name on the letter on the desk in the Peter Westhall's office. Recognising the handwriting as his father's, he hurriedly ripped open the seal in anticipation. He fervently hoped that he would be summoning him home. The only regret he would have about leaving Jamaica was not having the opportunity to get to know

Grace better. For the first time in his life he found himself interested in a woman who was neither a prostitute nor a slave. He didn't even know how to properly act with her as he had no experience in dealing with a virtuous woman.

She was the one woman who he found appealing enough, both physically and intellectually, to consider marrying, if she would ever have him. He smiled as he thought of their encounters since they had first met and he knew that she would take a lot of convincing. It was a good thing that he could be charming when he put his mind to it. He unfolded the single page eagerly.

The Acreage
Barbados
June 16, 1697

> *My Dear Son*
> *It is with deep regret that I write to inform you that I received a letter from your uncle in England yesterday (it will be several weeks by the time you get this) to tell me that your mother had passed away in England after a short illness.*

William stared in disbelief at the letter in his hand. His mother had died? He scanned the date. Months ago now? Shock gripped him and held him immobile for several minutes as he struggled to believe what he had read. His eyes reluctantly returned to the page and he had to blink several times before he could continue reading.

Apparently, she caught a cold and a persistent cough shortly after she arrived in England. Your uncle said that by the time she allowed him to summon a physician she had contracted pneumonia which she never recovered from.

I am so sorry to be the bearer of this sad news as I know that you and your mother had a very close relationship. She loved you dearly and though you will grieve, she would not want you to grieve for long.

I will be travelling to England as soon as I put things in order here so that I may be of comfort to your sisters and pay my last respects to my dear Elizabeth.

While the pain of her loss no doubt has you in its grip as you read this letter, take heart that "weeping may endure for a night but joy cometh in the morning".

William threw down the letter in disgust and pushed back his chair, causing it to crash to the floor. He ran his hands through his hair, struggling with the grief that needed an outlet. He paced the room as pain struggled with anger.

"Your dear Elizabeth?" he scoffed aloud. Was she his dear Elizabeth when he was bedding all the slave women on the plantation? When he took Sarah to be his mistress and paraded her and her daughter in front of his mother? Was he supposed to be impressed with the Biblical quote? Even the devil could quote the Bible. What a hypocrite!

"Mother," he cried in pain, sinking into an armchair. He had not even written to her since coming to Jamaica. He had only written his father asking him if he could return to Barbados. Even when he had returned from England he had not spent as much time with her as he could have. Now he would never see her again.

Pictures of her flitted through his mind. The rare occasions when she looked truly happy, the times when he unknowingly caught her with such sadness on her face that his own heart hurt, her tear-stained face the day he told her that he was being sent to England. The joy that made her look years younger when he returned home. And finally, the look of horror the day that he had stumbled home with dried blood on his cheek and a thin line of blood on his neck.

Tears ran unashamedly down his cheeks as he realised that a major chapter of his life was now closed. If he ever got married, his mother would not be there to meet his wife. Never would his children know a grandmother, if he ever had any. And yet Deborah and her mother continued to enjoy life. That could not be right. Justice had to be served.

❖

It was a week since William had received the letter from his father. After he had shared the news of his mother's death, Marsh had dragged up enough decency from somewhere to offer his sympathy and thankfully given him a wide berth for that week. However, he had now returned to his usual contemptuous self.

William's anger with his father and the unfairness of his mother's death was still simmering below the surface and he had no tolerance for the overseer's antagonism. Tension was building between them and he knew that a confrontation was inevitable.

Tiredness slowed his steps as he came in from the fields. He had been pushing himself to work hard in an attempt to block everything from his mind. The dirt and sweat that accumulated on him from the day's toil had him looking forward to a good soak in a tub. He would get Bella to scrub his back and, having denied himself any physical pleasure for the week as a mark of respect for his mother, he would have her tonight.

"Betsy," he called as he entered the house.

"Yes, Massa Edwards." She appeared almost at once from the direction of the kitchen. Betsy was the housekeeper who ran the Westhall's house efficiently. She was a mature woman with greying hair and a slight limp. The limp did not seem to deter her from carrying out her duties, though.

"Get two of the girls to bring up a tub for me and have them fill it with hot water. And send someone for Bella to scrub my back."

Her "Yes, Massa" hit his back as he climbed the stairs to his room. The Westhalls had told him to move into the big house in their absence and to entertain any guests who came to visit. That was another reason that Marsh hated him.

William stretched out across the bed and had almost fallen asleep when the noise of the tub being manhandled into the room roused him. Several trips later the tub was filled with steaming water and a bar of soap and a towel were left on a chair within reach. William barely had the energy to strip the clothes from his body before sinking into the tub with pleasure and leaning his head back on the rim.

The water had started to cool when he realised that Bella had not yet come to scrub his back or any other part of his body.

"Betsy!" he shouted and this time had to wait a few minutes before she appeared at the door. "Where the hell is Bella? I told you to send her to me ages ago."

"I tell she, massa, but I think Mr. Marsh call she to him."

"What? Does she know who the boss is here? Get out. I will deal with her myself."

"Yes, massa," she said in a tremulous voice.

William hurriedly washed himself in the now cool water, dried off and dressed in a pair of breeches and tucked a shirt inside before pushing his feet back into a pair of shoes. Waves of anger flowed from him as he strode down the stairs and out of the house. Adrenaline flowing through his veins replaced the tiredness and put him in a fighting mood. He hesitated in the yard, not sure if Bella would be in her hut or in Marsh's house. His decision was made for him when he saw her hurrying from the house clasping her unbuttoned dress to her.

"Bella!" His shout caused her to jump. "Didn't Betsy send someone to tell you to come to me?"

"Y-y-es, Massa Edwards." Her eyes refused to meet his.

"So why the hell didn't you come?"

"M-m-massa Marsh mek me come to him."

"What do you mean 'made you come to him'?"

The frustration of his whole time in Jamaica, Marsh's insubordination and his mother's death came to a boiling point with that statement and William lost control. He seemed possessed as he dragged Bella to the whipping pole, tied her hands with the rope and grabbed the whip that had been left there probably by Marsh after his usual evening whippings.

"I am the boss of this plantation. Not Marsh. When I send for you, you come to me. Do you understand me?"

"Y-y-yes, massa. I sorry, Massa Edwards. I didn' know what to do."

"Well, now you do and this is to remind you in the future…"

Stepping back, he took out his rage on the poor girl, hitting her over and over with the whip until his hand ached and her back was a mass of bleeding welts. Her screams had long since gone silent as she seemed to have passed out under the brutal punishment.

He dropped the whip and turned away. He would deal with Marsh next.

"Marsh!" he shouted, throwing open the door to the house that used to be his. There was no answer. "Marsh!" he repeated, heading for the bedroom. The smell of alcohol assailed his nostrils before he caught sight of Marsh, passed out on the bed. Anger returned in full force and he grabbed Marsh by the feet, pulling his half-naked body off the bed. He didn't care when his head thumped on the floor, jarring him out of his unconsciousness.

"What the h-?" Marsh started, rubbing his head sluggishly. The alcohol seemed to have dulled the pain of the fall.

William dragged him up by the shirt that he was still wearing and pulled him close to his face. Alcohol fumes fanned his face as he delivered his warning.

"I am the boss here. When I issue an order it is to be obeyed regardless of what you say. Do you understand me?"

"Wh-what you talking about?" Marsh's words were slurred.

"I am talking about Bella and about any other order I give around here. Bella is no longer your woman. She is exclusively for my use. I thought I had made that clear, but apparently you did not understand."

"Who do you think you are, coming 'bout here telling me what to do? I don't have to take orders from you. You don't know nothing about Jamaica or running a plantation here."

"You don't have to take orders?" William laughed mirthlessly. "Well, take this instead."

With that he threw a series of punches to Marsh's face, bloodying it before letting him go, only to follow with several punishing blows to the gut. Marsh crumpled at his feet and the vomit that spewed from his mouth barely missed William's boots. William looked down at him in disgust before storming out of the house. He walked blindly past Bella who was still slumped against the whipping post.

When he entered the house, Betsy timidly approached him.

"Massa Edwards," she began.

"What is it, Betsy?" he growled, rubbing his aching knuckles.

"I could move Bella?"

William paused before answering.

"Yes. Go and deal with her."

His rage receded as he watched Betsy limp towards the door to see after Bella and a twinge of conscience pricked him as the demon that had possessed him left until another time.

Chapter 4

Friendly Hall Plantation

The sun had barely lightened the sky when Grace was woken from her sleep by a persistent knocking at her door.

She buried deeper under her warm sheet and pulled a pillow over her head to block out the noise.

"Miss Grace, Miss Grace!" An urgent voice penetrated her sleep.

"Go away," she muttered.

"Miss Grace!" The door opened and the insistent voice was now right next to her bed.

Grace reluctantly pulled the pillow from her head and rubbed her eyes, trying to focus on who was disturbing her. The worried face of her housekeeper, Liza, caused the sleep to flee from her eyes.

"Has something happened to my father? Is the malaria starting up again?" she asked, pushing back the sheet and struggling to get out of bed.

"No. It is not Master George."

"Then what is it?" Grace demanded impatiently.

"It is Bella, a slave from Westhall. When we wake up this morning we find she on the back step. We ain' know how she get here but she look like she get beat real bad."

"My goodness! Is she-?" She trailed off, afraid to voice her worst fear.

"She still living. Moses carry she to the sick hut and Janey tending to she."

"Is she able to talk? Did she say who beat her?"

Liza went silent.

"You best come and talk to she you'self, Miss Grace."

"All right. Send up some water for me to wash with please and then I'll get dressed and go and see her."

Liza went out, leaving Grace with questions bombarding her mind. Who was this Bella from the Westhalls' plantation? Who could have beaten her and for what? She had heard horror stories of Colin Marsh's barbaric behaviour in the past. She wouldn't be surprised if this was the latest of his deeds.

Her thoughts reluctantly drifted towards William Edwards. She had been trying her best not to think about him, with some success, and had gone out of her way to avoid him as much as possible. However, when she heard that he had gotten word that his mother had passed away, she scripted a note on behalf of her father and herself and sent it to him. She knew what it felt like to lose a mother and even though she did not approve of him, she still felt sympathy at his loss.

She now allowed herself to remember when he came to dinner three months earlier. She could not help but notice how his large hands held the cutlery with ease and how polite his table manners were. He had even politely answered most of the questions her father asked him and made sure that he stayed away from topics that he and she would disagree on. Instead, he asked them about Jamaica, saying that he wanted to understand its history and the conditions that the country was facing.

She squirmed and blushed as she remembered him caressing the strands of her hair and pinning her against the sofa, but also how he left as soon as she asked him to. Surely the man who was so polite and mannerly wasn't capable of beating Bella like that. Was he? She was surprised at the sick feeling that such a thought evoked. No, it had to be Marsh.

She was glad when her maid, Lucy, came in with a pitcher of warm water for her to wash with. Automatically thanking her and then having a quick wash, she turned around for Lucy to button up her dress and then brush and pin her waist-length hair into a bun on the top of her head.

Her stomach growled, making its desire for breakfast known, but she ignored it.

"Has my father been told?"

"No, Miss Grace. He still sleeping. And you is the one who does deal with sick people anyhow so nobody didn' bother to wake him up."

"Just as well. He needs his rest anyway, especially after his bout of malaria this week."

Grace led the way down the stairs and out to the hut where the slaves were brought when they were sick. She was dreading what she would find. The slave girl, Bella, was lying face down with her back exposed and a light sheet covering her from the

Free at Last

waist down. Liza and Janey were standing silently beside the cot. It looked as if someone had smeared aloe on her back, but that did not disguise the countless stripes that marred her brown skin.

Grace was glad that she had not eaten breakfast, for her stomach lurched at the sight of the tattered skin and the smell of the dried blood. She was not usually squeamish as she was the one who looked after the sick slaves on the plantation, as Liza said, but this was beyond her experience and her comprehension.

"Who could have done such a thing?" she whispered in horror. She searched Liza's face for the answer.

"She say the master do it," Liza replied quietly.

"Marsh?" Grace asked hopefully.

"No, Massa Edwards, the one that come here to eat."

Grace sucked in her breath in disbelief. She looked from Liza to Bella's back and found it hard to reconcile what she was seeing with the words that Liza had spoken.

"Surely not!" She denied Liza's words. Surely the attractive and refined man that had sat at their table and eaten with such impeccable manners could not have brutalised the girl this way. Which was he? The polite well-spoken son of a wealthy Barbadian planter or a cruel, inhuman beast of a man? She had to know.

"Bella?" she called softly, moving closer to the cot. The girl stirred and moaned in response. "Sorry to disturb you. I know you must be in a lot of pain, but can you tell me who did this to you?"

"Massa Edwards." Grace had to strain to hear her words, but they were unmistakable. Her heard sank in disappointment

41

and then hardened as a righteous anger overcame her that a human being could treat another with such cruelty. That William Edwards could do such a thing to this young slave girl. She would pay him a visit and he would feel her wrath.

※

Westhall Plantation

A loud pounding at the front door caused William to pause with the cup of coffee on the way to his mouth. Who would be knocking at his door before he could even enjoy his breakfast? Although, looking at the crispy eggs and the blackened strips that could be bacon, it didn't look like anything he would enjoy. The house slaves were no doubt showing their displeasure with the way he had dealt with Bella yesterday.

He didn't know what came over him and he was still trying to come to terms with how he had lost control. Questions tortured him and pictures of Bella slumped against the whipping post had kept him awake most of the night. Was something in Jamaica causing him to become like the rest of overseers and planters that brutalised their slaves? Like the one who sent around the head? Or was there some demon already in him, maybe for years, which had been only waiting for the opportunity to fully reveal itself? Would he be able to control himself in the future?

"Excuse me, Massa Edwards," Betsy interrupted him. "Miss Grace from Friendly Hall say she want to see you."

"Miss Grace? What on earth does she want with me at this time of the day?"

His curiosity was more than aroused. He wondered if her father was ailing or something. Putting down his unfinished coffee, he pushed back his chair to rise from the table and got no further as a whirlwind in a blue flowered dress blew angrily into the room.

"William Edwards, what kind of animal are you?" she demanded furiously. He didn't even have to guess that she was talking about Bella before she stormed on. "How could you beat that girl so cruelly? There is nothing she could have done to deserve that!"

William could not reply. He had no answer. An uncharacteristic emotion washed over him which he recognised as shame. He ruthlessly pushed it aside as the demon stirred. The woman was not going to come here hurling accusations and telling him how to treat his slaves.

"How dare you come on this property accusing me of ill-treating my slaves?" he replied. "You are out of line!"

"Out of line?" she sputtered angrily. "You are the one out of line. The Westhalls would never condone this kind of treatment. They obviously did not know what kind of beast they were hiring when they brought you here. I can now see why you were banished from Barbados. You are worse than Colin Marsh!"

Even in her anger William found her magnificent. He knew that if she could read his thoughts she would no doubt seriously consider murdering him.

"The Westhalls left me in charge and I will run this plantation as I see fit. Now what have you done with my slave?"

"She came to our plantation for refuge and I will not return her to you, you animal. She will recover there. How much do you want for her? I will buy her from you."

"She is not for sale. Return her immediately or I will call the law out on you."

"You wouldn't dare!"

"Try me," he said coldly. He would not, but she did not need to know that.

Grace was at a loss for words. She had never encountered someone so demonic in nature.

"You are demon possessed. The Lord rebuke you," she hissed at him and turned on her heels, leaving him stunned.

William sank back into his chair in shock. Grace spoke with such conviction that he waited a few minutes to see if lightning would strike him down or some other judgement fall upon him. When nothing happened, he straightened up, chided himself for being fanciful and continued eating his breakfast. After one bite he pushed it away. Not only was it inedible, but he had lost his appetite.

It was bad enough that his own soul searching made him wonder if he had some sort of demon driving him, but to hear the words from Grace Fuller was extremely disconcerting. Could she be right?

❖

Grace took deep breaths to calm herself as Moses, the driver, helped her to climb onto the bench of the cart before shaking the stirrups to set the horses in motion.

"You all right, Miss Grace?" He glanced sideways at her.

"No, Moses, I am not all right. I cannot believe that man! I have never met someone so possessed by the devil. He needs deliverance. Under no circumstances am I allowing that girl to be returned to him. He can call the law for me if he wants to."

"I hope it wouldn' come to that, Miss Grace. You better start to pray that God will move him because you know that you really ain' got no right to keep somebody else slave."

Grace sighed. Moses was right. It was obvious that the devil had a hold on William Edwards and there would be no moving him with her words. She would have to call on the powers above to move his heart.

"You are right, Moses. He is desperately in need of prayer."

"Yes, ma'am," he agreed.

"Unfortunately, I do not think I can pray for him. I am too angry."

They fell silent, each lost in their own thoughts. Grace could not believe that William Edwards was so heartless and, worse yet, unrepentant about it. She could never be involved with a man like that, no matter how good looking he was. He would have to undergo a significant transformation first. She was disgusted with herself for even finding him attractive and that she had been tempted to allow him to kiss her.

As the cart took the final stretch to the plantation, Grace made a deliberate effort to calm herself and to mentally plan her day. She had already lost several hours to the disruption caused by the incident with Bella, but she would make the most of the rest. Today she had been planning to continue to teach some of the younger slaves how to read, but she would have to put that off for a while. First thing first, she had to check in on Bella and get some more information from her. She would also have to ask her father what to do.

Bella was sitting up and eating a little porridge when Grace entered the hut this time. She had a shirt thrown over her that was open at the back. Now that she could see her face, Grace realised that she was a very attractive girl with short tight curls and smooth brown skin. The realisation that her scarred back would never again be as flawless as the rest of her skin caused Grace to shiver as she thought of the pain that Bella must have endured.

"Bella, I am glad to see you eating. How are you feeling?"

She put down the bowl before answering.

"My back still paining me bad, but Janey give me something to drink to ease the pain and the aloe helpin'."

"Good. Bella, you said that Master Edwards did this to you?"

"Yes, Miss," she nodded with a faraway look in her eyes as if she was remembering the incident.

"But why would he do that?"

Bella was silent for a long time and then she looked up with shimmering eyes.

"Betsy, the housekeeper, send one of the girls to tell me that Massa William did want me to come and wash he back."

"Wash his back?" Grace repeated in shock.

"Yes, Miss Grace. But then Mr. Marsh tell me to come to the house with he. I could tell that he did drinkin' and I know how vex he does get when he drunk so I went wid he so that he wouldn't beat me."

Grace blushed at what Bella left unsaid. "When he finish wid me he drop sleep and as I was runnin' out of the house to go to Master William he meet me in the yard and start shoutin' at me that I is to obey he and do what he say, not what Mr. Marsh say." Her voice dropped and thickened with tears.

"You do not have to say anymore," Grace assured her, but it was as if Bella had not heard her and was in another place.

"Then he tie me to the whippin' post and start to beat me. I thought he woulda never stop. I think I faint because when I wake up Betsy did putting aloe 'pon my back. I never feel pain like that in my life," she whispered. Grace wiped the tears from her own cheeks.

"I'm so sorry, Bella," she whispered.

"I never thought that Master William woulda turn so. He call me to come to he bed nuff times and he never treat me rough, not like Mr. Marsh."

"Uh, thank you, Bella." Grace stopped her from sharing any more details as another blush stained her face and neck. "Has he ever beat anybody else like this?"

"Not when he first come, but when Massa Westhall left, he start beating the men nearly as bad as Marsh, but he never beat any of the women. I is the first," she ended in a whisper.

"I'm so sorry," Grace said again, feeling very inadequate. "How did you get here and what made you come?"

"One of the men bring me but I can' tell you who it is, Miss Grace. He say that he hear you and Master Fuller does treat you' slaves good and he borrow a horse and bring me here. I wouldn' want Master William to know who it is 'cause he would get a beatin' too."

"That's all right, Bella. I don't need to know. You rest some more. I need to talk to my father. And do not worry, we will look after you."

"Thank you, Miss Grace. Thank you."

Grace left the hut more determined than ever that Bella was never going back to Westhall Plantation. She was not ignorant of what went on at other plantations, but to hear first-hand how Bella had been used and abused by both men turned her stomach. Praying for William Edwards was going to be much harder than she thought, if not impossible.

Approaching the house, she couldn't help but admire the quaintness of it and the flowers that she and her mother had planted in garden beds along the front. It brought home to her just how vastly different her life was from Bella's. They could be around the same age, but while she lived a life of comfort and protection, Bella's life was one of powerlessness and abuse. She could not say no to the men who made demands of her, not without punishment anyway. And this only because of the colour of her skin and the inhuman laws that said people like her could be bought and sold like property and treated worse than animals. Well, she would make sure that she secured Bella's freedom, if it was the last thing she did.

"Father?" Grace called, knocking softly on the open door before entering his study. Her father still looked a little frail after his bout with the malaria so she did not want to burden him, however, this was important.

"Grace, I thought you were having a late morning in bed. I know how many nights you were up with me through this episode."

Free at Last

She crossed the room to kiss him on his weathered cheek before taking the chair in front of his desk. She paused, knowing that he would be upset when he discovered that Moses took her to Westhall. And maybe even more so when he heard what William Edwards was really like; the man he had trusted her to be alone with.

"I went over to Westhall Plantation," she confessed.

"Westhall? What on earth were you doing there?"

Grace explained what had happened, leaving out the fact that William Edwards threatened her with the law.

"That poor girl! I can't believe that of William. Grace, that was very dangerous! Anything could have happened to you."

"But it didn't. We have to buy her, Father. We simply cannot allow her to go back there. Something worse may happen to her."

Her father rubbed the back of his neck as he did when he was troubled, which was not very often.

"We can't make him sell her, Grace. And, as horrible as it sounds, there is no law that prevents a master from beating a slave or, worse yet, maiming a slave for any real or imagined offence. We will have to appeal to his humanity."

"Father, he has no humanity. We will have to appeal to his greed and make him an offer he cannot refuse."

"All right, but this time I will be dealing with him not you."

"I have no desire to see him or deal with him ever again, Father, so that is fine."

"I am so sorry that I left you alone with him that night."

"I was not in any danger from him, Father, so please do not feel guilty." Well, no danger of being beaten, but another kind of danger. "He is like two people. I feel that he could be a good person, but a demon seems to take possession of him and transforms him into a beast. There is no other explanation for the evil that is in him."

"Well, the Lord warned about casting out a demon and leaving the house empty. That only makes room for the demon to bring seven more worse than itself to take up residence."

"If this is only one and this is what it is capable of, I definitely would not want to see seven worse than this."

Chapter 5

Later that day
Friendly Hall Plantation

George Fuller sat in his office looking out of the window at the distant fields where some slaves were cutting canes. This was the end of harvest, the hardest time of the year, and tempers were usually short as everyone was tired. George's calm exterior belied the turmoil that was going on inside him. He was horrified to learn about William's treatment of the slave girl.

As a Quaker, they did not condone owning slaves, but he had inherited the plantation and saw coming to Jamaica as an opportunity to evangelize the slaves and teach them skills before setting them free. They had been here for ten years and had freed many already, but he felt that the time was coming to free the rest so that he could return to England. Since his wife died he no longer had any desire to stay in Jamaica. He was tired of the ill-treatment of the slaves in Jamaica and of the greed and lust that were prevalent among the planters. They needed evangelizing themselves.

He was disappointed in William because he had seen him as a possible husband for Grace and had hopes that they would get to know one another well enough that when the time came for him to return to England they would be ready for marriage. Now, he did not want his daughter associating with such a man. If he treated his slaves so badly, would he treat a wife any better? Would he continue to bed the slave women even after he was married as many of the planters did? He would never subject Grace to that.

He didn't even want to have to deal with William again, but Grace wanted him to buy the girl and he could not refuse in good conscience. He was sure that William would either refuse to sell her, which was in his right, or he would make him pay a significant amount of money for her. The plantation was certainly not as large or affluent as Westhall, but a life was more important than money so he was prepared to pay whatever he asked.

A knock at the door interrupted his thoughts.

"Come in."

"Excuse me, Master Fuller, but Master Edwards from Westhall Plantation here to see you." Liza's voice sounded nervous.

"Thank you, Liza. You can show him in." She nodded and went down the corridor to lead William Edwards to the office. The few seconds she was gone gave George time to compose himself and put aside his feeling of disappointment before William came in.

"Good day, George. I will not say it's good to see you again given the circumstances under which I am here." William got straight to the point.

George's good manners constrained him to offer William a seat which he refused.

"I can say the same. In fact, I am disturbed at my lack of judgement about your character. I am ashamed that I even trusted you to be alone with Grace."

"Rest assured that I would never hurt Grace in any way."

"So why would you hurt the girl Bella in that brutal manner?"

"Bella is a slave."

"She is also a human being! Would you treat your horse that way?" George asked, spearing him with a hard look.

William was the first to look away.

"What happened to Bella was unfortunate. I was out of my head with grief and I am afraid that she bore the brunt of it."

"Were you out of your head with grief from the time you took over running Westhall? I was given to understand that you received news of your mother's passing only last week. Yet, from what I have heard, this is not the first time you have beaten a slave nor is it the worst beating that you have administered."

William had no defence so he took the position of offence.

"I did not come here for your judgement. I came here to reclaim my slave and return her to Westhall. Have her brought to me, please."

"I am sorry, but I cannot in good conscience hand her over to you to await a worse fate. In any case she is not your slave, but the Westhalls'."

"They have left me in charge so the slaves are mine."

"I think I need to write Peter Westhall and let him know what has been going on at his plantation," George threatened.

"You are blind if you do not think that he knows what happens to his slaves, or even cares, as long as the plantation generates enough money to keep him and his family in comfort. Colin Marsh was ill-treating them long before I got there."

"Ah, so you admit that you have ill-treated them as well." George pounced on his words.

"I admit nothing."

"You do not have to; the stripes on Bella's back tell the story. It has also come to my attention that both you and Marsh have been using the girl for sinful purposes. I am reluctant to even speak of such things for 'it is shameful even to mention what the disobedient do in secret'," he quoted.

William barely restrained himself from rolling his eyes.

"Well, do not mention it. Just return my girl before I have to call the law out on you."

"The girl is very damaged and can barely move. Surely you would prefer to sell her."

"Why would I want to do that? She is a good, strong worker and as soon as her back heals she will be able to return to the fields."

"You can name your price." George could not believe that William could be so callous.

"You want to keep her that badly? Well pay me £100 pounds for her." George knew that William was trying to dissuade him by asking four times the price of a female slave, but how could he bargain with the girl's life when he was not sure if she would survive if she returned to the plantation.

"£100 it is. I will get my attorney to draw up the bill of sale and I will have the money for you as soon as it is done."

William was surprised. He did not think that Fuller would pay him that much for the girl. He had truly been expecting him to back down at the price. Now he could not go back on his word, for no matter what George thought, he was a man of his word. Maybe England had civilised him more than he realised.

"Shall we shake on it?" William asked.

"I don't think that is necessary. I am a man of my word. I will see you out."

George walked to the door and held it open for William before leading him to the front door.

"It would be the Christian thing to wish you a good day, but I would be a hypocrite if I did," George said.

"Indeed." William agreed. "And we would never want that on your spotless conscience, would we? Good day."

❀

William was about to untie his horse from the hitching post when he saw Grace walking towards the house from the direction of the slave huts. She carried what looked like a bowl and a spoon in her hand and he wondered if she had come from feeding Bella. She would probably be the type to feed a sick slave. Guilt stirred in his gut. He knew that he should mount his horse and leave the yard before she saw him but instead his feet carried him towards her as if he had no control over them. He did not know why he was even approaching her for they did not part well earlier and she would, no doubt, flay him with her tongue. Of course, it was no less than he deserved.

"We meet again, Grace," he greeted her as if he had not only hours before threatened to put the law on her.

Grace looked up at the sound of his voice, as if she had been deep in thought and had not heard him approaching. Her eyes hardened as she saw him and contempt shot from them, finding its mark in his gut where he keenly felt the loss of her regard.

"You are so much worse than I ever imagined," she spat at him. "I hope you have come to sell Bella to my father, for I could never let her go back to Westhall now that I know the full extent of your depravity."

"Depravity?" he repeated.

"You took an innocent girl and you forced yourself upon her then you beat her until she was senseless," she accused him angrily.

For a moment William looked at her in shock, wondering how she could have known about Deborah, before the rest of her sentence registered and he realised that she was talking about Bella.

"She was no innocent when she came to my bed. Marsh and God knows who else had her before me. Anyway, this is not a conversation for an innocent like you to be having."

"What a hypocrite you are!" exclaimed Grace, even as her face turned red at his words. "You disgust me! How could I even have found you attractive?"

"You found me attractive?" William repeated, smirking. Maybe all was not lost. Was it possible that he might still have a chance with Grace?

"This is not amusing! You are not even repentant of what you did. I have come to the conclusion that you are two men. One who is charming and polite and the other who is a monster controlled by the forces of darkness."

"Why Grace, you have quite an imagination. I will leave you to your fanciful thoughts," he joked. "You will be happy to hear that I have sold Bella to your father, but I am afraid you will have to do without a new dress or two for a while." With that, he gave her a mocking bow, strode back to his horse which he mounted and rode away without a backward glance. Grace stared after him in disbelief that he could be so cavalier about the situation with Bella.

William carried the weight of Grace's words with him but he would never let her know how they affected him. He had joked and called them fanciful, but inside he was afraid that she spoke the truth. Truly, he seemed to be two men. One who had the capacity to love and could love Grace if she gave him the chance. And the other who was a monster that could flog a slave woman almost to death just because she defied him. Could it be that he was really influenced by forces outside of himself? Grace called them the forces of darkness. Would they come upon him again and what evil he would do if they did?

❦

Grace admonished herself for looking at William's retreating figure. She would be happy if she never saw him again. The anger and hatred that she felt for him would require her to repent but surely the Lord did not expect her to pray for him now that she had found out the full extent of his sins.

For we wrestle not against flesh and blood, but against principalities, against powers, against the rulers of the darkness of this world...

The scripture dropped into her mind reminding her that it wasn't William whom she should be fighting against but the same forces of darkness that she had told him were controlling him. It was a lot easier said than done. It was easy to blame everything on the devil, but human beings were given free will. They could choose to do good or they could choose to do evil and William Edwards had chosen to do evil. Only God could help him now. She deposited the bowl on the table in the hall and went to find her father in his office.

"I hear that you managed to persuade William Edwards to sell Bella."

He looked up from a document he was writing. "As you said, I appealed to his greed. He accepted £100 for her."

"£100! No wonder he was taunting me about not being able to buy new dresses for a while. Thank you, Father."

"You ran into him when he was leaving?"

"Yes and, believe me, I have no desire to see him again."

"Did he threaten you in any way?"

"No, Father. He is not that way with me. I am convinced that he is in need of deliverance, for surely no-one can be that evil unless they were possessed."

"We must pray for him and for the slaves at Westhall as well," her father encouraged.

"Then we should not stop there, but we should pray for slaves everywhere or, better yet, for slavery to be abolished."

"I do not imagine I will see that in my lifetime, but until then we must do our part even if we only affect one life. In this case it is Bella's and it will mean a whole new life for her. She will be fertile ground for the gospel. All we need to do is sow the seed."

"And who will sow the seed in William's life?" she asked concernedly. She couldn't believe that she could actually feel concern for the man that only minutes ago she felt hatred towards. Perhaps she was two people as well. The one who was disgusted with William Edwards and the one who was still attracted to him despite all she knew of him. Surely she was an even bigger hypocrite than he was.

Chapter 6

September 27, 1697
Friendly Hall Plantation

Grace sat on a low stool with a piece of chalk and a large slate in her hand. Around her on the ground sat several of the slave children and some of the older ones like Bella with their own small slates. They met every other evening at this time to learn how to read and do basic reckoning. As she looked at the faces in front of her, eager and bright, Grace knew that she would defy anyone to tell her that slaves were not capable of learning. It was obvious that the planters wanted to keep them in ignorance so that they could control them, but at Friendly Hall their purpose was to help them to transition into freedom and be able to survive after they were free.

Her eyes were drawn to Bella whose back was now fully healed and who had blossomed since leaving Westhall. Grace had taken her into the house where it was discovered that she had an aptitude for cooking so the cook, who was getting on in age, had started to train her to help with the cooking so that eventually she would be able to take over her role. Looking at her now, head bent over her slate as she worked on the sum she had given them, Grace hardly saw any trace of the terrified, abused girl who was left on their doorstep three months ago. She thanked God for bringing her safely to them.

She wished that she could rescue all of them, especially the young girls. One day Bella had told Grace how Marsh had tried to force himself on a girl as young as nine years old and she had run to get Master William to come and save her. Her opinion of William improved slightly when she heard how he had pulled Marsh off the girl before any damage had been done and had given him a sound beating.

Grace warned Bella to be careful to stay away from Westhall Plantation, but she knew that she still liked to meet with her old friends on Sundays which was their day off. Afterwards she would return with tales of the happenings there. Grace tried not to show too much interest, but she could not help but listen to news of William Edwards and Westhall.

To Grace it sounded as if all hell had broken loose since the Westhalls left and she would not be surprised if the slaves revolted soon or made an alliance with the maroons to take over the plantation. She was also quite disturbed to hear that William had taken up with Bella's friend Susie, a slave girl a little younger than Bella. She told herself that she was disgusted with his ways and she was, but she refused to acknowledge that some contrary part of her was piqued that William was bedding yet another slave woman. Did she really expect him to suddenly change his ways?

"Who has the answer to the sum?" Grace asked the group, forcing her thoughts back to the task at hand.

"Me," Bella said, smiling confidently. "It is 24!"

"You are right, Bella. Very good." Grace smiled at her proudly. She felt good that she had been able to impact Bella's life and when they went back to England she would be able to survive on her own because she now had some skills. Maybe one day she might even have a husband and children and forget the abuse she had suffered at the hands of William and Marsh.

"I think we have done enough for today. I am very pleased with all of you. We will have another lesson tomorrow evening."

Everyone began to disburse and Grace gathered up her things. She suddenly noticed that the atmosphere had become ominously still and hardly a leaf stirred on the trees. Listening for the birds which would still be about at this time of the day, she was met with only silence. The absence of their noises was disturbing. She was about to hurry back to the house to tell her father about it when Moses approached her.

"Mama Sally say to tell you that something coming. She could feel it in the air."

Mama Sally was an old slave who was no longer able to work. Nobody knew how old she was because she had been there before Grace and her father came to the plantation and when they arrived she had already looked old.

"She is hardly ever wrong so I suppose we had better prepare ourselves for a storm of some sort."

"No, not a storm. She say it feel like a hurricane. You see how all the wind like it get suck up, she say that is how it does be before a hurricane strike."

The word hurricane struck fear into Grace. She had experienced her first and only hurricane three years after arriving in Jamaica. She had been twelve at the time and old enough to remember the terrifying sound of the wind as it blew over trees, blew away slave huts and even tore off a part of the roof of their house. The rain lashing against the roof and the windows, driven by the ferocious wind, was nearly as terrifying. The amount of water it had dumped in the gully that lay between Westhall and their plantation was enough to turn it into a river which soon burst its banks. Between the high wind and the rain, a hurricane could be disastrous, depending on the intensity of it and how long it stayed over the island. She immediately began to pray.

"I will go and tell my father. The children and the girls who work in the house will have to come inside because the huts will be no match for the wind. The rest of the workers should take refuge in the barn and the factory." Grace hoped she sounded confident because inside she was quaking with fear.

"I will go and let the rest know," Moses assured her. "Everything goin' be all right, Miss Grace. God gine keep we safe."

"I know he will, Moses. I need to remember to be anxious for nothing."

"Amen."

※

Westhall Plantation

William looked at the strange orange colour of the sky. It would have been a sight to behold if it was not accompanied by an eerie stillness; a silence unbroken by the call of birds or the rustle of the leaves on the trees. Something was brewing in the atmosphere. He could feel it as surely as he could feel his heart beating and it was not something good.

He hated to admit his ignorance to Marsh, but he set out across the yard to the overseer's house. It was Sunday and he was no doubt passed out from drinking or asleep after a big afternoon meal. This was the one day when both he and his whip rested.

"Marsh," he called, knocking at the door. He had to knock several times and was about to open the door and go in when it opened and a bleary-eyed Marsh appeared in the doorway.

"What could you be waking a man up for on a Sunday?" he complained.

"I feel something in the atmosphere, like a storm. What do you all do here when a storm is coming?"

Marsh came out onto the small patio and looked at the sky. He swore loudly.

"This ain't no little storm. I think we about to get a hurricane."

"A hurricane?" William repeated. Barbados had not experienced a hurricane in his lifetime but he had heard his father and mother talk about the one that hit the island the year before he was born.

"Yes. We have to get the livestock into the barns and secure the buildings as best as we can. There is not a lot you can do about a hurricane but pray."

If Marsh was suggesting they pray it must be very serious.

"We still need to prepare. We should get some of the slaves to harvest the provisions that are ready or near enough to ready.

We will have to store them so that we don't lose all the crops and so that we will have food after the hurricane."

"Aye. I'll round them up. We have to hurry. Hope it doesn't hit before nightfall."

"When was the last time you had a hurricane here?"

"The last bad one we had was seven years ago. It came early in August and it was devastating. The island took a pounding for four hours, with the wind coming first from one direction and then from the other. We better pray that this one only brushes us."

"What do you do with the slaves?"

"The slaves? They will have to take shelter in the outbuildings because their huts will probably blow away." He sighed. "If we survive this, it will probably set the plantation back quite a bit."

William realised that this was the first time he and Marsh were speaking civilly to each other. It had taken an impending hurricane for Marsh to lay aside his animosity and cooperate with him. He wondered if Grace and her father knew what was coming and if they were preparing for it. If the last one was in 1690 like Marsh said, they would have been here when the hurricane hit so they would know what to do.

He was surprised at the strong desire to ride over to Friendly Hall to see how Grace was faring. The only thing that restrained him was his need to prepare his own plantation for the expected onslaught. That and her parting words to him when he left there three months ago that he was possessed by the forces of darkness.

He now lived every day with the forces of darkness that she had spoken about. They no longer left and came back; they appeared to have taken up residence and he had no control over them. They caused him to shout at the slaves and order whippings for the smallest infraction. He seemed to have lost himself and what was even more frightening was the fact that he had no sense of guilt or shame any longer. Grace seemed to have been his saving grace (the side of his mouth flicked up at the pun) and now that he no longer saw her it seemed as if all the light in his life had been snuffed out, leaving him in total darkness.

He wondered if they would survive the hurricane. A part of him almost wished that it would take his life so that he would be out of the hell called Jamaica. But then, if the Bible was to be believed, based on how he had lived his life so far, he would simply be exchanging one hell for another.

❖

The sky had turned black within an hour of sending the slaves to harvest what they could. They had come back in with a few sacks as it soon became too dark to see properly. Another gang was working to secure the main house and the outbuildings as best as they could. Whereas before there was not a gust of wind to stir the leaves, now it began to pick up, causing the branches to dip and sway together in a teasing dance.

When the rain changed from a light drizzle to a serious downpour, he called a halt to the boarding up of the windows and shut himself in the main house. Betsy, the other house slaves and Susie, who had taken the place of Bella, settled themselves on pallets to one side of the hallway. Since there were no windows in the hallway they would be safer.

Susie looked terrified and tried to follow William to his room until he barked at her to go with the other slaves. Although she was not as appealing as Bella, she served her purpose and she obeyed his orders without question. However, he had other things on his mind tonight, like what he would do if the house lost its roof or if one of the nearby trees fell down and crashed into the house. He would not borrow trouble. After all, if it was true that the devil looked after his own, he and Marsh should be very safe.

The wind began to howl as it forced its way through small cracks in the house and under the doors. He could hear the branches of the trees lashing against each other with the force of the wind. As the wind increased to a seemingly impossible speed, branches broke under its force and became dangerous flying objects.

Lightning flashed, forcing its way through the spaces in the boards that had hurriedly been hammered into place to cover the windows. A few seconds later thunder roared in the distance, promising that when it grew closer it would shake the house.

William was restless. As much as he wanted to, he could not lie down and sleep until the hurricane passed, so he remained fully clothed and alert in case he had to deal with any damage to the house. He prowled about the rooms with a lantern, checking to see how the windows were faring under the abuse of branches that had broken off and anything that had not been secured. He almost stumbled upon one of the slaves as he turned into the hallway where they were huddled together on their pallets. As he lifted the lantern to throw the light further, he saw Susie curled into a ball against the wall between Betsy and an older slave, whimpering every time the thunder roared.

The sound of glass shattering from the direction of his office caused everyone to jump and sent him hurrying down the hallway, dreading what he would find. He threw open the door just as lightning lit the room, revealing pieces of glass strewn across the floor in front of one of the windows. The tell-tale sign of the boards, which had been hastily affixed across the window, hanging by a few nails needed no explanation. Wind was now howling through the broken glass and forcing the rain inside, wetting everything in its path. William's gaze swept the room frantically looking for something to cover the opening, without luck. Making sure that he swept everything from the top of his desk into its drawers, he left the room, pulling the door closed. He could do nothing more until there was a break in the hurricane.

As he pulled the door closed, he turned to find Betsy behind him.

"Master William, what happen?"

"One of the windows broke. I can't do anything about it now. I'm going upstairs to check on the rooms."

"Master William, this like it worse than the last hurricane. You think the roof could blow off the house?" Betsy asked worriedly, voicing his worst fear.

"I doubt that, Betsy. I'm sure that the house was built strong enough to withstand a hurricane."

The words had hardly escaped his lips when a terrible, wrenching noise from above them made a liar out of him. William raced to the stairs, taking care not to drop the lantern. Betsy was on his heels with the other slaves swarming around the bottom of the stairs like disturbed bees. All eyes were focused upwards as if they would be able to see what caused the disruption from there.

William wasn't sure which direction to head in until another tearing sound guided him to the room that he had taken over as his. It was in one corner of the house and as he cautiously pushed the door, he felt a force pushing it back causing him to lean his weight against it to open it. Lifting the light towards the roof, his eyes widened in horror to see the roof being peeled back like the skin off a mango.

Wind and rain poured through the widening gap. In a few minutes the whole room would be completely open to the fury of the hurricane. He dared not advance any further, not that there was anything he could do except look on helplessly. Just as he moved to close the door, a particularly violent gust of wind threw something against the house and the window beside his bed flew in under the pressure, revealing a large tree, which crashed onto his bed creating a gaping hole in the wall. It was then that he began to petition heaven for divine intervention.

Chapter 7

Next Day
Friendly Hall Plantation

The gentling of the wind brought with it an easing of the tension in the house. The hurricane had lashed the plantation for hours, there had been stillness for fifteen minutes as the eye passed over, and then the wind and rain had started up again for several more hours, this time from the opposite direction. To Grace it had felt like the longest hours of her life. Every branch and piece of flying debris that hit the house sent shivers of fear into its occupants, causing prayers and petitions to go up to the heavens.

She had never liked thunder, not that she knew anyone who did, but the thunder that accompanied the hurricane was unlike any she had ever heard. When it was right over the house it literally shook the roof, causing her to cover her ears in terror. At one point her father sat on the sofa hugging her to his side to give her comfort as he had when she was a child.

How the children managed to sleep through the storm she did not know, but she was glad that they did while the adults kept vigil, too terrified to join them in slumber. During the most violent part of the hurricane, Grace's father gathered them into the sitting room and shared the story of Noah in the ark. They were greatly comforted to think that in the same way God kept Noah and his family safe in the ark during the flood, he would take care of them in the hurricane. Towards the early hours of the morning, the strong gusts of wind gave way to the gentler breezes that they were now experiencing, signalling that the hurricane was over.

"I think it is finally over, thank the Lord," her father said, glancing at her as she joined him at one of the windows in the sitting room. They peered through the gaps that were not covered by boards and were greeted by the sight of the yard littered with all kinds of debris. There were even a few dead chickens that must have been blown there by the wind. Most of their plants and trees had been uprooted and taken by the wind, leaving empty holes in the earth that were now filled with leaves and grass.

"Amen to that," agreed Grace. "That was the most terrifying experience of my life."

"But God brought us through."

"He did promise us that he would command his angels concerning us to guard us in all our ways."

"Yes, he did." Her father moved away from the window to shrug into his jacket which he had thrown over the arm of the sofa. Grace watched his movement absently, blushing as she remembered how William had pinned her against the same sofa. She hoped he had survived the hurricane. Despite how contemptible he was, she didn't wish him dead, especially not before he had time to change his ways. After all, nothing was too difficult for God, not even freeing William from his demons.

"Are you going outside?"

"Yes. It looks like the worst has passed. It is a miracle that our house has not been damaged, at least not that we can see. You stay inside until I let you know when it is safe to come out."

"Be careful, Father. And put on your hat before you go out. It is still drizzling a little bit."

"That I will, dear," he assured her as he dropped a kiss on her cheek before heading for the door. Grace was a good daughter; she looked after him and the household well. She would make some man a fine wife. He hoped that he lived to see her married to a good man and give him some grandchildren before he went home to be with the Lord.

"Do you think that Westhall fared as well as we?" Grace asked concernedly.

"I don't know, but I certainly hope so. As soon as I assess our damage, I will send Moses over to see."

George turned away to open the front door, hiding the concern in his eyes that the first thought on Grace's mind had been of Westhall Plantation and William Edwards. That was not the man he had in mind when he thought about a good husband for Grace. He admitted that he may have at first but not now, after what he knew of the man.

The plantation was a disaster, but it still fared better than he had expected. While part of the roof of the barn had blown off and the slave huts were totally destroyed, the main house was virtually unscathed. The same could not be said of the yard, for the smaller trees had been torn up from the roots

Free at Last

and those that managed to withstand the fierce wind had nary a branch or leaf to show. The canes in the distance were flattened and where the plantain and bananas used to be, the patches were empty.

George looked at the devastation in shock. This was even worse than the one they had experienced in '90 where the eastern part of the country had been hardest hit. Still, he was grateful that no lives had been lost and that there was not worse damage to the buildings. That could only be because of the grace of God. But, knowing the repairs that would have to be made to bring the plantation back to order and the money that he would have to invest, he felt drained. He did not know if he had the strength or the will to start over again. Maybe now was the best time to go back to England. But what would he do with the plantation? Who would want to buy it now? Maybe he could sell it to Westhall so that he could expand. He would no doubt lose money on the sale and while there were more important things in life than money he had to look out for Grace's future as well. He felt as if he was carrying a great weight on his shoulders.

❖

William was glad to ride away from the devastation at Westhall, at least for a short while. Once the rain had held up sufficiently he ventured out of the house to be greeted with a scene that surely gave a picture of what hell looked like. The roof of the main house had been nearly blown off and the walls of the room he had slept in had collapsed. Furniture has been tossed around like toys by the vicious wind and bits of splintered wood lay strewn around. They had been relatively safe downstairs.

Some of the slaves had not been so fortunate as one of the outbuildings had collapsed, killing five slaves and injuring others. Their huts, which were made of wattle and daub, had been completely demolished and lifted by the wind and deposited miles away, leaving the slave yard as bare as if nothing had ever been there.

Worst of all was the storeroom where they had kept the food that had been hastily harvested. It had been blown down and most of the crops were either crushed under the weight of the stones or had been blown away by the wind. He did not know how all of them would be fed in the next few weeks.

Marsh had survived the hurricane since the house that was once William's seemed to be surprisingly sturdy and was also in a more sheltered area. William left him to arrange for the burial of the slaves and the initial tidying up, saying that he was going to see how the Fullers had survived.

He hoped all was well with them. After the death and destruction at Westhall, he needed some light and hope as he felt that he didn't even know how to start over. Somehow, he knew that he would find them in Grace and God knew he desperately needed to see her now.

The ride to Friendly Hall took twice as long as usual since the road was littered with fallen trees, dead animals and parts of houses and other buildings that had blown from distant places. He could hardly recognise the route he had taken to the plantation only months before. Walking his horse slowly, turning it this way and that to avoid branches and other obstructions, he couldn't help but wonder if this was not indeed the judgement of God as it was said he had judged Port Royal. But if that was so, Grace and her father would also have been affected and where was the justice in that. He urged his horse to walk a little faster as his anxiousness to see her increased.

The first site of the plantation, with the house still standing, gave him his first feeling of hope since he had left Westhall. Most of their trees and plants had suffered the same fate as his but the plantation looked to be in a better position to be restored to normal more quickly than Westhall was. The yard was busy with slaves dragging debris and branches to one pile and doing their best to clear the grounds around the house.

As he approached the house, the front door was flung open and Grace hurried out, followed a few seconds later by her father. He wondered if they had seen him approaching, in which case he was encouraged by the urgency with which she had rushed out to greet him.

She was wearing a house dress that had seen not only better days, but better years by the looks of it. Her long hair was bound in an untidy bun at the back of her head but a few wilful strands escaped and hung down one shoulder. There was a smudge of dirt on her cheek and sweat on her brow as if she had been working. To William she had never looked more beautiful.

"George, Grace, I am very glad to see that you survived this terrible hurricane," he greeted them as he dismounted.

Grace glanced over her shoulder, surprised that her father was so close behind her. Her eyes drank in William's face, noting the dark circles under his eyes and the tiredness that made his lids heavy. He looked defeated, which was so unlike William that she was moved by compassion. She was surprised at how relieved she was to see him unhurt.

"Yes, we did, thanks to the good Lord," her father said, coming to stand beside her. "How are things at Westhall?"

"Fairly bad. We lost five slaves and there is a lot of damage to the main house and some of the outbuildings. It will take a considerable investment of time and money to get the plantation up and running again. I will have to send a letter to Peter Westhall as soon as possible to let him know what has happened."

"I'm so sorry to hear that," Grace sympathised, meeting his eyes.

William basked in the comfort she offered, happy that the hurricane had laid to rest the contempt she felt for him, even if only temporarily.

"How was it for you?" he asked with his eyes on Grace. Grace noticed that for once there was no desire in his gaze and no flirtation, just a gentle regard, causing her heart to soften towards him.

"It was terrifying, especially as I hate thunder. I never want to experience another hurricane again."

"I know what you mean. You will be happy to hear that even I was moved to pray."

The smile that lit Grace's face at his teasing confession brought light to his day.

"We will make a believer out of you yet," she promised.

"Yes, well, I have to get back to Westhall. I just wanted to make sure that you were all right. George, if you need any help send one of your men over and let me know. We have a lot of rebuilding to do ourselves, but we have a good number of slaves and can spare some."

"Thank you, William. I appreciate the offer, but we should be fine, as we haven't sustained too much damage. To tell the truth, the hurricane has made me think that this might be a good time to start seriously planning our return to England," George announced. "I do not feel that I have the will to start over."

Grace looked at him quickly in surprise. This was news to her and for some reason, in spite of saying that she never wanted to experience another hurricane, she was not quite ready to leave Jamaica.

❈

Bella was hovering by the front door when Grace came in. Her face, which in the last few months had been free of worry, was now wrinkled with concern. It did not take Grace much effort to work out that it was because she had seen her talking to William Edwards.

"Miss Grace, what Master Edwards want? He come for me?"

"Of course not, Bella. I have explained to you that my father bought you so you are no longer owned by Westhall Plantation so he cannot take you back. He came to see how we had fared in the hurricane."

"What?" Bella looked unconvinced. She had experienced the wrath of William Edwards first hand so she was not quick to believe that he was there to ask how they had fared. Grace could not really blame her, truth be told, for if she had not seen his concern herself she, too, would be unconvinced.

"Westhall had a lot of damage and a few of the slaves were killed."

"Oh dear! I wonder who dem is. I hope none of them was Susie," she worried. "Marsh ain' one of the people that get kill?" she asked hopefully.

"Bella. We should not wish bad things for people, even if they deserve it."

"Miss Grace, Master William evil and Marsh evil. I don' believe that he any different even if he come to see how you fare."

"Bella, people can change."

"Not he. He is the devil. I will always hate he for beating me and scarring up my back. And now he come over here actin' like he good to fool you. That is only for now. Watch and see that he gine soon be back to hi'self and sharing licks again 'til he hand tired."

"I hope not, Bella."

Grace really hoped that William had changed. He had seemed so genuine and concerned about them, about her, and there had been no sign of the flirtatious man that she had seen before. Granted, they had all been through a traumatic experience which was bound to change them. Surely having survived the hurricane and even prayed through it, if he was to be believed, William would not revert to his old ways. Would he?

Chapter 8

October 2, 1697
Westhall Plantation

> Dear Peter,
>
> I have only now had the opportunity to sit down and write to you of the events of five days past as I have been working day and night before falling into my bed in utter exhaustion. By the time you get this letter you may have heard of the devastating hurricane that hit the island on the night of September 27th. I have never seen the likes of it before as we have not had a hurricane in Barbados in my lifetime.
>
> I do not mind telling you that it was a terrifying experience for man, woman and beast alike. Westhall sustained severe damage, with the main house losing part of its roof. The walls of the room that I slept in also collapsed after a tree fell through one of the windows, causing considerable damage and giving the wind an opening to complete the rest. I am grateful that I was unable to sleep and was checking on the house or I would have been lying in my bed and therefore would not be here today.

Five slaves lost their lives and several others were injured when one of the outbuildings that they were sheltering in collapsed. Surprisingly the overseer's and manager's houses were largely intact and needed only a few minor repairs which have already been done. The slave village is entirely gone so some of the slaves are living in the overseer's house while others are having to sleep in makeshift huts, while the house slaves are in the main house. It is fortunate that you and Julia are not here. I have Marsh overseeing the clearing of debris and restoring of things to order as far as is possible given that we lack material.

Of great concern to me is our lack of food. We had managed to harvest some provisions before the hurricane hit, but a substantial amount of it was destroyed when the storehouse collapsed. We have salvaged as much as we could, but based on what we had in store before and the little that is left of what we harvested, we will have to start rationing food soon. I will go to Black River in a week or so to see what I can purchase, but the roads are currently impassable and it will take some time to clear them.

The cost to restore the plantation to its former state will be significant as I will need to acquire materials to fix the main buildings and for the slaves to reconstruct their huts. I do not know yet how the rest of the country has fared, as the west seems to have borne the brunt of the hurricane, so we may have to get goods from as far as Kingston and have

> *them shipped here to Westhall. In the meantime, we will continue to do our best under the circumstances. Please write to me as soon as possible and let me know how you will arrange the money to rebuild. I still have a fair amount here to cover our immediate needs.*
>
> *Your faithful servant*
> *William Edwards*

William sealed the letter with a bit of wax, wrote the address that Peter Westhall had given him and set it aside to be mailed as soon as he could arrange it.

❖

October 10, 1697

> *I have hardly had time to write anything recently. A hurricane struck the island on September 27th and ever since then I have been working day and night trying to restore the plantation to some sort of order. However, we are running low on food and three days ago I started to ration it. If I don't we will soon starve. Never in my life have I had to eat less food than I wanted!*
>
> *Things have gotten very bad and tempers are short. The slaves are having to sleep wherever they can as their huts were destroyed, so between the*

sleeping conditions, the hard work and the lack of food, they are becoming rebellious and harder to control. Yesterday I caught Mingo stealing a yam and some salt fish so I ordered 100 lashes for him. I can tell that the other slaves would have liked nothing more than to cut my throat, but I cannot allow stealing food to go unpunished when we are all on the brink of starvation.

Tomorrow I have purposed to take the cart and one of the slaves and go to Black River to buy some provisions there. One of the neighbouring planters passed by only yesterday and told me that he had just come from there and there is food to be bought as ships from America and Hispaniola started bringing supplies there as soon as they heard that the hurricane had hit Jamaica. I will stop at the Fullers and see if they have heard that or if they need anything, although they seem to have survived very well.

I have not seen Grace since the day after the hurricane when I visited to see how they had fared. She had looked glad to see me and even smiled when I told her that the hurricane had driven me to pray. Even now I can picture the curving of her lips as she smiled. Her smile brightened my day which, to that point, had been very dark as I realised the extent of the damage to the plantation. I can only hope that she is softening towards me.

She would be happy to know that I have not bedded Susie or any of the other slaves since the hurricane. Nearly two weeks! The truth of the matter is that I have been too tired to even entertain such a thought. Of course she does not have to know that.

I got Betsy to pack a few clothes for me because I expect to be gone for about a week and I will leave as soon as the sun rises tomorrow. Marsh will be happy to be in charge once again and I am sure that he will be well able to keep the slaves in line with his own particular form of brutality. Despite what Grace thinks of me, I am not half the monster that Marsh is for, though I have ordered whippings, I have never mutilated a slave.

❈

Next Day

The day dawned clear and bright. Looking at the sky no one would imagine that is was covered with heavy black clouds that released inches of rain on the island just two weeks earlier. William climbed up on the bench of the cart, placed the pistol that he had taken from the office under the seat and gestured to Cudjoe to get the horses moving. He did not know if he considered him to be one of the more trustworthy slaves, but he preferred to have the big strapping slave at his side if they ran into trouble on the way and to load the provisions they were going to buy.

He was a man of few words which was fine with William because he had no desire to carry on a conversation, far less with a slave. He used the opportunity to enjoy the quiet of the morning, broken only by the sound of the horses' hooves on the road and the birds which had returned to the area and were now calling to each other.

He was surprised at how fast the grass and shrubs that had been uprooted were being replaced by new plants as nature began to repair the same land that it had damaged with the fury of the hurricane. The day was still cool and unspoiled, but the sun would soon be climbing in the sky and it would get uncomfortably hot. He almost envied Cudjoe in his thin shirt and calf-length pants.

As they drew alongside the gully halfway between Westhall and Friendly Hall William felt the hairs on the back of his neck raise. He did not know what caused the strange sensation, but he tensed and looked around him. The sudden flight of a flock of birds was followed by a high-pitched warble which seemed out of place since the birds had taken flight shortly before. The dream he had had on the way to Black River flashed across his mind, making him shiver.

"Anything feel strange to you?" he asked Cudjoe, still looking around.

"Strange, Massa? Wha' you mean?"

What was strange to William was that Cudjoe had called him 'Massa' since he never addressed either him or Marsh that way. Looking at him out of the corner of his eye, William could swear that he saw the glimmer of a smile on his face. That alone caused his heartbeat to begin to accelerate and the thought of an ambush flashed across his mind. Could he have somehow connected with the maroons? He had been told that they did not frequent this area, but now that the hurricane had brought hardship to everyone, had they begun to move into new territory?

The amount of money he carried in his jacket made him uneasy and he instinctively patted the place where it was pressing against his side. He started to reach for the pistol that he had placed under the bench in case of trouble, when Cudjoe stayed his hand.

"Don't worry with that, Massa." Rather than reassure him, the words gave him cause to worry especially since Cudjoe stopped him from reaching for his pistol. William shook his hand off.

"What do you mean, don't worry with that? I sense danger."

Cudjoe pulled on the reins to stop the horses and replied, "You right massa, but not fo' me." With that he dropped the reins and grabbed the pistol from under the seat. William froze, expecting to feel a bullet pierce his chest, but instead the slave jumped down and disappeared into the bushes, leaving him in stunned disbelief.

Before William could grab the reins, from the corner of his eye he saw three figures rush from the bushes that Cudjoe had disappeared into. Fear made his hands clumsy and he fumbled with the reins, dropping them twice before he could pick them up. That was enough time for the first man to reach the cart and pull him from the bench.

William hit the ground with enough force to jar his shoulder from the socket and knock the breath out of him. Before he had time to struggle to his feet, a blow across his back with what felt like a limb flattened him to the ground. Pain exploded in his ribs as the limb slammed into his side causing him to arch in pain. He curled himself into a foetal position instinctively to protect his internal organs, only for the piece of wood to smash down on his exposed leg. He did not know if the cracking sound he heard was from the wood breaking or his leg. All he knew was pain. It forced a shout from his mouth.

A blindfold was roughly tied around his eyes and a gag covered his mouth, terrifying him because he was unable to see what his captors would do next. Would they kill him? Was this how he was going to die? Why would they blindfold him if they were going to kill him? That gave him some hope despite the pain that wracked his body, but the hope soon died as his jacket was jerked from his shoulders, causing him to shout in agony against the gag as his bruised ribs and shoulder were jarred. The back of his shirt was ripped open and he was forced face down into the mud.

There was a terrifying silence as he waited to discover what his captors would do next. The sound that broke the silence was chillingly familiar to him. It was the sound of a whip whistling through the air, but this time he was not the one wielding it. In the few seconds that it took for him to register what it was, the sting of leather, like a thousand ants, landed across his back leaving a gash. His back arched instinctively and he sought to crawl away, but a foot was planted on each of his hands, holding him in place. It was only the gag that prevented his shout from echoing among the trees as the whip fell again. He did not know how many times the leather came down across his back for he passed out after twenty lashes.

❈

The heat of the sun on his bloodied back and the buzzing of flies roused William out of his blessed state of unconsciousness. He could not name a part of his body that was not in excruciating pain except for his face, for they had not touched his face for some reason. Then it dawned on him through the haze of agony that they had not wanted him to see their faces so they were possibly men that he would know. Could they have been his men? Did Cudjoe plan the ambush with them? He realised that his hands were not bound so he could remove his blindfold and the gag, if he was able to move his hands.

Gingerly testing the right one, he froze with the pain and figured that it must be broken or the shoulder dislocated. He inched the left one towards his face. Every movement shot pain through his body and he struggled not to empty his stomach with the gag still in his mouth as he would strangle on his own vomit. Manoeuvring his hand to remove the gag from his mouth caused indescribable agony to his back and forced a hiss of pain from his mouth. He pulled the blindfold over his head and squinted in the bright sunlight. When his eyes adjusted to the light he looked around. From what he could see, he was in the grass on one side of the road and there was no sign of his horses or the cart.

The brightness of the sun caused him to close his eyes again and he lay quietly waiting for his heart to stop racing from the effort it had taken to free himself from the gag and blindfold. His tongue felt swollen in his mouth and all he could think about was water; even a drop would do. He was powerless to chase the flies that he could hear buzzing around his back and sipping on the blood that had not dried as yet. As he lay in the dirt under the tortuous sun, William prayed, not for his life to be spared, but for death to take him.

He didn't know how long he had lain there drifting in and out of consciousness when the sound of a horse approaching chased away thoughts of death and raised his hopes of being rescued. He forced himself to lift his head slightly. Cracking an eye open, he saw a white man riding towards him. He did not recognise him so he may have been an overseer from another plantation. Feebly raising a hand, he tried to call for help, but no sound came from his parched throat. He did not know if the man saw him or not, but he passed by on the other side of the road leaving William once again in despair.

Sometime later, he had no idea how long or short it was, the sound of gravel being crushed under someone's feet gave him renewed hope. By this time, he was too weak to even raise a hand to attract their attention. Although the footsteps slowed they did not stop. William knew that if he did not get help soon he would die on the side of the road in Jamaica. Tears of pain and regret stung his eyes, but did not even ease his thirst by trickling down to his mouth. It was no less than he deserved.

❖

Sammy raced into the yard of Friendly Hall Plantation shouting, "Murder! Murder! A white man dead up the road."

The first person he ran into was Bella who was coming around the side of the house.

"Wha' that you saying, Sammy?"

"They got a white man by the side of the road not too far from here. I couldn' see he face good but he back look like somebody beat he wid a whip and left he to dead."

"I gine get Moses to carry me in the cart to see. Come so you could show we where he is. You sure he dead?"

"I ain' stop to look but he didn' moving. He near the gully between here and Westhall."

Within minutes, Bella, Sammy and Moses were on their way with Bella sitting in the back of the cart. As they got near to the gully Bella began to get frightened and wished she had not come with the men as she did not want to see a dead man.

"We shoulda tell Miss Grace or Master George," Moses said.

"Master George ain' feeling so good today and Miss Grace looking after he," Bella told him. "I hope he ain' dead," she added fearfully, referring to the man that Sammy had seen.

"I hope so too," Moses agreed.

"Look, that is he on the side of the road over there." Sammy pointed to what looked like a lump from there.

Guiding the cart nearer, Moses handed Sammy the reins and jumped down to look. He could see that it was indeed a white man whose back was a mass of bloody, torn skin that looked as if someone had whipped him. His hair was dark and tied back with a leather thong. As he walked slowly around the body to see the face, he jumped back, causing Bella and Sammy to jump too.

"Who it is, Moses?" she asked from the safety of the cart.

He looked up and met her eyes.

"It is Master Edwards from Westhall." Bella gasped in horror.

"Master Edwards? He- he still alive?"

Moses bent down and saw the faint movement of his back. "Yes!"

"Lift he up and put he in the cart on he belly," she instructed.

"He shoulder look funny, though, like if it brek or out of place. I hope he don' wake up when I moving he because this gine hurt he bad. Sammy, come and help lift he feet."

Moses and Sammy struggled to lift the unconscious body as carefully as they could while Bella made room so that they could put him in the cart on his belly. Thankfully he remained unconscious. In a few minutes Moses had turned the cart around and was heading back to Friendly Hall. Bella kept looking at her former master as if she could not believe it was him lying bleeding beside her in the back of the cart.

"I wonder who do this to he?" she whispered, as if fearing she would wake him up.

"You ain' glad after wha' he do to you?" Moses asked, testing her.

Bella was silent for a few minutes before she answered quietly with her voice full of compassion.

"No. I feel sorry for he."

Moses smiled slightly. Miss Grace's teachings were bearing fruit.

Chapter 9

"Miss Grace! Miss Grace!" Bella shouted, frantically running into the house as soon as Moses had pulled the cart up to the front door.

"Bella! What is it?" Grace met her at the bottom of the stairs where she had run from her father's room. He had not been feeling well and she hoped it was not another malaria attack coming on.

"It is Master Edwards," she panted.

"What about him?" Grace's voice rose in anger, wondering what he had done now.

"He half dead in the back of the cart."

"What? Bella, you're not making any sense," she said, already hastening to the front door. Bella chased after her.

"Sammy find he beside the road. It look like somebody beat he and left he for dead."

Grace felt the blood drain from her face and she had to hold firmly to the front door that she had just pulled open. Steadying herself until the faintness passed, she cautiously approached the back of the cart where Moses and Sammy were standing as if she was afraid of what she would find.

The sight of William's lacerated back and his shoulder twisted in an unnatural way caused her to gasp and cover her mouth with her hand. She forcibly swallowed the vomit that rose in her throat and pulled herself together.

"Where to put he, Miss Grace?" Moses' question shook her out of her frozen state and stirred her to action.

"Bring him to the sitting room and put him on the floor. We can take him upstairs later. Bella, go and get a blanket quick and put it on the floor."

Bella rushed off to find a blanket, almost bumping into Liza and the other house slaves who had come running when they heard the commotion and were gathered around the door.

With Moses carefully lifting William's shoulders and Sammy carrying his legs, they mounted the few stairs to the front door and inched their way to the sitting room, trying to keep from bouncing him too much.

Grace followed them, issuing instructions as she went.

"Liza, I need some water that has been boiled and cooled down and some clean cloths. Send somebody to see if they can find any aloe in the yard if the hurricane didn't uproot all. And steep some willow bark in hot water. He will need it for the pain."

As the men carefully placed William on the floor on the blanket that Bella had spread out, George staggered into the room looking pale.

"Bella told me that William has been beaten!"

"Father, you should not be out of bed!"

"I am all right, Grace. His shoulder looks to be dislocated."

"Yes," she agreed, assessing it. "We will have to set it first."

"It is a good thing we had to do this for Little Jack last year. Moses, you will have to do it." George instructed him what to do and he and Sammy held William up while Moses pushed his shoulder back into the socket.

William's scream of agony caused them all to jump and his eyes flew open as the pain jerked him out of consciousness. His haunted, pain-filled eyes scanned the faces around him wildly, as if he thought he was still being attacked, before settling on Grace's. The look of relief that filled his eyes before they drifted closed again touched a place in Grace's heart.

"Lay him on his stomach now. I need to clean his back off and put some aloe on it. Then I'll have to try to get some willow bark tea in him."

"You want anythin' else, Miss Grace," Moses asked.

"Yes, get a knife and cut off the rest of his shirt so that I can get at his back properly. Father, you should go back to bed. Bella and I can deal with this. I will let you know how he is later."

Her father nodded, leaving the room unsteadily. Grace knew that he still was not feeling well, despite what he had said. Now she had not one, but two patients on her hands.

Within minutes Moses had come back with a knife and removed the tattered remains of the bloodstained shirt, leaving William's back exposed for Grace's ministrations. Grace's stomach heaved at the sight of his mutilated back although she was not generally squeamish.

"I wonder who did this?" she mused, as she waited for Liza to bring in the water and cloths.

"Somebody with a whip," Bella offered.

"Yes, I can see that, Bella. Did Sammy see anything or anybody?"

"I didn' ask he, Miss Grace, but when we get there we ain' see no horse or cart or nothing. I don't know if Master William was walking or if somebody t'ief he horse. Now I study it, he didn' have on no jacket or hat neither, so he like he get rob."

Liza came in with the water and cloths and put them next to Grace.

"The willow bark steeping, Miss Grace."

"Thanks, Liza. Bring it in when it is ready with a spoon. We will have to try and get some in him to help with the pain and to stave off any fever in case his back gets infected. Did you get any aloe?"

"Janey ain' come back in yet. I goin' and look for some myself."

Grace knelt next to William and soaked a piece of clean cloth in the water. She squeezed out some of it, leaving it wet enough that she could moisten the dried blood and remove the bits of dirt and grass that had become embedded in the flesh. She tried to be as gentle as possible, but William groaned and stirred. Bella winced next to her, knowing first-hand what pain he was in.

"I am sorry, William, but I cannot help it. I need to get the dirt out of the cuts before I put on the aloe so that they don't get infected," she whispered in his ear.

He moved his head faintly in acknowledgement and whispered, "Water."

"Oh, of course! I should have thought of that. Bella, go and get a cup of water for me please."

"Yes, Miss Grace."

William felt movement next to him as Bella got up to go. The pain in his back reminded him that he had inflicted a similar punishment on her. How she must be enjoying seeing him suffering. Anger stirred in him at Cudjoe's deception and the memory of all that had been done to him, making him tense up.

"Relax, William, or you will hurt your back more," Grace advised him, feeling his tension. "Your shoulder was dislocated as well but Moses set it back in place. They did not touch your face at all so you are still quite passable," she teased him, talking to distract him from the pain she was no doubt causing.

Bella came back with a cup of water and a spoon that she had thought to bring. Grace put down the cloth and took them from her.

"Can you turn on your left side a little?" she asked William. "I need to feed you the water."

He tried to inch over on one side, only to hiss in pain and drop back on him tummy.

"Is something else hurting? Grace asked worriedly.

"Ribs," he whispered. "Leg."

"Oh dear. Bella, come around to this side and lift his head a little so that I can try to get some water into his mouth."

Some of the water trickled down William's chin, but they managed to get a few spoonfuls in his mouth, earning a small sigh of gratitude from him.

"Here, Miss Grace, we manage' to find a few aloe plants and I cut them open and tek out the inside. I goin' bring the tea now."

"Thank you, Liza," Grace said, taking the bowl with the slimy mixture from her. "I will smear this aloe on your back as gently as possible," she told William. "It will help heal the cuts and keep away infection."

"All right," William murmured and braced himself.

"It goin' make the cuts feel better," Bella advised.

Grace applied the aloe as quickly and carefully as she could before turning her attention to his other injuries. She gently prodded his ribs and was rewarded by a tortured groan.

"I pray that your ribs are bruised and not broken because if they are broken they should be wrapped up tightly, but I cannot do that because of your back." Grace was distressed, but tried to hide it from William, for she knew that a broken rib could puncture his lungs.

"Which leg is hurting?"

"Left."

The time for modesty was long past so Grace carefully pushed the leg of his pants up and found a huge black and blue bruise on the side of his leg and his calf. She smeared some aloe on it and made a bandage with another of the clean cloths and wrapped his leg tightly, hoping that the bone wasn't broken. By that time Liza had come back with the tea.

"William, I need you to drink some of this willow bark tea. It will help ease the pain. Bella, help me again."

William was taken aback that Bella was helping Grace to care for him. From the way Grace treated her slaves he knew that she would not force her to help if she refused and Bella had good reason for not wanting to help him. After drinking about half the cup of tea, William indicated that he had had enough.

He was exhausted and could feel himself sinking into oblivion once more. He closed his eyes, silently thanking God for sparing his life and for somehow delivering him to Grace's house. He would ask how he got here later.

❊

Next Day

William woke up with a start. He had been dreaming of being beaten by four men who had rolled him into the gully after they had finished with him. The sensation of falling had woken him up before he hit the bottom and he was relieved to find himself lying on his belly in a soft bed. His back was one mass of throbbing pain and now he also had an ache in his lower back which was probably caused by sleeping in the same position for several hours.

Knowing that any movement would be agonising, but unable to stay on his stomach any longer, he carefully levered himself up with his good arm and eased onto his side. He was surprised at how little strength he had in his arm and wondered how much blood he had lost.

He realised that he was shirtless since his shirt had been ruined and lifting the sheet that covered him from the waist down, he saw that he was still wearing the same pants, but his boots had been removed.

The bed he was lying on was very comfortable and now that he was on his side, he could see a part of the room as well. There was a small table next to the bed with a book on top that looked like a Bible. Knowing the Fullers, he would not be surprised. A sizeable window faced the bed, letting in a nice breeze and, looking behind him, he saw another window. A wash stand with a pitcher and bowl stood to one side of the window with the door towards the foot of the bed. The room was tidy but sparse so he assumed that it was the guest room.

His stomach growled, making him wonder how long he had slept. He was surprised that he did not need to use the chamber pot by now but he had not had very much to drink at all the day before. Tired of lying down, he tried to ease his feet off the bed so that he could at least sit up. He succeeded, but the movement jolted his ribs, causing him to gasp and hold his hand against them.

Getting up was obviously not going to be an easy task, but his dry mouth drove him to try and find a drink of water. Judging the distance to the door, he wondered if he had the strength to make it without falling over. He was still eyeing the door when it opened quietly and his eyes met with Bella's. Hers widened in shock to see him sitting up and she began to back out of the door as if she was afraid he would do her some sort of damage. Not that he was capable of doing anyone damage, even if he felt inclined to, which he did not.

"Bella!" he said, stopping her.

"Yes, Master William?" she answered fearfully.

"Uh, can you bring me a cup of water?" He hesitated over asking her for the water rather than telling her to bring it as he would normally do.

"Yes, Massa." She started to retreat again.

"And, Bella." She paused uncertainly in the doorway. "Thank you for helping Miss Grace tend to me." Her eyes widened and she nodded uncertainly before pulling the door close behind her.

William thought of sitting back against the bed but the tightness across his back reminded him of the freshness of his injuries. He wondered how long they would take to heal. Their slaves were expected to be back in the fields the day after a whipping. He stirred uncomfortably.

His thoughts swung back to Bella and the way he had beat her so unmercifully and something akin to pain gripped his heart. He did not know if he had received as many stripes as he had given her, but if her back had pained her half as much as his was paining him, he did not know how she could ever forgive him for what he had done. He was at a loss as to how she could even find it in her heart to help him. That did not make any kind of sense to him.

The door opened again and William looked around, expecting to see Bella with the water, but instead Grace entered, leaving the door open. She seemed to be avoiding looking at his bare chest as she approached the bed to give him the water, so he obligingly pulled the sheet up under his arms, which still left his shoulders bare.

"Bella told me that you had woken up. You slept for a whole day."

"A whole day?" he repeated in disbelief, taking the water with a word of thanks.

"Yes, indeed. How are you feeling?"

"Sore, aching and weak."

"I'm sure you are," she sympathised. Perching at the foot of the bed, she asked, "What happened?"

"I was on my way to Black River with one of my men driving the cart." He stopped suddenly remembering something. "Where is my cart and my jacket?"

"Bella said that they did not see anything when they found you. If you had the cart it must have been stolen, along with everything else. One of our slaves named Sammy was walking past and saw you. Apparently, he came running into the yard shouting 'Murder' and he took Bella and Moses to where he had seen you and they brought you here."

William closed his eyes. He was in pain on so many levels. There was the physical pain which was now compounded by the pain of the loss of the plantation's money and something that surprised him. It was the pain of guilt that Bella, of all people, had helped to bring him here.

"I have to get back to the plantation," he said frantically. "I was going to buy supplies and food because there is not enough food to last them more than a week. I had already started to ration it."

"You cannot go anywhere for a time," Grace admonished him. "I will talk to my father and see if he would be willing to send Moses, who is our most trusted slave, to buy the provisions you need. In the meantime, we can send a few things over as we have more than enough for ourselves."

"I would be forever in your debt. In truth, I am already in your debt."

"What happened to the slave who was driving you?" she asked, ignoring that.

"I know not. I started to feel uneasy as we approached the gully between our plantations and rightly so, for he stopped the cart when we drew near, grabbed the pistol that I had under the bench and took off into the woods."

"It is God's grace that he did not kill you," Grace said, horrified.

"Before I could grab the reins, three men appeared from the bush and approached the back of the cart. One dragged me to the ground, which is probably how I dislocated my shoulder, and they started to beat me. Then they blindfolded me and tied a rag across my mouth so that I could not shout. I will spare you the details of what followed."

"That must have been horrible!" Grace exclaimed. "The fact that you were blindfolded must have made it even worse. Maybe they thought you would have recognise them, or they did not want you to, if you ever saw them again."

"Yes, that is what I think as well. I am sure I will never see Cudjoe again. He must have joined the maroons by now."

"You are very fortunate not to have been killed or to have died from your wounds."

"You know they say that the devil looks after his own." His attempted humour failed to amuse Grace, as he should have known.

"William Edwards, you may have been used by the devil in the past, but you do not have to continue to live your life that way."

With that, she stood up and headed to the door.

"I will have some chicken soup sent up to you and I will be back later to tend to your back."

"Grace," his voice stopped her before she reached the threshold. She turned around to face him. "Thank you for saving my life," he said solemnly.

"You are not yet out of danger of succumbing to an infection," Grace reminded him and closed the door behind her.

Chapter 10

Grace expelled her breath as she walked down the corridor to her father's room. She had no right noticing the width of William's shoulders or the light dusting of hair on his chest although he had attempted to pull up the sheet, presumably to preserve her modesty. She should have asked him if he needed more willow bark tea for his pain, but she completely forgot. She hid her face in her hands as she stood outside her father's door. What manner of a caretaker was she to get so distracted that she was negligent about her patient's care? She would have to get one of the girls to take some for him shortly. She just needed to check in on her father.

"And how is my other patient doing?" she asked him, poking her head around the open door. He beckoned her to come in.

"I am fine, Grace. Time for me to get out of bed. Fortunately, it was not malaria, thank the good Lord, and whatever it was seems to have passed. Besides, I need to use the necessary."

"Oh, goodness!" Grace exclaimed, catching her father by surprise.

"What is it?"

"I forgot to ask William if he needed to relieve himself as well."

"Well, I am glad to hear that. A young lady like yourself should not be asking a gentleman such things." Grace rolled her eyes. "Get Sammy or Moses to see after his needs. And how is he faring? That is the first question I should have asked."

"He is still in pain, but he will survive, providing his cuts do not get infected. I hope his ribs are not broken because I cannot bandage them due to his back and he has a bad bruise on his leg."

"Sounds like he will need a while to recover."

"Yes and he will need some clothes because his seem to have been stolen and his shirt was completely ruined."

"Send Moses over to Westhall to tell them what happened and get his housekeeper to send some for him."

"Of course, I completely forgot to do that. I do not know what is going on with me," she chided herself.

"You are doing too many things. I am well so you may cease worrying about me. Look after William and see that he recovers soon."

"That reminds me, he was on his way to Black River to buy provisions, as they are running short. I told him that we could send over some to help out, but I would ask you if we could send Moses and another of the slaves to buy food for them. I am sure he will repay the money when he gets better."

"Yes, that would be the neighbourly thing to do. However, we should get Moses to take him back to Westhall before he leaves."

"No, Father," Grace said hurriedly. "We do not know if there is anyone there to care for him or if he will have sufficient food. He may even be in danger if he returns right now."

"Danger?"

"Yes. He told me that he was ambushed and his slave ran off and left him to be beaten. It was horrible. We do not know if slaves at Westhall were involved so we cannot return him there until he is fully recovered."

"Well, yes, that is true. Perhaps while he is here we can share the gospel with him," he added with a smile.

"Indeed. We have a captive audience so to speak, and since his room is right over our meeting place, he cannot help but hear the good news," Grace smiled in agreement.

❃

William was never so glad to bathe and change into clean clothes. Grace had sent her slave, Moses, to help him use the chamber pot before going over to Westhall to tell Marsh the news and get clothes from Betsy. There was money secreted away there, but he would never trust Marsh with it so he would arrange to pay George back later. When Moses brought back the clothes, he had helped him with a sponge bath since he was still weak and aching. It was rather humiliating, but he was so glad to be clean he endured it silently.

He had quietly thanked Moses, first for rescuing him and then for everything he had done since. He could not name one of his slaves who would have done what the slaves at Friendly Hall had done for him. No-one, save Susie, had apparently asked how he fared and, if he knew Marsh, he was sure he would have been happy to hear of his demise. Moses had said that all he asked him was if he knew what was to be done about getting provisions. William was not surprised. After all, he was not a master the likes of George Fuller.

A knock at the door announced Bella who came in bearing a bowl of steaming soup and a chunk of bread.

"Master William, Miss Grace say that you must be hungry."

"I certainly am. Thank you, Bella. Please put it here on the table." It was getting surprisingly easier to say 'please' and 'thank you' to the slaves.

As she put down the soup and turned to leave, William struggled with himself momentarily before he said: "Bella?" She turned around but did not make eye contact with him.

"Yes, Massa William?" She waited expectantly.

"I am very sorry for beating you as I did. After being beaten myself, I now realise that no-one should be whipped like that, especially not a woman. I am sorry," he repeated.

"All right, Master William. I could go now?"

"Yes, Bella."

As she left William picked up the spoon to eat, but he didn't feel as if he had done enough to communicate what he had wanted to say. Did Bella forgive him? Could he expect her to? He knew that he would never forgive the men who stripped and beat him until he was nearly dead. If he ever found out who they were, they would be dead men.

❧

After drinking the delicious chicken soup, with the yams and sweet potatoes in it, he used the bread to sop up the last of the liquid so that when the housekeeper, who said her name was Liza, came to get the bowl it looked as if it had been cleaned already.

"You eat that good, Master William," she commented. "You want some more?"

William was full from the first helping and was getting tired again, so he refused. He was a bit frustrated with how weak he still was and although he was looking forward to seeing Grace, he was not looking forward to her cleaning his back and putting fresh aloe on his cuts. He knew it was important to keep them from getting infected, but his back still pained him as did his ribs and his leg.

"Miss Grace say to tell you that she goin' come up as soon as she finish eatin'."

"All right. And Liza, can you ask Master George or Miss Grace for some paper and a quill and ink for me? I need to write a letter."

"Yes, Massa. I goin' bring them right back."

Within minutes, she was back with the promised writing material. She helped William to prop some pillows against the bedhead and carefully lie back so that he could write his letter. It was a little awkward since he had to keep reaching over to the bedside table to dip the quill in the ink, but being able to lay back, even though his back was not yet healed, was a great relief.

October 12, 1697
Friendly Hall Plantation

> *Dear Father*
>
> *You may be wondering why I am writing to you from a plantation other than Westhall. It is a long story and I do not rightly know where to start.*
>
> *I received your letter informing me about mother's passing in July, but I have to confess that I had no desire to reply. I have now come to terms with her death and I hope that the girls have as well. My main regret is that I did not spend enough time with her when I returned from England and before I had to leave for Jamaica.*
>
> *We had a hurricane about two weeks ago which devastated this part of the island. Westhall sustained considerable damage and we lost five slaves. I was on my way to a near-by town to buy supplies when I was ambushed and attacked by three men. They blindfolded me, beat me mercilessly and left me for dead.*
>
> *Fortunately, some slaves from Friendly Hall Plantation, which is the nearest plantation to Westhall, found me and brought me here and*

tended to me. I had met the owner, whose name is George Fuller, at the Westhalls' house. His wife died a few years ago and he has a daughter, Grace, who looks after the household. They are Quakers (I know your opinion of Quakers) but they are good people and have looked after me well. Grace would make any man a good wife as she is a gentle, caring person, though she can be roused to anger, which I have managed to do on several occasions. She is the first woman, who is not of ill-repute, that I have considered in terms of marriage. However, I am sure she would never entertain marriage to me, as she thinks I am of the devil. You may share her opinion.

Jamaica is a hard country. In the short time I have been here it has changed me and not for the better. Or perhaps it has only brought out more clearly what was already in me. The incident in which I was beaten and almost killed caused me to examine myself and I discovered that I am disgusted with the person that I have become. I do not think that I can remain in this country much longer and not completely lose my soul, assuming it is not already lost.

I will oversee the repairs to Westhall and give Peter Westhall until June next, or hopefully before, to find someone to take my place. If you are still opposed to me returning to Barbados, I will go to

America or perhaps to England and make a fresh start there.

I look forward to hearing from you soonest.

Your son
William

❈

George Fuller poked his head around the door to William's room as he had not seen him since the day before when he instructed Moses how to put his shoulder back in the socket. He was pleased to see him looking considerably better than he did the day before but, to tell the truth, he would be even happier when he was well enough to return to Westhall.

As far as he was concerned, he did not want Grace forming an attachment to him. As it was, she would not hear of sending him home. He had no idea of what William's intentions were towards Grace and even if they were honourable, William would have to be completely transformed to have a chance with his Grace. Still, he was a guest and he would treat him with the courtesy deserving of such.

"William, I am indeed glad to see you looking so much better. I am sorry that I am only now coming to visit you, but I was not very well myself."

"That is quite all right, George. I am being well looked after. I am indebted to you for your hospitality and for the use of your slaves to get supplies for Westhall, especially in light of our last meeting. There is money in a safe place in the main house, but I do not trust Marsh with the location of it, so when I return to Westhall I will see that you are repaid."

"I am happy to help. After all, the Good Book says: 'Do unto others as you would have them do unto you'. That speaks not only of doing good but refraining from doing evil if you don't want it returned to you," he continued.

William did not have an answer to that, so he simply nodded. He fully understood the message that George was preaching. He was relieved when Grace joined her father at the door. She was carrying a bowl with water and some clean cloths while Bella came behind her with another bowl which most likely contained the miracle-working aloe.

"Hello, William. It is time to tend to your wounds," she announced. "Will you be needing some willow bark tea? I can get Liza to prepare some for you."

"If it would not be too much trouble, but I know that after your ministrations, no matter how tender they are, I will need it."

"I am sorry, but I cannot help it. Your back has been very badly damaged."

"I do not want to overly impose on your hospitality and your time. I can return to Westhall and get Susie, one of my salve girls, to tend to me."

"That won't be necessary, William," Grace said decisively, ending the discussion. Bella had told her that Susie had taken over her place as William's woman so no way would she encourage William to have Susie tend him. She would look after him herself.

"Please take off your shirt so that I can tend to your back."

"This is straining the bounds of propriety, Grace." George protested rather weakly.

"It is a trifle late for that now, Father. I have seen William without a shirt on and I have not swooned. I daresay I can gaze upon his bare chest without lustful thoughts." *I will repent of that lie later,* she thought to herself.

I cannot claim the same, William admitted to himself, observing how well Grace filled out the dress she had worn to dinner that evening. With those unholy thoughts stirring in him, he must surely be on the road to recovery.

"Since you have Bella here to help you, Grace, I am going to retire to my room now, as I am still feeling rather tired. Goodnight, everyone."

There was a chorus of "Goodnights" in response.

William unbuttoned his shirt and struggled out of it, favouring his ribs which were still very tender. Grace had to forcibly restrain herself from offering to help because she knew from dealing with her father that men did not like to admit that they needed help, especially from a woman.

"Please lie down," she invited him as she rested the bowl on the table. Did her voice sound husky to him or was it only she who noticed it?

"I would love you to lie with me," William murmured, turning his face into the pillow.

"What was that?" Grace asked, leaning closer.

"Nothing, Miss Grace."

"Humph. Most of your back is looking better, but I am concerned about one area that has some particularly deep cuts.

It is not healing as well as I would like and it is looking as if it is beginning to fester. I will have to prepare a special salve for it tomorrow, as I do not have any already made."

She began to gently clean his back with a very dilute solution of salt water which would hasten the healing. William lay without flinching as she moistened and then patted dry his back before applying the aloe that Bella proffered.

"All finished," she announced. "You can put your shirt back on now, although it may be best to leave it off so that the aloe does not ruin it. Let me look at your leg. Have you tried to stand on it?"

"I did earlier but I cannot put any weight on it yet. Moses had to help me to stand."

"Oh dear, I think that the bone may be fractured. You will have to keep off it. We have a crude pair of crutches downstairs that I will have Bella bring up for you."

"I very much appreciate all of this, but I need to be getting back to work soon," William fretted.

"I don't see how you will be able to work with bruised ribs and a fractured leg, even if your back is healing. I would say you need two weeks' rest at least."

William did not argue. To tell the truth, he was not looking forward to going back to Westhall. He quite enjoyed having Grace look after him for one, and he did not think he could stomach Marsh's brutality any longer. He knew for sure that he could never wield a whip against a slave again. How was he going to survive at Westhall until next year?

After Midnight

Grace had only been in bed a few hours and had not gotten into a very deep sleep as yet, when something disturbed her. She was not sure what it was so she strained her ears to see if a noise could have woken her up, but she heard nothing unusual. Yet she felt disquieted in her spirit. Throwing off the sheet, she got up and pulled on the dressing gown that was at the bottom of her bed. She lit the lamp on her bedside table and walked cautiously to the door.

Once in the corridor, she found herself heading towards the end where William was staying in the guest room. She stood with her ear to the door, hoping that no-one would wake up and see her, especially her father. She did not know why, but she felt as if William needed her. Turning the knob, she pushed the door open quietly and raised her lamp slightly to throw light into the room.

As the light reached the bed, she saw William. The sheet had been thrown off him and he lay tossing and turning. Hurrying over to his side, she put her hand on his forehead and found it much hotter than it should be. As she had feared, it looked as if his cuts had become infected and brought on a fever.

She hurried from the room, down to the kitchen to get some cold water and a cloth to cool him down. She needed some feverfew tea as well and debated whether to wake up one of the slaves to make it while she was wiping him down or do it herself. In the end she did not have the heart to wake anyone so she struggled until she got the fire lit under the kettle and waited for it to boil.

The waiting was agony, for she longed to go up and check on William and start to work on bringing down his fever but she knew the tea would help. After what felt like an hour, but was in fact only a few minutes, the water began to bubble in the kettle and she swung it off the fire, grabbed the handle with a thick cloth and poured it over the leaves in a pot. She barely remembered to bank the fire before she grabbed the bowl of water and hurried back to William's room.

He was still moving restlessly on the bed and was hot and dry. She put the bowl down on the side table, wet the cloth and squeezed it out. Pushing back the hair from his forehead, she sponged it with the wet cloth. The cloth was hot when she removed it to dip it in the water again. She repeated the process several times, then pushed aside his shirt to wipe his neck and the top of his chest. The cloth still came away hot. After a brief hesitation, she raised his shirt and wiped down his entire torso and then pushed up his sleeves and cooled down his arms.

When the water began to get warm, she rushed back downstairs to empty it out and fill the bowl with cold water again. After wiping him down for nearly an hour his temperature still had not broken. She stifled a sob of frustration and tiredness as she climbed the stairs again, taking the feverfew with her. Somehow she would get it into him and between the tea and sponging him down, the fever would break. It had to!

Chapter 11

Early morning

Grace felt a hand gently stroking her hair. It was wonderfully comforting, but she couldn't figure out why someone would be stroking her hair or why the rest of her body felt so stiff and cramped. As she drifted into awareness, the cause of her stiffness became apparent. She was sitting on the floor with the top part of her body draped across a bed. William's bed! Her eyes flew open and met his heavy-lidded gaze. It was his hand that was idly playing with her hair!

Grace blushed to the roots of her hair before scrambling to her feet and making sure her dressing gown was securely tied, before smoothing down the hair that William's fingers had been entangled in.

"Uh, good morning."

"Good morning, Grace. Your hair is as silky as I imagined it would be."

"William –," she began. He held up a hand to stop her protest. "Uh, thank you." She seemed incapable of saying much more than 'uh'.

"It looks like we spent the night together. Does that mean that we have to get married now?" William teased her in a husky voice.

Grace was so relieved that he seemed to be feeling better that she did not have the heart to scold him.

"You would be a most fortunate man if that was the case," she threw at him, regaining her composure.

"I would indeed," he agreed, leaving her momentarily speechless.

"I see you are feeling better this morning. Your fever broke sometime in the wee hours of the morning." She thought it would be safer to change the subject.

"You looked after me all night?"

"You were burning up with fever, and I had to sponge you down with cold water." Grace tried to keep her face impassive and hoped that she would not blush as she recalled sponging off his face, strong arms and muscular torso.

"And I slept through the pleasurable experience of having your hands all over my body?" he baited her. "I am deeply distressed that I cannot recall any of your caresses."

"They were hardly caresses," Grace protested, turning red. "Perhaps you can recall the wonderful experience of me forcing feverfew down your throat to break the fever?"

"Alas, I cannot say that I can, but it seems to have worked. Thank you, Grace," he said seriously. "I really should not tease you so, but I cannot help it."

"You could help it if you tried, but you enjoy it."

William laughed. "Life is to be enjoyed, Grace. You need not be so stuffy."

"Stuffy! I am not stuffy," she insisted.

"No? Well come over here and let me see how adventurous you are," he challenged.

"William Edwards, I believe you are well enough to return to Westhall. You are back to your usual objectionable self."

"You wound me, Grace."

"I *will* wound you if you continue with your suggestive comments."

"Surely you would not turn me over to the mercy of the slaves at Westhall. Unlike yours, mine hate me and would be happy to see me succumb to fever and die. With the possible exception of Susie, and I cannot even be too sure about her."

"If you treated your slaves the way we treat ours they would be loyal to you."

"On the contrary, they would think that I have gone mad. But you are right to a point. I cannot go back to how I treated them in the past. Something in me has changed. I am a different person."

Grace had never seen William so serious and she silently rejoiced at the change.

❖

Grace quietly closed the door behind her and turned, almost bumping into her father. He was fully dressed in a suit even at this early time of the morning.

"Grace, did you spend the night in William's room?" he asked sternly, taking in her appearance. The dressing gown had come loose again and most of her hair had worked its way out of the long plait that she tamed it into every night.

"Yes, Father, I did," she replied almost defiantly, moving a little way down the corridor. The last thing she wanted was for William to overhear their conversation. Besides, she was tired and all she wanted was to lie down and sleep for a few hours. "And before you say anything, you know me well enough to realise that if I spent the night in his room it had to be for a good reason. He was burning up with fever and I was up most of the night wiping him down and trying to get him to swallow feverfew tea."

Her father had the grace to look ashamed.

"My apologies, Grace. I should know better, but I cannot say that I trust that man."

And with good reason, Grace agreed silently.

"But you can trust me, Father," she assured him. I think.

"Yes. I am sorry I made such a ridiculous accusation. Will you be able to join us for service this morning?"

"Service?" she repeated vaguely.

"It is Sunday, Grace."

"Oh dear, I forgot," she exclaimed. "I will go and get dressed and have a quick breakfast." To tell the truth, she would like nothing more than to fall into her bed. "What are you teaching today?"

"I thought I would teach on the Good Samaritan," he said with a smile. Grace's smile was wide. "I will stop and ask William if he would care to join us."

"I would be shocked if he said yes," Grace said, heading to her room. Although she had seen a change in him. Maybe he would surprise her.

However, Grace was not surprised when she got downstairs in the garden and saw only her father and the slaves. They did not enforce many things on the plantation, but attending Sunday service was one of them.

It was a truly beautiful day. The sky was a brilliant blue, but populated with enough clouds for it not to be too hot and there was a cooling breeze from the South West. The benches that they used for the services had been stored in one of the outbuildings during the hurricane and had escaped damage, so they were brought out and set up in a large square so that everyone could see each other.

There was a tall tree nearby that normally provided shade, but most of its leaves had blown off, as well as some of its branches and new ones were only now reappearing so shade would be limited. Still, Grace felt a well of contentment rise in her as she looked around and silently thanked God for the beauty of their surroundings and for sparing their lives and the plantation during the hurricane.

"Grace? What will you sing for us this morning?" She brought her thoughts back to the service. A hymn immediately sprang to mind and she stood up.

William heard voices below his window but he was not curious enough to fight his way to the window with the crutches that Grace had sent up for him. However, the sound of Grace's pure, sweet voice, unaccompanied by any instrument, froze him in position. He could imagine that this was how the angels sounded as they sang in heaven and this was probably as close as he was going to get to hearing an angel in this life or the next. He could have lain there and listened to her all day. Her voice soothed something in his soul and flooded him with a peace he had never known before.

"Thank you, Grace," he heard George say. The sounds coming through the window were so clear that he may as well have attended the service. That was probably why George did not insist when he politely refused his invitation to join them, excusing himself on the basis that he was not ready to attempt the stairs.

"This morning I am reading the story of the Good Samaritan."

William rolled his eyes. Now he was going to have to sit through a sermon. He could not remember the last day he had darkened a church door and now it seemed that the church had found him. They had a captive audience as he could not leave his room, not without much difficulty anyway, and it would have been inexcusable to close the window. Given that they had been so hospitable to him, the least he could do was endure their church service. While he could not see out, he could just imagine that they had all their slaves seated on benches to hear the gospel, as Grace called it.

> *"And, behold, a certain lawyer stood up, and tempted him, saying, 'Master, what shall I do to inherit eternal life?' He said unto him, 'What is written in the law? How readest thou?' And he answering said, 'Thou shalt love the Lord thy God with all thy heart,*

and with all thy soul, and with all thy strength, and with all thy mind; and thy neighbour as thyself.' And he said unto him, 'Thou hast answered right: this do, and thou shalt live.' But he, willing to justify himself, said unto Jesus, 'And who is my neighbour?' And Jesus answering said, 'A certain man went down from Jerusalem to Jericho, and fell among thieves, which stripped him of his raiment, and wounded him, and departed, leaving him half dead. And by chance there came down a certain priest that way: and when he saw him, he passed by on the other side. And likewise a Levite, when he was at the place, came and looked on him, and passed by on the other side. But a certain Samaritan, as he journeyed, came where he was: and when he saw him, he had compassion on him, And went to him, and bound up his wounds, pouring in oil and wine, and set him on his own beast, and brought him to an inn, and took care of him. And on the morrow when he departed, he took out two pence, and gave them to the host, and said unto him, Take care of him; and whatsoever thou spendest more, when I come again, I will repay thee. Which now of these three, thinkest thou, was neighbour unto him that fell among the thieves?' And he said, 'He that shewed mercy on him.' Then said Jesus unto him, 'Go, and do thou likewise.'"

William was unaware of the tears rolling down his face until one dropped onto his shirt. He could not even explain why he was crying, but somehow the words carried him back to the place where he had been beaten. He was the "certain man" who was travelling, not from Jerusalem to Jericho, but from Westhall to Black River, when thieves fell upon him, beat him, stripped him and left him half dead.

He remembered lying bleeding on the dirt and trying to attract the attention of the white man who went past on a horse. One of his own kind, but he passed by and left him to die. Then there were the footsteps that he had heard approaching him. That must have been the Fuller's slave, Sammy. He did not abandon him but ran and got Moses and Bella. Bella, who had every cause to hate him and to leave him to die in the dirt. But they brought him to the plantation and Bella took care of him and fed him. Bella had showed him mercy.

George's voice broke into his reflection and he heard him ask the slaves: "Does this story remind you of anything?"

"Yes, it like wha' happen to Master Edwards," he heard a voice say. It sounded like Liza.

"Yes," agreed George. "And who showed mercy to him?"

"Bella," she answered. "Even after the way he beat she so bad."

William covered his face in shame.

"Yes. Bella was like the Good Samaritan. You see, in those days the Jews and the Samaritans hated each other, but it was a Samaritan who showed the Jewish man mercy. Jesus said: 'Go, thou, and do likewise.' He is telling us that no matter if someone hates us and treats us badly, we are to show them mercy. That is what it means to be a good neighbour."

"Bella." William now heard Grace's voice. "When you brought home Master William and cared for him, you were being a good neighbour. I am sure that Jesus was well pleased with you."

"With me?" Bella's voice rose in surprise.

"Yes, with you. You have done well." Grace praised her.

But I have not, William silently condemned himself. I am the lowest of men and I will no doubt die in my sins.

"Before we finish today, let us pray for the safety of Moses and Sammy who have gone to Black River and for healing for Master William," George invited. "Bella, would you lead us in prayer?"

William's eyes opened in surprise. George was allowing a slave to pray? In all the times he had been to church in Barbados and even in England, the priest had never invited anyone else to pray. He strained to hear Bella's voice.

"Father God, please sen' angels to watch over Moses and Sammy and help them get to Black River safe. And please heal Master William quick and take 'way all the pain that I know he in. In Jesus name. Amen."

William heard the simple prayer from Bella's heart and he was gutted.

Chapter 12

Later that evening

William felt that he would go crazy if he did not leave his room. Although it had only been three days since he had been in it, he was not accustomed to the confinement. It was almost as bad as being cooped up on the boat to England and then to Jamaica. One of the slaves, not Bella, had brought his lunch, but he had not seen Grace or her father since that morning. He was glad that he had had some time to compose himself after listening to the service and was even happier that Bella was not the one to bring his lunch. He did not think he could look her in the face just yet.

Washing himself as best as he could at the wash stand, he managed to change into a clean shirt and pants, slip on a pair of shoes and wedge the crutches under his arms. That was the easy part, although getting dressed still left him breathless. He was obviously still weak from the blood he had lost and the fever the night before. Truth be told, he should not even be attempting to go down the stairs on his own.

In the end he found that it was easier to use one crutch so he left the other at the top of the stairs and worked his way slowly down the flight. He was amazed at the thrill he felt on accomplishing that small feat. The house was not that big, so he found the front door and let himself out, not quite sure where he was heading. It felt good to be outside in the fresh air while the sun was still around to shine on his face, but close enough to setting for it to lose its sting.

He had no plans of where to go so he decided to walk around the house a little to get some exercise. He saw several men and women in the slave yard, chatting with each other and relaxing. Some were working on rebuilding their huts while others were obviously more intent on observing the Lord's Day. Friendly Hall had a lot less slaves than he did at Westhall, as the plantation was considerably smaller. He had discovered that in Jamaica they needed fewer slaves per acre since they did not have the need to fertilise as the planters did in Barbados where quite a lot of manpower was used in fertilising the fields to increase yields. He idly wondered that he did not see any children, but as he walked around to the side of the house opposite his room, he discovered why.

Grace was asking questions and he could hear children's voices vying to answer. The sound of Grace's voice made him draw nearer, while trying to keep as quiet as he could so that he could observe her without her seeing him. She was sitting on a stool with about twelve slave children on the ground in front of her and she appeared to be teaching them how to read. William wondered if that wasn't against the law, for the slaves at their plantation in Barbados were never taught to read, except Deborah, whom their father encouraged to be in the room when they were being tutored. That was probably what contributed to her rebelliousness. He had always heard that teaching slaves to read fuelled their rebellious natures and gave them ideas about freedom.

His eyes were drawn to Grace's face which grew animated when one of the children recognised a word that she had written. She was beautiful. Her hair, which he had stroked that morning, was now tamed into its customary bun at the back of her head, but he knew how wild and wonderful it looked when it was loose. How he would love to see it strewn across his pillow, unrestrained and free, the way he would like Grace to be. The way he knew she could be, given the glimpses of passion he had seen in her.

"You have all done very well today so you can have the treat that I promised you. Go to the kitchen and the cook will give it to you." She finished her teaching and began to pack away her slate and chalk to the cheers of the slave children who streaked past him to get their treat.

William hobbled towards Grace, catching her off guard.

"William! What are you doing out here? How did you get down the stairs?"

"I did not know that I was under house arrest," he teased. "Besides, I had to come outside and get some fresh air. I am not used to being inside for such long periods of time."

"Of course you are not under house arrest, but you could have fallen on the stairs," she said worriedly.

"Grace, I am touched that you are worried about me. That must mean you care for me a little. Do not worry. I took my time and watched each step carefully. I certainly do not want to break my neck when there is so much to live for." He looked at her intently to make his point clear.

"Please," Grace dismissed him. "Anyway, I am glad you got out here without incident. And so you know, I care about all of my patients. I have never lost one yet and I do not want you to be the first."

"Touché," William conceded. "And I thought I was special. Is this how you spend your Sunday evenings? Teaching the slaves' children?"

"Yes, why?" Grace sounded defensive, making William wish he'd never mentioned it.

"You may think it is an admirable thing to do, but are you sure it will not be more of a hindrance than a help?"

"How could teaching them to read possibly be a hindrance?"

"It will only give them knowledge and make them wish for freedom."

"But that is our aim, to give them freedom. As you can see they are just as capable of learning as we are." William never doubted that, for he knew that Deborah showed far more aptitude for learning than his sisters. It had nothing to do with the colour of a person's skin or their status; it was simply if they had the opportunity to learn.

"Yes, I see that," he conceded, earning him an approving smile from Grace.

"Would you like to go for a short walk about the yard?" she asked.

"If it will prolong the time in your company, then certainly," he replied gallantly, making Grace roll her eyes. "I am surprised that the hurricane did so little damage to your property," he observed, looking about.

"Yes, we are grateful, but then God did promise to command his angels concerning us." William could see that she really believed what she said and he wondered what it would be like to have that assurance.

Grace wanted to ask him if he had heard the service that morning and what he had thought of it, but she wanted him to bring it up. They walked for a little while in silence, with William concentrating on manoeuvring with the crutch on the uneven ground until he became more comfortable with it. The sun was beginning to set, turning the sky into a canvas of pinks and oranges.

"Beautiful," Grace breathed in awe, looking at the sky.

"I quite agree," William murmured, but when Grace turned to look at him, he was gazing at her, not the sunset. She lowered her head demurely to hide her blush.

"I meant God's creation," she chided him.

"So did I," William smiled at her.

"So you believe in God, then. I was not sure. You certainly don't live your life as if you do."

"I believe that God exists, but I do not believe that he gets involved in the affairs of men any longer."

"Why, then, did you pray during the hurricane?" she challenged. He laughed that she caught him out based on his own words which she obviously had not forgotten.

"All right, I suppose at some level I believe that he does get involved. For I would certainly not be alive if Bella and Moses had not shown me mercy and brought me here." It would seem that he had heard the message. "After what I did to her, it would have to be God to cause her to have mercy on me. I still do not know why he allowed me to live for I am a worthless man. My life was certainly not worth saving."

"Because of what you have done since you have been at Westhall?" Grace asked quietly.

"That is only part of it. If you knew the things I have done you would have nothing to do with me."

"Worse things than beating Bella and the slaves at Westhall?"

"Some people might not consider them worse, but you would." Grace felt that she did not want to know, but something was pushing her to find out the depths of his depravity. Maybe so she would lose her attraction for him once and for all.

"Is it the reason you were sent to Jamaica?"

William stopped walking and turned to look at her. Gently taking her chin in his free hand, he looked into her innocent eyes.

"Grace, believe me, you do not want to know. You will hate me more than you do now." He released her chin and began to walk back towards the house.

"I do not hate you."

He laughed softly, almost a mocking laugh. "Well if you do not now, you certainly would if you heard my confession."

"Confession is good for the soul," she told him. "You can tell me anything. I promise not to judge you."

"Grace, you are too good and pure to hear of the things I have done in my life. Leave it be."

"William, there is nothing you could have done that God will not forgive. There are many people in the Bible who —"

"I raped my sister!" William's blunt confession interrupted Grace and shocked her into silence.

"You what?" she whispered in disbelief.

"My half-sister. Not that it makes it any better."

They had reached the place where the service had been held that morning and William dropped down on one of the benches, leaning his crutch up next to him. Grace sat a little way from him, close enough to hear him but not close enough to touch. William was not surprised that she had distanced herself from him, whether she realised it or not. He looked straight ahead and began to talk, glad for the fading light that would hide the disgust on her face when she heard the whole story.

"Deborah is the daughter of my father and his mulatto mistress, Sarah. From the time she was born my father favoured her, especially since she looks more like him than my sisters do and because he loved her mother. He made sure she was in the classroom when our tutors taught us and she learned how to read and write. She used to play with my sisters until she got older and then she started to take her place and serve us." He chanced a quick glance at Grace but her face was expressionless.

"When I got older I found out that her mother was my father's mistress and he slept with her openly, even though my mother was in the house. When visitors came to the plantation I would see them looking at Deborah and then at my father and they would realise that she was his child, to my mother's shame. Many nights I would hear my mother crying in her room. She was never truly happy and that made me hate Sarah, Deborah and my father.

"As Deborah got older she became very beautiful and I was determined to have her. My father turned a blind eye to me bedding the other slave girls, but he warned me to stay away from Deborah." Again he glanced at Grace whose face now looked drawn. He continued. "That only made me more determined than ever to have her, so when my friend Harry suggested a plan I heeded it. He told me to wait until my father went to town overnight and pretend I was sick and ask for her to bring me food in my room so that she would be at my mercy. I grasped the idea." Grace looked at him and murmured what sounded like "Amnon and Tamar".

"Pardon?" William asked confusedly.

"There is a story in the Bible just like that. Sorry, continue."

"Well she brought up my dinner and I trapped her in my room and told her I was going to have her because I had waited long enough. She told me to stop, saying that it was wrong because she was my sister. I told her that she was not my sister, she was my slave. And I took her innocence."

Grace was silent. Tears were now running down her cheeks. William wanted to wipe them away, but he knew she would not welcome his touch. He was not sure of the cause of her tears. Was she crying for the girl that she did not know or to discover he was such a reprobate?

"My father called me to his office when he got back the next day and demanded to know why I had bedded Deborah. I suppose Sarah could not wait to go running to tell him. I asked him if he was saving her for himself. He hit me across my face and snarled at me: 'I don't sleep with my offspring and neither should you.' It was the first time he openly acknowledged that

Deborah was his child. I have never seen him so angry. And then he shipped me off to England for two years to see if I would come back more civilised.

"When I came back from England I was still full of resentment towards Deborah for I felt it was her fault that I had been sent away. By this time, she and her mother had been freed and my father had set them up in town with a house and their own businesses. I could not stand it! So I watched her house until one day, when I was certain that she was alone, I knocked at the door and she opened it before she realised it was me. I pushed my way in and told her that we had some unfinished business that I had come to take care of. It was my intent to have her again." William's hand came up to absently rub the scar on his cheek.

"Is that how you got that scar?" Grace asked, her voice heavy with tears.

"Yes. She had a knife in her pocket and when I tried to take it from her, she slashed at me and cut my face. Her fiancé, Richard, who is my cousin (that is a story for another day) ran in and rescued her. He threatened to kill me if I did not leave Barbados, so my father sent me here to run the plantation for Peter Westhall. So now you know the whole sordid story."

"Yes, I do," Grace agreed, wiping her cheeks. She got up and turned to leave.

"So, can you still say that you don't hate me?" William asked, stopping her, although he was reluctant to hear her answer.

"I cannot honestly answer that right now," Grace admitted quietly and hurried away, leaving William in the dark, alone and dejected.

Chapter 13

"William, I am glad to see that you are up and about. Were you out for a walk?"

"Yes, I was getting a bit of air."

"I was just about to have dinner and it seems that Grace has deserted me. She sent Lucy, her maid, to say that she was not feeling well and that she would have something in her room, so please join me and take her place."

William forced his face into a pleasant mask and followed George to the dining room, murmuring something about being sorry to hear that Grace was ill. He would not be surprised if Grace was truly not feeling well, for his story was enough to make any innocent woman sick. He was angry with himself for bearing his soul to Grace only to have her run off without saying anything. She was clearly too distressed to speak to him. He should never have given in to her insistence that he tell her his story. Now he was forced to sit with her father and make small talk over dinner when all he wanted was to be alone. He would have liked some response from her. Anything would be better than not knowing how she truly felt, although it was not hard to guess.

"Thank you. I appreciate all you and Grace have done for me. However, I am feeling much improved and I can get around with this crutch, so I believe I will return to Westhall tomorrow. Do you by chance have another cart that could transport me?"

"Yes, certainly, but do you think it is wise to return to work so soon? Does Grace know of this?"

"No, I have not told her, but I am sure that she will be in agreement. She is probably eager for me to leave so that she can get back to her usual duties. Besides, I do not think it fair of me to be here eating my fill every day while they are on rations at Westhall."

"But you need to eat well to build up your strength," George protested. He did not even know why he was trying to get William to stay when he had told Grace that he did not trust him. Truth be told, it was because he felt guilty that he had not made any effort to share the gospel with William and the boy certainly needed to hear the good news. He had thought he would have him for a week at the very least. Had something happened?

"I will be fine. Besides, your men should be back with the supplies in a few days and I will be there to send the money when they deliver them."

"I am not worried about the money," George dismissed. "God always provides. But do you have someone who can see to your needs?"

"Yes, Susie will see to my needs." *And I have some pressing needs for her to see to*, William added in his mind. *A stiff drink would also be welcomed. This pious living is not easy.*

"If you insist, I will arrange for one of the men to take you over in the morning. But I would like to extend an invitation for you to join us next Sunday for our service since you were not able to come today. It would be a good opportunity to thank the Lord for saving your life and giving you another chance."

"I would be happy to," William forced the words out with a polite smile. What could you really say to that?

"Good, good. We begin at about 8 o'clock before the sun gets too hot. I am looking forward to having you join us. And you may bring any of your people."

William nodded noncommittally and picked up his fork to eat. He was sure that Grace would not be happy to see him and the last thing he needed was for his slaves to be getting religious.

❖

Early Next Day
Westhall Plantation

William climbed from the back of the cart with help from the slave who had brought him over. He walked slowly to the front door, leaning on the crutch that he had borrowed, while the slave followed behind him carrying his bag. He mounted the steps carefully and pulled open the front door.

"Betsy!" he bellowed and waited for a moment. After there was no response he shouted again.

Betsy and Susie appeared at the top of the staircase, looking surprised to see him.

"Master William, we didn' know you was coming back today. We was just cleaning the bedrooms upstairs." They came down the stairs so that he would not have to look up at them.

William noticed that Betsy did not seem overly glad to see him, but what did he expect? This was not Friendly Hall. Susie at least looked a little pleased. She was probably thinking of the coins she would be getting now that he was back.

"You can leave the bag there and head back home," he told the slave, pointing to the floor just inside the door. As he turned away to head upstairs to his room, he belatedly realised that he did not say thanks. If he was at Friendly Hall he would have thanked him without a second thought. The Westhall way was firmly back in place as if he had not left.

"You need anything, Master William?" Betty asked, stopping him.

"Not right now. How have things been here?"

"The same, Massa."

"Any sign of that traitor, Cudjoe?"

"No, Massa."

"Not that I expect to ever see him again. I suppose that Marsh is out in the fields?"

"Yes, Massa."

"All right, I will see him later. Susie, come and help me get up the stairs and into bed. I need to rest."

Betsy and Susie exchanged glances. They knew what the master meant.

"Yes, Massa," Susie said, obediently following him up the stairs that he was managing well on his own. It was obvious that he didn't need any help, at least not with the stairs.

A little while later William shifted away from Susie and lay face down on the bed, waiting for his heart to return to its normal pace. Parts of his body felt good after the much-needed release, but his ribs were hurting like the very devil and his back was beginning to pain him again. Susie rose up on her elbow and curiously peered at his back. After all, she had never seen stripes on a white man's back before, far less the master's.

"Massa, you' back painin' you?" she asked hesitantly.

"Yes, Susie, it is. Can you find some aloe to put on it? And do you know if we have any willow bark here?"

"I should be able to find some aloe but wha' is willow bark? I never hear 'bout that."

"Never mind. Just bring me a bottle of rum and a glass."

She stood up and hurriedly dressed to go and do his bidding.

"And, Susie," he said, dragging himself to sit up.

"Yes, Massa?" she waited expectantly.

"Thank you." He dug into the drawer next to the bed and handed her a few coins.

Susie stared at him in shock before mumbling her thanks for the coins and rushed from the room.

William pulled his clothes on and lay back against the bed-head in pain. Was bedding Susie worth the pain he was now in? Grace would definitely say no to that and would no doubt rebuke him for his ways. He smiled a little at the thought and the picture of her face that came to mind. He had tried to force his thoughts away from her, but it seemed he had little control of his mind where she was concerned.

He had hoped to see her before he left, but she had been conspicuously absent when he ate breakfast and then eased himself in the cart, after thanking George for his hospitality again. He assumed that George had told her of his departure and yet she had not appeared to wish him safe journey or to give him any of her miracle-working teas. He had asked George to convey his thanks which prompted him to offer excuses for her, saying that she had not recovered from her illness of the night before.

It was clear that she had no desire to see him again and with good reason. She was far too good for him anyway. How could he have thought any differently? As soon as he was back at Westhall he had bedded Susie and was about to drown his pain in a bottle of rum. He hoped it would dull not only the pain in his back and ribs, but also the pain in his heart, for surely Grace was lost to him before he even had her.

Downstairs

"Betsy, something like it wrong with Master William," Susie whispered to her.

"Wha' you mean?"

"I see he back and it cut up like a slave own after a beating, but something like it happen to he head too."

"Like wha'? You think he get hit in he head?"

"Must be because he just tell me 'Thank you'."

"What?" Betsy exclaimed. "He thank you? For what?"

"I ain' certain. It could be for the time in the bed or for getting the aloe he ask me to pick to put 'pon he back. He like he come back different."

"Sound like he different better. I hope it last."

"Me too. You got anything here name willow bark?"

"No. Wha' is that?"

"Don't worry. I forget he tell me to bring a bottle of rum instead."

❖

William opened the drawer of the bedside table where he had moved all his things after the hurricane. He took out his journal and opened it to the last day he had written. He was surprised that it was only four days ago, for it felt as if a month had passed. He opened a bottle of ink and dipped his quill in it.

October 14, 1697
Westhall Plantation

> *I have just come back to Westhall after spending three days at Friendly Hall under the care of Grace. On my way to Black River, that traitorous dog Cudjoe led me into an ambush and abandoned me. He must have planned it, for three men appeared from the bush, blindfolded me, stuffed a gag in my mouth and beat me until I passed out. Never have I felt such pain as that whip falling across my back again and again. Never did I know the pain that I was inflicting on my slaves until I felt it myself.*
>
> *Bella and two other slaves from Friendly Hall found me and carried me there. To tell the truth, I could have stayed there forever but I had to leave. I*

could not stand to see the look of hatred and disgust that I knew I would see in Grace's eyes when we met again for I told her the whole wretched story about Deborah. I would not have told her except that she kept pushing me and the fool that I am, I could not deny her. But now it has robbed me of the very thing I hold most dear; her presence.

I have not seen her since and I know that she was avoiding me but I cannot blame her. What has light to do with darkness? I am even quoting scripture now after just three days at Friendly Hall. Anyway, I am glad to be back at Westhall, where I can sin without my conscience, Grace, bothering me.

I just bedded Susie in the Westhalls' bed and it was a great relief as I had not bedded her since the hurricane nearly three weeks ago. I cannot remember the last time I have denied my body pleasure for three weeks! I will numb the pain in my body with a bottle of rum if Susie would hurry with it and I have asked her to put some aloe on my back, but I doubt she will be as gentle as my Grace. Oh, that she was really mine.

❈

Friendly Hall Plantation

The house seemed empty without William, which was quite silly since it was full of people, as it had been before he came and disrupted her life. Grace knew that she couldn't pretend illness any longer, as her father would soon be asking questions and she did not wish to lie to him. To tell the truth, she did feel sick. Sick that William, whom she had been starting to soften towards despite all he had done, was worse than she had even imagined. He had done something that was detestable.

That he beat his slaves was bad enough, but now that she knew he had raped his own sister and taken her innocence, she did not know how she could ever look him in the face again. How she could ever respect him, far less contemplate a relationship with him? How she wished she had never forced him to confide in her. But would she truly have preferred not to know the truth about him?

She pushed back from her vanity and stood up, mentally preparing herself for the meeting with her father. He would want to know if she was feeling better and he would no doubt tell her that William wanted to thank her personally for tending to him. She would have to do her best to school her face lest her disgust for him be evident to her father. He would never know from her lips the truth about William for it had been told to her in confidence. Though what he had done was reprehensible, she would keep his unspeakable secret to herself.

Minutes later she sought her father out in his office. He was seated at his desk reading his Bible. He looked a lot healthier than he had a few days ago, of which she was glad. A surge of love flooded her as she watched him pause in his reading to close his eyes and pray. Why could William not be a man of God like her father, a man that she could admire and love?

Opening his eyes, George saw Grace standing silently by the door. He was not embarrassed to be caught praying, for prayer was part of their lives.

"Grace, are you feeling better?" He rose from his desk to greet her with a kiss on her cheek. "You still look a little pale."

"I am much improved, Father."

"You missed William's departure, but he sends his thanks. He felt that he should get back to the plantation."

"Hmmm," Grace murmured. *I'm sure he did.*

"I was just praying for him. That boy needs prayer."

"Yes, indeed." *You have no idea how much!*

"He has allowed the devil to use him most evilly, but there is nothing he has done that God will not forgive."

Grace stared at him for a moment. She had been so appalled by what William had confessed that she had not thought about God's mercy. Even though she had used that reasoning to get him to tell her his story, she could not truly have believed it. Especially after she heard what he had done as if there were big sins and little sins. The fact that she, who had been so named, was so far from exhibiting that quality, shamed her. William had warned her that she would judge him and he had been right. What a hypocrite she was. She had been his judge and jury as if she was without sin.

Chapter 14

That Evening
Westhall Plantation

William heard the mournful song of the slaves coming in from the fields and sent one of the house slaves to tell Marsh that he was back and that he wanted to see him in the office. The slave returned to tell him that Mister Marsh said he would come as soon as he finished his evening whippings. Hearing that, William grabbed the crutch that he had borrowed from the Fullers and limped out to the whipping post where he seized the whip from Marsh's hand and snarled at him: "There will be no more whippings at Westhall!"

"What? Are you mad, man? Do you want a rebellion on our hands?"

"This is not the place to have this discussion, which is why I sent for you to come to my office. Now follow me."

Marsh gestured at one of the slaves to untie the one at the whipping post and grudgingly followed William inside.

William had barely closed the door behind them when Marsh erupted. "Did you get hit in the head during the attack?

How do you expect me to control these Negroes without the whip? We may as well prepare ourselves to be slaughtered in our beds," he mocked.

"The Fullers do not use the whip at all on their plantation and their slaves are hardworking and loyal. In any case, after what I just went through I could never lay a whip across another slave's back."

"Well you may have developed slave-loving ways but that does not mean that I have to abide by them."

"If you value your position here, Marsh, you will do as I say," William advised him coldly.

"So how am I supposed to control these slaves? How will I get them to do any work?"

"Find a way."

Marsh stomped out of the office and banged the door on his way out. William dropped his hands onto his head in frustration. He needed to get out of this job and off the island. He did not even know how he would last until June, by which time he hoped that Peter Westhall would be able to find someone to run the plantation for him. The only ray of light in Jamaica was Grace and that was assuming she would eventually speak to him again.

Maybe attending their service would earn him some points with her. He could not very well tell her father no, so if he had to go surely he should derive some benefit from it.

❈

The Following Sunday
Friendly Hall Plantation

Grace dressed with care for the service that morning. She told herself that she just wanted to look nice for herself, but she knew that it was because her father had told her that William was attending. How he had gotten him to agree, she could not imagine, but she knew that her father was not above using guilt when a person's soul was at stake. Taking one last look at herself, she was satisfied that she looked her best so she picked up her Bible and went downstairs.

William was already standing by the benches talking to her father. He looked particularly handsome in a black jacket and breeches, with a crisp white shirt underneath it. His hair, which had been long enough to tie back in a queue when he was there, was now cut short and was slicked back. He was also clean shaven and, looking at him, no one would be able to tell the things he had done. She had better keep her eyes off him and on the word of God.

She could not delay any longer so she approached the two men with a cheery, "Good morning."

William looked at her cautiously as if he was trying to determine her mood. When he could detect no sign of hostility or reserve, he opted for the same approach and said, "Good morning," pleasantly. Truth be told, he would rather be in his bed getting some much-needed rest or something else.

He had crawled out of bed barely an hour ago, leaving Susie to sleep since it was her day off. However, the sound of him shaving and getting ready woke her and she asked if he was going out. When he said that he was going to the Sunday service at Friendly Hall, she excitedly begged to come. Apparently, Bella had told her about the services. He saw no harm in her attending since she was not working that day anyway. He should have known better.

"You are looking much better," Grace commented.

"Thank you. I am feeling a lot better and will soon be able to give back the crutch."

"We are in no hurry for it," Grace assured him.

"It is time for us to begin," George said and Grace started to usher the slaves to take their places while George invited William to sit.

Grace noticed an attractive slave girl, whom she did not recognise, talking to Bella. Grace gestured to Bella to come over and sit.

"Miss Grace," Bella said excitedly. "This is my friend Susie from Westhall. She ask Master William if she could come with he and he say yes."

"That is wonderful. Welcome, Susie," Grace smiled.

As she moved to a bench to sit, the name Susie began to register. She was the one who William had taken to bedding after Bella had come to Friendly Hall! He had the gall to bring his slave woman to the church service. Grace seethed with anger as she deliberately sat on a bench far from William rather than share one with him, although the way they were arranged she could not avoid seeing him. She hoped that her father did not ask her to sing today for she did not know how she would be able to force a joyful noise from her lips. It was with great relief that she heard him tell everyone that they would start with a time of silent communing with the Lord. William had no idea what he was supposed to do so he sat with his eyes closed like everyone else and had a little nap.

After a few minutes, George took his Bible and stood up.

"Last Sunday I taught about the Good Samaritan and how he had mercy on the Jew who was beaten by robbers and left for dead. Today I am sharing a story that shows the mercy of Jesus.

> "*And the scribes and Pharisees brought unto him a woman taken in adultery; and when they had set her in the midst, they said unto him, 'Master, this woman was taken in adultery, in the very act. Now Moses in the law commanded us that such should be stoned: but what sayest thou?' This they said, tempting him, that they might have to accuse him. But Jesus stooped down, and with his finger wrote on the ground, as though he heard them not. So when they continued asking him, he lifted up himself, and said unto them, 'He that is without sin among you, let him first cast a stone at her.' And again he stooped down, and wrote on the ground. And they which heard it, being convicted by their own conscience, went out one by one, beginning at the eldest, even unto the last: and Jesus was left alone, and the woman standing in the midst. When Jesus had lifted up himself, and saw none but the woman, he said unto her, 'Woman, where are thine accusers? hath no man*

> *condemned thee?' She said, 'No man, Lord.' And Jesus said unto her, 'neither do I condemn thee: go, and sin no more.'"*

Grace squirmed in her seat. Her father was no doubt preaching to her. It was as if God was using him to remind her how quick she had been to judge William.

"Sometimes, we are quick to judge others when we ourselves are sinful. While God is not expecting us to condone sin, he does expect us to extend grace and mercy. How much easier it is to see other people's sins and not our own."

William looked over at Grace and found that she looked most uncomfortable and well she should. She had done nothing but look down on him and condemn him since they met. She set such a high standard that no-one could reach it. He certainly did not think that he could so why would he even try?

"The scribes and Pharisees were always trying to catch Jesus doing something against their law. Here is another instance. It says in Luke chapter 5:

> *"And after these things he went forth, and saw a publican, named Levi, sitting at the receipt of custom: and he said unto him, 'Follow me.' And he left all, rose up, and followed him. And Levi made him a great feast in his own house: and there was a great company of publicans and of others that sat down with them. But their scribes and Pharisees murmured*

> *against his disciples, saying, 'Why do ye eat and drink with publicans and sinners?'*
>
> *And Jesus answering said unto them, 'They that are whole need not a physician; but they that are sick. I came not to call the righteous, but sinners to repentance.'"*

"Now a publican was a tax collector. They were the most hated people because they were Jews who worked for the Romans who were oppressing the Jewish people. Sometimes they took more taxes from the people than they were supposed to and kept it for themselves. The scribes and Pharisees were accusing Jesus and his disciples of eating and drinking with these hated people.

"What would that be like today? It would be as if Jesus was having dinner with the drivers, overseers and managers from plantations. The people who oppress and ill-treat slaves. And we might be wondering why would Jesus have anything to do with those kinds of evil people?"

It was now William's turn to squirm as he heard himself included among the evil people. He could not deny it. Did George forget that he was there?

"But Jesus said only people who are sick need a doctor. In other words, you cannot do God's work by only being around people who are righteous. You also need to be friends with sinners in order to lead them to repentance.

"This is a challenge to all of us today, myself included, to be more like Jesus. That means having more compassion and being among those who we would normally want nothing to do with.

"Today I am glad to welcome Master William and Susie, our neighbours from Westhall. I hope you will practice what you heard today and make them feel welcome. We hope that you will come again," he said to them.

I hope you won't come again, Grace thought and immediately felt ashamed. Had the message today fallen on deaf ears? Or on a hard heart?

❈

At George's invitation, William agreed to stay for an early lunch. He was looking forward to the meal at Friendly Hall, as their meals always seemed better than the ones at Westhall. Maybe it was the care that the cook put into making them because of the way she was treated by the Fullers. He needed some advice from George about that.

"Make yourself comfortable, William. One of the girls will bring out some juice shortly." George had led William to the small patio at the front of the house. He wondered if Grace would join them but she had escaped into the house as soon as the service was finished. William figured it was either to oversee the preparation of lunch or, more likely, to avoid him.

"What did you think of the message this morning?" George asked him.

"It was interesting," William prevaricated. He wondered what Grace thought of it. He almost wanted to thank George for the timeliness and accuracy of his message given how Grace had treated him. "I would actually like to talk a little about the second part, when you likened the publican to overseers and managers."

"I hope I did not offend you," George interrupted hastily.

"No. You did not say anything that is not true. We are seen as evil and to tell the truth we are very evil. Before my incident, I was just as bad as the rest, except maybe Marsh, who has his own brand of evil."

"And now?" George prompted him.

"And now, after experiencing being whipped, I cannot bring myself to lift a whip against another slave. I have told Marsh that there is to be no whipping at Westhall, and of course that did not go down too well. He has accused me of being a Negro lover and asked how he is supposed to control the slaves. I could use your advice on that."

"William, I am very pleased to hear you say that. You know, of course, that we do not use the whip here and our slaves are hardworking and loyal. What we do here is based on the instructions of your very own Henry Drax from Barbados, or at least most of them."

"My father also follows his instructions, but to tell the truth I have never paid much attention to them."

"Well, my boy, they were written by a man who not only used them but was able to demonstrate that they work. Not only does he give every detail of how to run the machinery of the sugar plantation, but how to treat the slaves. I have my own copy here, which is precious to me but I am persuaded that I need to lend it to you."

"I would be most grateful," William said humbly.

"Mr. Drax was a man of many virtues. His instructions stated that 'slaves are not to be treated with too much severity and they must not by any means be in want'. So in order to make sure that they 'work with cheerfulness' as he called it, he advised that they should be well fed with a wide range of provisions. He mentioned cassava, plantain, corn and peas as well as molasses and fish. He also had certain workers who he favoured to have extra provisions because of their role on the plantation."

"So are you saying that he did not condone punishment of his slaves?"

"No, that is not the case. There was punishment for stealing food but it was light and there was severe punishment for stealing sugar, rum or molasses. However, he condemned punishing slaves to satisfy the anger or the passion of the overseer."

"It is known in Barbados that when we had the slave plot in 1675, none of his slaves were involved."

"When you treat slaves well, it breeds loyalty and if you feed them well, they need not steal."

"I have been doing many things wrong, both in Barbados and here," William admitted.

"Admitting that you have been doing wrong is the first step," George commended. "Go and sin no more."

"That reminds me of your sermon this morning." George nodded encouragingly. "You also said that in the same way Jesus associated with publicans and sinners, righteous people should not shun people who they consider to be sinners."

"That's right."

"Then you would have no objection to my courting Grace?" William asked with a challenging smile.

"You have me there. Indeed, I must practice what I preach. I have no objection, so long as you treat her with respect. However, what happens will be entirely up to Grace."

Well, he never backed down from a good challenge and Grace was definitely a challenge.

Chapter 15

"Grace, where have you been?" her father asked as she appeared on the patio.

"I've been overseeing the preparations for lunch as we have a guest." Her eyes briefly swept over William.

William would not be satisfied with such a brief glance at her so he took his time, taking in her smooth hair and tight bun at the back of her neck. She had obviously taken time to go to her room to fix her hair and make sure that it was firmly in place. His prim and proper Grace was back. How he would love to ruffle that calm exterior and see her face filled with passion, and not the passion that came from anger either. He smothered a smile.

"Grace, may I tell you how beautiful you look today?"

She was wearing a flowered dress that did wonderful things for her full figure.

"Why thank you, William." She tried unsuccessfully not to blush with pleasure.

"I think I will lie down for a short while before lunch," her father announced, rising from his chair.

"Father, are you unwell?" Grace asked, alarmed.

"I am fine, but I woke very early this morning to finish my message and I am feeling somewhat tired now. Please excuse me."

"Certainly." William hoped he did not sound too eager, but to have an opportunity to be alone with Grace was more than he expected. Grace, however, looked less than happy.

"What were you and my father conversing about for such a long time," she asked, more to make polite conversation than anything else.

"I was asking him about how you handle your slaves. You will be happy to know that I have outlawed flogging at Westhall. After being on the other side of the whip, I cannot condone the use of such an instrument of punishment."

"William, I am delighted to hear that."

"Yes, well it has been quite a challenge, especially trying to control Marsh. I expect that he will leave soon and find some other plantation to run. I have been talking to your father about Henry Drax's Instructions on the treatment of slaves."

"Does it cover the abusing of female slaves?"

"What do you mean? Are you accusing me of abusing the female slaves?"

"You are bedding Susie, are you not? The girl that you brought to the service with you today." Her voice dripped with disapproval. "That is abuse."

"Apart from my lapse with Bella, I assure you that I do not abuse the female slaves and certainly not in bed."

"Then you have certainly changed!" she said maliciously.

William had no difficulty in understanding that she was referring to what he had told her about Deborah.

"'He who is without sin cast the first stone'," he quoted at her. "Did you even listen to your father's message today? Or were you too busy judging me?"

Grace blushed with shame. William was right, she admitted grudgingly, but she blamed it on the shock of hearing Susie tell Bella in the kitchen that she woke up when Master William started to dress for the service and asked if she could come with him. That he was bedding Susie was bad enough, but that she spent the whole night in his bed was shameful. Neither Susie nor Bella had seemed to think that anything was amiss.

She had told Susie that she did not need to submit to Master William's advances, only to be told that Susie preferred him bedding her far more than Marsh who was cruel and especially since he also gave her coins afterwards.

"Jesus also told the woman to 'go and sin no more'. Does that mean you do not intend to bed Susie anymore?"

William had to admire her persistence. "Would it bother you if I did?"

"Why would it bother me, other than the fact that you are encouraging the poor girl in a life of sin." Surely that was the only reason and she could not possibly be jealous of the slave girl, Grace persuaded herself.

"For you, Grace, I will no longer have relations with Susie, or any of the other women on the plantation."

"I am shocked! Can your word be trusted?"

"Certainly! You can get Susie to tell Bella if I renege on my word."

"I am pleased that you would do this, but what is your motivation?"

"Grace, you constantly wound me with your suspicions and accusations. My only motivation is to please you in hopes that you will someday forgive my past indiscretions and come to realise that I am a man who would make you a fine husband."

"A fine husband?" Grace repeated in shock. "You are the last man I would marry, William Edwards."

William laughed confidently. "I look forward to making you change your mind."

❈

Lunch was an ordeal that Grace could not wait to get through. William sat opposite her and hardly took his eyes from her, except to respond to something her father said or to make sure the food did not fall off his fork before it reached his mouth. And what a fine mouth it was. Grace was beginning to think that she would be perpetually red from the looks William was giving her and her own traitorous thoughts.

Her father seemed oblivious to the undercurrents between them as he talked about replanting cane and other topics that Grace had little interest in.

"I remember you saying that you were thinking of selling the plantation and returning to England," William commented.

"Yes, but until I get someone to buy it I am forced to continue to maintain it otherwise the slaves would have nothing to do and it would be worth less if it had no crops planted."

"I am planning to leave Westhall myself." Grace's head shot up.

"You are?" The words flew out of her mouth before she could stop them.

William was tempted to tease her that she would miss him, but held back only because of her father's presence.

"Yes, I plan to write to Peter soon to tell him that he will need to find someone else to run the plantation by June next year. That is as long as I intend to remain in Jamaica."

"And where do you plan to go?" George asked him. Grace waiting expectantly for his answer, while trying not to look too interested.

"If I cannot go back to Barbados, I will go to America or maybe even back to England as my sisters are living there and we have other family."

"That is unexpected," Grace commented quietly. She was surprised at the loss she felt at the thought of William leaving Jamaica.

"Do not worry, Grace, I will not leave you behind. We shall be married by then."

Grace rolled her eyes. "Your arrogance knows no bounds!"

Her father laughed at the exchange between the two of them and seemed not in the least bit concerned.

"You would think you would have the decency to ask my father's blessing first. Not that I take you seriously for one minute," she huffed.

"But he already has, my dear," her father announced, shocking her into silence.

"What ever happened to not being yoked with unbelievers?" she asked, amazed.

"I am persuaded that William will not remain in that state for too long. Soon he will learn to commune with God."

Well, you are more persuaded than I, thought Grace. William was suspiciously quiet and when Grace chanced a glance at him he was looking thoughtfully at his plate as if it had the answers to life. She would pay money to know what was going through his head.

❈

"Why don't you young people take a turn around the garden?" George suggested after lunch. Grace looked at him in dismay. He was encouraging her to go for a walk with the rogue William? Surely he did not think that one church service could have changed him.

"That is a wonderful idea, George. I need to walk off some of that lunch. Thank you, Grace. It was indeed delicious."

"You are welcome. Not that I cooked any of it."

"But your selection of the dishes and your supervision of the preparations were outstanding." Grace had to laugh at his ridiculous praise.

"All right, I will go for a short walk." After all, what could he possibly do in broad daylight?

They walked in silence for a while as Grace led him to her favourite part of the plantation. Before the hurricane, it had been a beautiful garden with a small pond and a stone bench overlooking it. The pond used to have fish but they had been killed in the hurricane and it had not been restocked yet. The flowers and shrubs had also been uprooted and she had only just begun to clear the beds and replant seeds. The hurricane had devastated everything. Surprisingly, the stone bench had remained intact, probably because the wind blew right through it.

"This is my favourite spot on the plantation. It was truly beautiful before the hurricane. I often come here when I want to relax and enjoy being outside."

"Well, I am honoured that you brought me here," William said solemnly. She glanced at his face to see if he was being sarcastic but he looked sincere. "It is very peaceful. Even romantic, one could say." Now he was back to his flirting ways.

"I never thought of here as romantic," Grace said, tilting her head on the side as if to look at it from another angle.

"That is because you were never here with me." William's husky voice said from right behind Grace.

"And how does that make it romantic?" she challenged him boldly, turning around.

"Well, if you have to ask, then I'm doing something wrong," he laughed. "I will have to correct that right away."

Grace knew that she should move but William's eyes on her lips held her in place. He gently grasped her shoulders and drew her closer. He seemed to hesitate for a second as if to give her a chance to back away, but Grace remained. That was all the invitation William needed. He lowered his head and rubbed his lips against hers. They were as soft and plump as they looked.

Grace closed her eyes to savour her first kiss. William's lips were firm and confident as he increased the pressure against hers. Her heart took off in response, then almost stopped when she felt the tip of his tongue moisten her lips. He didn't make any further overtures for which Grace was glad, because she was sure that her knees would buckle, but sorry because she wanted more.

William fought to control himself from tasting all the delights of Grace's mouth, but he wanted to take things slowly with her. He wanted her to trust him and to know that she meant more to him than a few minutes of pleasure. He brushed his lips against hers once more before stepping back.

Grace opened her eyes in bewilderment. William had kissed her and she had not wanted him to stop.

"You kissed me." she stated the obvious. William thought she would rail at him, but instead she shocked him by saying, "Why did you stop?" She sounded unsure of herself. She wondered if he did not enjoy kissing her because of her inexperience.

"Oh Grace, believe me when I say that it was hard to stop. I would like to keep on kissing you, and so much more, but I promised your father I would treat you with respect and I intend to honour that."

"How is kissing me disrespectful?" she flirted, regaining her confidence. William stared at her for a second and then he burst out laughing. He never knew what to expect with Grace.

※

William climbed up on the bench of the cart with a wince as his ribs and back reminded him that they were not quite healed. Susie pulled herself up without any help and turned to wave at Bella as he jerked the reins and led the horses to the road that would take them back to Westhall. George and Grace stood on the front steps to see him off. Grace had an unreadable expression on her face. He wondered if she was thinking about their kiss as he was. How he would have loved to pull her in his arms before he left and show her what a real kiss was like. Next time, perhaps.

Grace watched William ride off with Susie sitting beside him as if they were a couple. She was perturbed at the fit of jealousy that came over her. What was wrong with her? Just because William had kissed her did not mean that they had made any commitment to each other. But he had better not even think of touching Susie anymore!

"Master William, thank you for takin' me to the service. I was glad to see Bella and I was glad to be able to eat my belly full too."

William laughed at her honesty. "Me too, Susie. Moses should be back with the supplies tomorrow if all goes well and we will be able to eat our bellies full again at Westhall." William could not believe that he was carrying on a conversation with a slave. Grace was really rubbing off on him.

"I didn' understand all of what Massa Fuller was sayin' but I would still like to go back."

"We will go next week." William was surprised at how eager he was for next week to come, not so much for the message, but to see Grace. He wondered if he could find some excuse to see her before. He smiled to himself. How had one kiss from this woman made him so besotted? And not even a proper one at that!

William guided the cart into the yard and called for one of the stable boys to unharness the horses and put it away. He tried not to jar his leg as he climbed down and headed for the front door.

"Massa?" Susie's voice stopped him.

"Yes?" he answered, turning.

"You want me to come to you this evening?"

Most Sunday evenings Susie would come to William's room and stay for several hours. William's body reminded him of how pleasurable those hours were. He reined in his thoughts.

"No, Susie. Not this evening." He groaned silently. Or any other evening, he added to himself.

"All right, Massa."

William opened the door with a sigh. It was going to be a long night, not to mention a long eight months. Grace Fuller had better marry him soon!

Chapter 16

The next Sunday

William did not have to remind Susie about the service, for she was dressed and waiting for him when he came downstairs for breakfast. Life at Westhall had improved considerably during the week since Moses had returned with the cart full of goods and had arranged for other supplies to be delivered the following week. With full plates of food once again, everyone was in good spirits, even Marsh seemed somewhat mellower. William wondered how long it would last.

He had not gone back out to the fields yet as he was not able to sit on a horse for any length of time or his ribs and back began to pain him. He spent time in the office tallying up the damages to the plantation so that he could send it to Peter Westhall to put in an insurance claim. The little bit of book work did not occupy him enough to keep his mind from drifting to Grace and the brief kiss he had given her. He cursed himself many times for stopping when he did, especially since she had asked him why he stopped.

For the first time in his life he had done the honourable thing. Never had he treated a woman with such care and respect. Surely this must be love. Susie could not understand why he had not sent for her during the week and had asked if he was feeling sick. He knew that it was the coins she missed and not lying with him so he gave her a few coins anyway.

A little while later he had heard her telling Betsy that she was sure he must have gotten a blow to his head during the attack, because he did not want her to come to his bed but he still gave her coins. He could understand her bewilderment, for he also found his behaviour reason for astonishment. No longer was he concerned with pleasing himself and doing what he wanted, but he found himself wanting to please Grace. He wanted her to look at him with something other than disgust, and he was beginning to see signs of interest when she looked at him. That was a start.

Hurrying down the hallway to grab his hat and be on his way, he came upon Betsy and Susie. It seemed that they were always whispering about something, probably him.

"Betsy, the breakfast was very good. Thank you. Let us go, Susie, before we are late."

From the corner of his eye, he caught Betsy and Susie exchanging shocked looks before Betsy remembered to stammer her thanks. He knew that they were thinking that he had lost his mind and he stifled a smile. Grace would be pleased to hear him. Grace. He could hardly wait to see her again and he hoped that George would invite him to stay for lunch. He wouldn't mind seeing how her garden had progressed since the week before and he definitely intended to taste Grace's lips again. He should probably be thinking more about the service and what George would find to share that week, but his mind was far from the things of God.

❖

As soon as William drove the cart into the yard he saw the boy Sammy who had found him and called for help. He climbed down from the cart and handed it over to him with a murmur of thanks. Susie was down and across the yard, eager to find Bella, before he had even gotten down properly. William stopped Sammy before he climbed up to move the cart.

"Sammy, I did not see you before you went on the trip with Moses, but I want to thank you for going for help when you saw me on the road and for helping Moses to bring me here." He reached into his pocket and gave Sammy a small bag, heavy with coins.

Sammy's eyes opened wide when he felt the weight of the bag and he thanked William heartily before climbing onto the bench and driving the cart away. William followed Susie to the meeting place but a quick glance around did not reveal Grace's presence. He made his way towards George to greet him and thank him for the invitation. Somehow, he knew that Grace was deliberately taking her time to join them. Glancing at his pocket watch, he saw that she had two more minutes before she would be late.

"Is Grace joining us this morning?" he asked George.

"Yes, of course. Grace never misses a service. In fact, I am surprised that she is not down here already."

"Maybe she is hoping to avoid me for as long as possible," William said with a smile.

"Well she will not be able to avoid you forever and I have told her to set another place for lunch. I hope that is all right with you. I'm afraid I am being a bit presumptuous."

"Not at all. I would be delighted to join you for lunch. As I have said before, your cook is a lot more talented than mine."

"Glad to hear that. Let us get ourselves ready to worship the Lord."

William was getting himself ready for Grace's appearance and he was not disappointed. This week she was wearing a green dress with lace about the elbow length sleeves and the neckline which was very modest. After all, it was Grace. It was a lot less revealing than what the women he usually associated with would wear, yet seeing Grace in it stirred him, forcing him to remind himself that he was at a church service.

"Good morning, William," she said pleasantly.

"Good morning, Grace. You look lovely as usual." His eyes dwelt on her lips long enough to remind her, in case she had forgotten, that he knew what they tasted like. The tell-tale colour along her cheek bones told him that her memory was just fine. He smiled as he took his seat, noting that once again Grace chose the bench opposite his. That was fine with him; he would have time to be close to her later.

"Grace, would you bless us with a song this morning?" George asked her.

William glanced at her and was sure that he saw her smother a groan before she obediently rose and began to sing. He had heard her sing the day he listened to the service from his room, but sitting right in front of her was completely different. Grace had a voice that would melt the hardest of hearts. As he sat captivated, he realised that it was more than her voice. It was something that he could not identify and he was powerless to resist it. It made him ready to hear what George would say.

"Today I am reading from Luke again. As you may have realised, it is my favourite of the gospels."

> "And when much people were gathered together, and were come to him out of every city, he spake by a parable: 'A sower went out to sow his seed: and as he sowed, some fell by the way side; and it was trodden down, and the fowls of the air devoured it. And some fell upon a rock; and as soon as it was sprung up, it withered away, because it lacked moisture. And some fell among thorns; and the thorns sprang up with it, and choked it. And other fell on good ground, and sprang up, and bear fruit an hundredfold.' And when he had said these things, he cried, 'He that hath ears to hear, let him hear.'"

"If you are wondering what this parable is about, you are not alone. The disciples also asked him, saying, 'What might this parable be?'"

William was glad to hear that he was not the only one who had no idea what the parable was about. He supposed that Grace would no doubt understand it. They were poles apart in the things of God. She was a saint and he was a sinner. How would they ever get together? What was it she had asked her father about being unequally yoked? He wondered what that meant.

"The seed represents the word of God. They may be messages that you hear when you come on Sundays. Several things can happen to that seed. It can fall by the wayside and get stepped on or eaten up by birds so that it never produces fruit. That is when you hear a message but as soon as you get up you forget what you heard, the message was snatched away, so that it does not bring about any change in your life."

William stirred guiltily. He was trying to remember what the message was last week, without any success.

"Then some of the seed fell on rock and it sprang up quickly but it didn't last because it had no moisture. That is when you hear a message and you get excited about it, but as soon as hardship comes along you fall away. The seed that fell among the thorns that choked it means when you hear a message and you want to do what it says, but then worry and other things come to distract you. And finally, the word that falls on good soil is when you hear a message and your heart receives it and it brings about a change in your life."

William began to feel a little better. The word must have brought about a change in him, for he had not bedded Susie or any of the slaves for the whole week. What was it that he and Grace had been talking about when she challenged him to change? Oh yes, it was that message where Jesus told the woman to go and sin no more. Maybe he had begun to bear a little fruit after all. But he had not really been tested in this yet.

One week was nothing, but would he still be able to keep his word after one month?

❖

Moses came to greet William and to ask if the other supplies had arrived yet. William was still a little surprised that a slave would approach him to speak, but he knew that this was not unusual at Friendly Hall. He saw Grace speaking to Susie a little way off and he would dearly have loved to be a fly buzzing around them to hear what she was saying. If he was still keen on gambling, he would bet that she was subtly trying to find out if he was still bedding her or if he had kept his word. He would find out from Susie later.

He was surprised how offended he was that Grace might not trust him but, truthfully, he had not been very trustworthy in the past so how could he blame her. He would just have to show her that he was worthy of her trust, even if it killed him and after only a week, it was beginning to look like a real possibility that he might die soon.

He decided to join them and see if Grace looked guilty as that would tell him what she had been talking to Susie about. Granted, she could have been explaining the message to her as well but somehow, he doubted it.

"Hello, Grace. Sorry to interrupt your conversation, but I was wondering if you might be willing to have a look at my back. There is a spot that is still sore, but I cannot see it and I would like to know if it is healing well." All right, that was not completely untrue as there was a spot that was a little sore.

"Look at your back? You are no longer my patient. Surely you can get Susie or one of the women at Westhall to look at it for you."

"But you have forbidden me to show my back or anything else to Susie," he reminded her. Grace rolled her eyes. That was hardly the same thing. "Susie, I hope you told Miss Grace that I have not asked you to come to my bed for the whole week."

"Yes, I just tell she so."

William looked at Grace pointedly and she had the decency to blush guiltily.

"Susie, why don't you go and find Bella," Grace urged her.

"Grace, Grace. I am deeply hurt that you could not trust me and had to go behind my back searching for evidence of my deception. My non-existent deception." William enjoyed seeing Grace squirm as she was discovered.

"I am sorry, William. I should have trusted you, although I find it hard to do so, given what I know of your past."

"I hope that you are prepared to make it up to me, for I would not want our relationship to go forward with this between us." William delivered this with a straight face, although he was dying to burst out laughing at the expression on Grace's face.

"What relationship? We have no relationship."

"Do you make it a habit of kissing people with whom you have no relationship?" Grace snapped her mouth shut. What could she say to that? If she said yes, then he would call her a hussy, but if she said no, then she would be admitting that they had a relationship. She chose not to answer and was relieved when her father distracted William.

"William, come and have a drink on the patio with me," George invited him. "You can tell me what you have been doing this week."

"I have been doing nothing really worthy of discussion, George." William said, following him.

"Well, perhaps we can discuss the message from this morning," he suggested. William could think of nothing he would like less. Maybe he could find out more about this unequally yoked business instead, if it was going to be a hindrance to getting Grace to marry him.

"It was a good message as usual, George, but I have to confess that I am more curious to find out more about being unequally yoked. What exactly does that mean?"

"It is from 2 Corinthians. It says: 'Be ye not unequally yoked together with unbelievers: for what fellowship hath righteousness with unrighteousness? And what communion hath light with darkness? And what concord hath Christ with Belial? Or what part hath he that believeth with an infidel...'"

William held up his hand. "Thank you; that is more than enough. I understood from the righteousness and unrighteousness part." Those verses definitely described him and Grace. She was light and he was darkness. How could they ever be together?

Chapter 17

November 30, 1697
The Acreage Plantation, Barbados

Thomas closed the ledger where he had just recorded the latest slave birth on the plantation. November 30th. The date haunted him. Not that there was anything significant about it in itself, at least not to anyone else. But to him that date would always remind him of the worst day of his life. It was not when he found out that his wife, Elizabeth, had died in England. No, it was the date that he had come back from England a year ago, after paying her his final respects, and had rushed to see Sarah to let her know that he was finally free and could marry her. And she had refused him.

Sarah. He wondered if the ache in his heart when he thought about her would ever go away. He remembered writing in a very similar ledger the date he had bought her from Jonathan Holdip. It had been the fifth day of August in the year 1677, twenty years ago when she had been seventeen.

From the time he had seen her at Holdip Manor, he had wanted her and had refused to take no for an answer. He had not cared that she was a companion to Jonathan's wife from the time their daughter died, or that his wife did not want to part with her. He did not even mind parting with the exorbitant sum of fifty pounds that he had offered for her, for it got him what he wanted: Sarah, a beautiful untouched mulatto girl.

At first, what he felt for her was just physical desire. He had wanted to possess her body and be the one to take her innocence. After all, she was his property and he had bought her for his pleasure. He had been so eager for her that first time that he had been like an untried boy, quickly gaining his pleasure at the cost of hers. His friends, who shared similar tastes in bedding slave women, would have laughed if they knew how guilty he felt at the sight of her tears. It should not have mattered if she received no pleasure from their coupling. She was just a slave. But to him it mattered and when he left her room that night, he had felt like the lowest of men.

Perhaps it was his male vanity that wanted the satisfaction of knowing that he could give her pleasure. So on his next visit to her room, which was more than a week later, he held himself in control to ensure that she received the pleasure that had been denied her the first time. That satisfaction turned to anger the next day when he found Jethro kissing her. Jethro, his trusted slave whose only fault was that he loved Sarah and said he could not help himself. Such a blind fury had come over him that he would have flogged Jethro to within an inch of his life without any feeling of remorse. It was only Sarah's intercession for him and her assurance that the kiss meant nothing that had saved him.

In the months and years to follow, what had started out as physical desire alone became love. He still felt guilty that he loved Sarah more than he loved his own wife, but he had made his peace with Elizabeth. Theirs had been an arranged marriage and although she had loved him, he had never felt that deep passion for her. Unfortunately, she knew it and it became even more apparent as his feelings for Sarah deepened.

The day that Sarah gave birth to their daughter, Deborah, was one of joy for him but pain for Elizabeth, for she looked more like him than their daughters did. He loved his daughters, Rachel and Mary, and his son William, but Deborah had a special place in his heart because she was the child born of his love for Sarah. When William took her innocence at sixteen he had been so livid that it had taken great restraint not to beat him senseless, so instead he sent him to England for two years.

He had received a letter from William a few weeks ago asking him once again to come home and telling him how he had been beaten and left for dead in Jamaica. Tears came to Thomas' eyes again as he grieved for the pain his son must have endured. He had been deeply concerned to read that William had feared the person he was becoming. He had said that Jamaica was making him even worse than he had been before and if that was the case Thomas needed to get him out of Jamaica. After reading the letter he had decided that he would sail to Jamaica in a few months and arrange for William to come back.

It would be good to have him back home. Perhaps this time they could get to know each other as father and son, something they had not done before, due to his neglect. He was lonely. He lived in a big plantation house, on seven hundred acres and he had no-one to share it with. It was pointless. What did anything mean without his family? Without Sarah? He had freed her more than a year ago after Elizabeth insisted that he get rid of her and bought her a house in town.

At least she had not married Jethro as he had feared she would. When he freed Jethro so that he could marry Sarah, it was then that he knew he loved her more than he loved himself, for he had wanted her to have a chance at happiness and he was still married at the time. It was a twist of fate that Elizabeth had died soon afterwards, leaving him free, but Sarah had still refused him. She had said that he would regret it if he married her and, although it was not illegal for them to marry in Barbados, she believed that his friends would no longer associate with him. He was willing to live with that but she was afraid that in time he would grow to resent her.

He had not seen her for a long time, several months in fact. He could not bear to see her and know that he could not be with her, so he made fewer trips to Bridge Town or if he could not avoid going, he made sure that he went nowhere near High Street where her shop was.

He had heard from Deborah that she was doing well, enjoying teaching girls how to sew and running her business. He had used his associations to help her get business initially and by all reports it was thriving. He wondered if she was truly happy. Did the profits from her business and the satisfaction of sharing her skills keep her warm at night? Did she remember his touch and lie in her bed longing for him as he longed for her? Did she ever wonder how he was doing? Did she care that he was so lonely for her that it was like a physical pain? He did not even have the desire for any other woman. How pathetic he had become.

He was now fifty-five years old and still fit. He forced himself to go out on the plantation every day to keep active and his mind busy, although he found little joy in that anymore. He did not know how many years he had left in him but he would make sure that he made the most out of whatever remained. The first thing he intended to do was write to William.

He took a piece of paper from his desk drawer and sat staring at it for a while. What could he say? How could he ask for forgiveness for the part he had played in what William had become? He had hardly spent any time with him when he was growing up, being too busy making the plantation a success. He had not intervened when his mother spoiled him, giving him his every wish. So how could he expect him to be any better than he was?

The Acreage
November 30, 1697

> *My Dear William*
>
> *I hope that this letter finds you in better health than you were when you wrote to me. I was deeply troubled to hear of your suffering in Jamaica. The thought that you could have lost your life distressed me greatly. I thank God for sending those slaves to save you and take you to their plantation. When I sent you there to work for Peter Westhall, I thought it would be for your betterment, but it was never my desire to see you suffer.*

I trust that you have been able to get the plantation back in order after the hurricane, although I know it will take some time, as I remember from the one that hit Barbados soon after we moved here. It does put you back several years. However, I am sure that Peter will put in the money that is necessary to restore the plantation to good working order because Jamaica is poised to take over Barbados as the greatest producer of sugar and he is not one to let such an opportunity pass him by.

I found it quite interesting that you wrote at length about the young lady Grace. It sounds as if you are already quite taken by her. You are right that I do not have time for the Quakers here, but she and her father sound like good people and the fact that they took you in and tended to you put me in their debt. Please extend my sincerest thanks to them. I hope that your relationship with Grace develops into a lasting one.

I am very pleased that you have been examining yourself and that it is your desire to be a better man. I too have been examining myself and I am less than pleased with what I have found. One of my biggest regrets is that I did not spend enough time with you when you were growing up so that we never had a close relationship. I would very much like to rectify that and I am giving thought to coming to Jamaica next year to spend some time with you. Perhaps when you leave the plantation, we can take a trip to Carolina together to visit your mother's family there. I look forward to getting to know my son better and I can only hope that you will feel the same.

*Your loving father
Thomas Edwards*

❦

Thomas had barely sealed the letter to William, when there was a knock at the door of his office. Cassie, one of the senior house slaves, opened the door at his answer to come in.

"Excuse me, Massa Thomas, but Massa Bowyer here to see you."

"John Bowyer?" Thomas asked in surprise.

He and John, who owned a neighbouring plantation, had been good friends. In fact, William and his son Henry had also been good friends and had been of a similar nature, which was not a good thing, for together they had spent much time in Bridge Town gambling and visiting establishments of ill-repute.

He had not spoken to John in over a year since the day that he had ridden over to The Acreage when he had heard that Thomas had freed Jethro just months after Deborah and Sarah had been freed. He had accused Thomas of causing problems with his slaves because of the manumissions and had called him a slave lover and a Quaker before riding off.

When Elizabeth had died, his wife had written a letter to send their condolences to which he had replied thanking her. He could not imagine what John would want with him now.

"Show him in, Cassie."

Before he had time to compose his thoughts John Bowyer came through the door. Thomas stood and the words of greeting froze on his lips at the state of his friend. He looked as if he had aged five years, his eyes were red and he looked as if he had not slept. His unshaven and dishevelled appearance was so uncharacteristic that Thomas knew something serious must be wrong.

"John, this is a surprise," he managed to get out.

"Thomas, Margaret passed away yesterday," he said baldly, sinking into the chair in front of Thomas' desk.

"My God, John. I am deeply saddened to hear that. What happened?"

"It seems to have been her heart. We have been together for so many years that I am at a loss as to what to do."

"I know what you mean," William sympathised, although his situation had been somewhat different. "Here, let me get you a brandy."

He went around to a small table near his desk and poured two glasses of brandy, handing one to John.

"Her death made me consider how short life is and I thought about our friendship and how foolish I was to let decisions that you made on your plantation come between us. I apologise for my behaviour last year and I ask your forgiveness."

"You have it, John. I too have been sitting here looking at my life and the mess I have made of it, particularly with

William. I had just put the seal on a letter to him when Cassie told me you were here."

"We have not done well by our sons, have we?" he commiserated. "Thankfully, Henry has settled down and is planning to get married to the Newtons' daughter, Mary-Anne, early next year. Or he was. I am not sure if he will put it off to observe a period of mourning for his mother. My poor Margaret will not even be here to see him wed and she was so excited when they announced their betrothal." His eyes started to well up and Thomas discreetly turned his head to give him some privacy.

"My congratulations to Henry, although this is indeed a sad state of affairs in which to be offering felicitations. I am determined to make sure that the latter part of my life is much better than the former. I want to leave a legacy that is more than just the plantation that I own. I hope to see my son be a better husband than I was and do a better job of raising his children than I did."

Thomas was well aware that he had failed miserably as a husband to Elizabeth, but he hoped for a second chance to be a good husband, this time to Sarah. He had also failed as a father to William. He could not deny it; William was the man he was because he had been absent for most of his life and what he did see of him was a poor example. He hoped that he had become a better man as he had said in his letter.

Chapter 18

December 28, 1697
Jamaica

Vineyard Plantation was hosting a party for the twelve days of Christmas celebrations. Granted, it was the fourth day of Christmas, but since work did not cease in order to celebrate the days of Christmas in Jamaica, Saturday was the best day for a party. Vineyard was the closest plantation to Westhall and Friendly Hall, but it was still a good few miles away.

William had met the Dorrills, who owned the plantation, the night of the Westhalls' party and he, along with the Fullers, had been invited. He offered to take the Fullers in the Westhalls' carriage which had hardly been used since they had left. One of the slaves from Westhall would drive but they had offered one from Friendly Hall to accompany them. In any case, he had taken the other pistol from the office and this time he would keep it very close to him.

As soon as the carriage stopped by the Fullers' front door, William jumped out and knocked to announce his arrival. He was looking forward to seeing Grace. He had seen her almost every Sunday and he was quite pleased with how their relationship was progressing. He had learned a lot about her and her desire to help people in general, but the slaves in particular. Watching her with the children especially, he could see that she was a natural teacher and that she would be a good mother. He hoped that he could convince her to have his children someday.

He had kept his word to Grace and had not so much as looked at Susie or any of the other slave women, but the only way he had been able to survive was to work himself to a state of exhaustion each day so that all he could do at night was drop into bed. Sundays were the hardest for him because not only was there no work, but he saw Grace, who looked particularly alluring every week. The messages were interesting most times but it was Grace who drew him to services each week, not George's messages.

Although he often walked with Grace or sat in her garden, which was now almost back to its original state, he rarely did more than kiss the back of her hand or her cheek. The restraint was killing him, but he wanted to show Grace that he wanted more from her than her kisses. The only good thing about it was that he knew Grace wanted his kisses, but she would never be so forward as to say so, or God forbid, make the first move.

This party would be the first formal occasion that they would be going to together since the Wetsthalls' party. He had been told that there was usually a lot of socialising in Jamaica but the hurricane seemed to have diverted the funds that would have been used for throwing parties and the like. He was therefore looking forward to this party with great anticipation as there would no doubt be dancing and he would have an excuse to hold Grace in his arms.

The door finally opened and George greeted him before stepping back to invite him into the foyer.

"William, it is good to see you. Since you have two sisters you will no doubt appreciate that ladies need more time than us men to get ready. However, hopefully Grace will soon grace us with her presence." He laughed at his pun on Grace's name as he always did whenever he had cause to use one.

"It has been quite a while since I saw my sisters I am afraid, so I have forgotten the ways of women. But I am sure the result will be worth waiting for," he said graciously.

The words had barely left his mouth when Grace appeared at the top of the stairs. William had seen her look beautiful many times, but tonight her beauty left him speechless. Her auburn hair was piled on her head in an elaborate style with curls left out to frame her face. Her dress was of a dark blue satin with short puffed sleeves and a neckline more daring that anything he had seen her wear. William managed to tear his eyes from Grace for a moment to glance at George's reaction to Grace's décolletage. His eyebrows were almost touching his hairline and as he was about to open his mouth to comment, William spoke quickly.

"Grace, your beauty has rendered me speechless. I can see that I will have to fight off all the eligible bachelors tonight."

She blushed, as he had expected. "Thank you, William. I am sure that the bachelors will be too taken in by the beautiful women there to notice me."

"Grace, if I did not know you better, I would think that you are fishing for compliments," William teased, earning another blush.

"Grace, I hope you have a shawl or something to cover you up," her father interjected, somewhat disapprovingly.

"Yes, Father," she said obediently.

"We had better go then."

William stepped forward to offer his arm to Grace and escorted her to the carriage. He could hear George muttering behind them about scandalous dresses and immodest necklines and smothered a smile. If George had not already prepared his message for the next day, William was sure that it would be something appropriate.

❈

Vineyard Plantation

The carriage ride took about an hour. William did not know if he preferred to be sitting across from Grace as he was or if it would have been better sitting next to her. George had chosen to sit beside Grace, perhaps so that William and Grace would not be too close to each other, but while William was spared having his thigh rubbing against Grace's, instead he had to contend with trying to keep his eyes off the considerable amount of bosom that her neckline exposed. He could well understand George's displeasure, for it was certainly not a dress that a pious young lady would normally wear. He wondered if Grace had worn it for him. If she had, was she aware that she was playing with fire?

He had had to use all his powers of concentration to focus on making conversation and not on Grace's cleavage, especially as George had his eyes trained on him throughout the trip. The sight of Vineyard Plantation was a very welcome one and he was out of the carriage almost before it came to a stop. He helped Grace down while George brought up the rear.

There were already quite a number of people there. William and the Fullers were greeted by the hosts and invited to join the other guests in the room where the party was being held. William was impressed to see the size of the room, which was almost as large as some ballrooms he had seen in England. There was a small band of musicians in one corner of the room and some of the guests were already taking advantage of the music.

The double doors that opened on to the long veranda allowed gentle breezes to cool the dancers and keep the room at a pleasant temperature. William and the Fullers saw several people that they knew and were introduced to several new people. William noticed that quite a few of the young men were also having trouble keeping their eyes off Grace, and he resolved not to move too far from her side during the night. George seemed to have come to the same decision and stuck to them very closely. William found it rather ironic, considering how he allowed them to go for walks alone on Sundays. Granted, Grace did not dress like this on Sundays.

"Grace, may I have this dance?" William asked, as a lively tune started.

"Certainly."

William led her to the dance floor, glad for his years in England and the numerous balls and parties he had been to. Grace was truly graceful on the floor. He mentally cringed as he realised that he was picking up George's habit of making puns with Grace's name.

"Where did you learn to dance?" he asked her when the music ended.

"My mother taught me. We used to dance together when she was alive and sometimes we would get my father to join us."

"Would you like a drink, after expending all of that energy?"

"Thank you. I am parched."

William did not want to leave Grace unescorted, with so many men ready to pounce on her, but it would look rather silly to ask her to accompany him to get a drink. He had not taken more than a few steps before two fellows approached her. One was the son of an estate owner he had met before and the other was the overseer of a plantation. He still found the Jamaica way of socialising between the different classes strange. It was also strange to see free coloured people mingling with the white.

By the time he got their drinks Grace was on the dance floor again and appeared to be having a great time by the smile on her face. He had to bite back a growl when he caught her partner with his eyes glued to her bosom. Did she really not think that she would attract unwelcome attention with that dress? Where was George when he was needed?

As soon as the dance finished William made his way to Grace and handed her the drink, which she took gratefully. He led her near to one of the open doors where the breeze coming in was quite chilly.

"My, it is certainly cold tonight," Grace remarked.

"Perhaps you should put on your shawl," William replied drily. Grace ignored him.

"I have not had such an outing in a very long time. I am enjoying it tremendously."

"I am sure you are." Was that jealous-sounding man really him?

"Excuse me, but may I have this dance?" They were interrupted by an older gentleman who had to be close to George's age.

"Certainly," Grace said politely, handing her glass to William.

Am I one of the slaves? William fretted silently as he took the glass. It was not as if he had any claims on Grace, as he would if she were his fiancée, so he could not stop her from dancing with whomever she wanted to. He was just annoyed that she would want to dance with so many other men. He had no desire to even look at the women who outnumbered the men at the party. Although some were quite attractive, none of them stirred him like Grace. How pathetic he had become.

Rather than dwell on Grace and her constant presence on the dance floor, William made an effort to talk to some of the other guests, deciding to feel out some of the overseers to see if they were looking to move on to another plantation, but he did not meet with any success. The guests were more interested in gossiping about Peter Beckford, the younger, who had been accused of killing the Deputy Judge Advocate, a Mr. Lewis, a few weeks earlier. He had reportedly fled to nearby Hispaniola to escape arrest. The Beckfords were among the wealthiest landowners in Jamaica, with thousands of acres and hundreds of slaves. No doubt their money would soon erase the scandal.

When the musicians changed from the lively tunes and slowed down the music, William approached Grace and asked her to dance before any of her admirers could do so.

"Why, Grace, I have hardly seen you all evening," he chided her.

"You could have sought me out as the others have done."

"Am I just one of the others?" He sought her eyes with his. Her face was flushed from dancing and there was a faint sheen of sweat glistening on her bosom. She was beautiful. Heat stirred in him.

"Did I give you cause to think that you were special?"

William almost choked at Grace's words. Who was this woman? Where was the demure girl that he saw every Sunday?

"Unless you usually kiss all the men that you know, then yes I had cause to think I was special."

Grace looked around quickly to see if anyone had overheard him.

"What? No answer to that?" William taunted her.

"I'm feeling rather flushed. I would like to go out to the veranda."

"I would be happy to escort you," William offered.

William guided her to the farthest door and led her outside where the temperature had dropped since earlier in the night. Grace rubbed her hands up and down her arms to warm herself. Quickly shedding his jacket, William draped it around Grace's shoulders.

"Thank you. Mrs. Dorrill told me that she has a beautiful garden. I would love to see it," Grace told him.

"You should come during the day."

"I'm sure I could see some of it now. There are lanterns scattered throughout."

William could not believe what he was hearing. Grace was inviting him to take her into a dark garden? Was she allowing herself to be used by the devil to tempt him, as she had accused him of doing during their early encounters?

"I would be happy to escort you, so that no harm comes to you."

"What harm could possibly come to me?" she asked recklessly. William did not bother to dignify that with an answer. Surely she was not that naïve.

They slipped unnoticed down the steps at the far end of the veranda and headed towards a stone bench that they could see in the distance. Grace held on to William's arm so that she did not trip on the pathway. Her hand felt hot through his shirt, in contrast to the cold night air. Instead of sitting on the stone bench William led Grace, without protest, behind a tree that blocked them from the house. Perhaps she was tired of his restraint and had decided to push him to take things a bit farther. He would be happy to oblige.

"Grace, do you know that in certain circles in England, just being caught together out here would be reason enough to force a marriage between us?"

She laughed. "But we are not doing anything, are we?" That was a challenge if he ever heard one and William did not back down from a challenge.

"I can change that," he murmured, drawing her closer. "You better stop me now if you want to, Grace, because I want to kiss you."

"I am not stopping you," she said boldly.

William needed no further invitation. He lowered his head to meet Grace's lips, kissing them once, twice before parting them to taste her mouth fully as he had been dying to for all these weeks. He forgot that Grace was inexperienced as he passionately devoured her mouth and when she sank her fingers in his hair and gave a small moan of pleasure, he lost all conscious thought. He forgot that they were at a party, in the garden and that her father was somewhere in the house and could possibly be looking for her.

Grace enjoyed the texture of William's hair in her fingers and the pleasure that his mouth was giving her. She could not have imagined such bliss. She moaned in protest when his mouth left hers, but her moan turned to one of pleasure as his mouth found a sensitive spot on her neck. Grace shuddered as William's lips moved lower, kissing her shoulders and the base of her throat. She felt herself being lifted and held against him so that he could bury his face in the softness of her bosom. Grace thought that she would burst into flames. She craved more but did not know what it was she craved. A small part of her mind was whispering that this was wrong, but the desires of her flesh smothered the warning.

William knew that he should stop, but Grace's skin was creamy and soft with a mixture of a floral scent and the faint smell of sweat from her dancing. He licked the skin just above her neckline enjoying the slight taste of salt and Grace. As he buried his face in her softness again a voice behind him said, "Grace Fuller!"

They sprang apart guiltily. William turned and blocked Grace with his body. George Fuller stood before them like an avenging angel. Never had he seen such a look of anger, somehow mixed with disappointment, on George's face. Grace moved a little to the side so that she was not hidden behind William. After all, she could not allow him to protect her when she was as much to blame.

"You have shamed and disgraced yourself and this family. This is one time that I am grateful that your mother is no longer with us for she would have been horrified to see you act like a harlot with this man." Grace hung her head in shame. Tears began to stream down her face.

"And you, William Edwards, I trusted you with my daughter and this is how you treat her? Like a common harlot? You are not worthy of her! Come along, Grace. I will tell our hosts that you are feeling ill and ask if they can provide a carriage to take us home."

Grace stepped past William and followed her father. How could she feel such delight only a few minutes earlier and such despair now? William watched them leave, overwhelmed by shame and disappointment in himself. He did not even need

George's words to make him despise himself, for he already did. Now he fully understood the words of the scripture George had shared: "What does light have to do with darkness?"

He slid to the ground against the trunk of the tree, grabbing his jacket which had fallen from Grace's shoulders to bury his face in it. A feeling of such disgust came over him as he recalled George's disappointment and the tears that streamed down Grace's face. He was responsible for that. He had taken Grace's light and tainted it with his darkness. She was right; he was possessed by some force of darkness and he could not live with it any more. He thought it had gone but it had just been dormant.

"Lord," he whispered, "free me from this darkness. Forgive me for the evil I have done and for the shame I have brought to Grace. Deliver me from evil and change me forever. Amen." He hoped that his prayer, as simple as Bella's had been, would be answered.

A fit of coughing came upon him and then he felt a peace such as he had never known before and a feeling of joy swelled in his heart and burst from his lips as laughter. God's grace was as easy as that. He was free at last.

Chapter 19

December 31, 1697
Needham's Point, Barbados

The sunlight streaming through the window highlighted the red in Deborah's brown wavy hair, which was strewn across the pillow in wild abandon. Richard lay on his side and admired the woman that had been his wife for a whole year. He picked up several strands of her hair and ran them teasingly across her lips. Deborah twitched and made a shooing motion in her sleep as if to get rid of a fly. Richard repeated his action, with a wicked smile. Deborah twitched again and mumbled something incoherently.

"Wake up, wife of mine. Do you not know what day this is?" Richard whispered in her ear.

"No," Deborah grumbled, turning on her side to get some more sleep. Richard smiled at the back she presented to him. After years of having to be up before dawn when she was still a slave at The Acreage, Deborah now refused to get out of bed before the sun was up for at least an hour.

He leaned over and pushed the hair away from her ear so that he could tickle it with his tongue before he whispered, "It is our first anniversary."

He felt Deborah grow still as her brain worked out what he had said. Sleep fled and she turned over with a huge smile. "Happy anniversary, husband of mine. I cannot believe we have been married for a whole year!" She threw her arms around him in delight.

"Neither can I. Happy anniversary, Deborah. This has been the best year of my life."

"Oh, Richard. Mine too. You totally and completely changed my life and I could not be any happier. On second thoughts, I would be much happier if I used the necessary first," she said, scrambling out of bed. Richard laughed at the sheer joy of being married to such an unpredictable and feisty woman like Deborah.

"I have already done my business and had a quick wash," he informed her.

"Not fair," she murmured from the room next door.

"It is not my fault that you will not get up in the morning."

A few minutes later she was back and dived under the sheet to snuggle against Richard, who was blissfully warm.

"Brr, it's freezing," she groaned, absorbing his warmth.

"Deborah, we are in the tropics. If you want to feel freezing you should come to Carolina."

"Yes, well that is not likely to happen. You would probably be charged for marrying a coloured woman."

"That may be so, but I would not change that for the world."

"Or at least not for a rice plantation," she teased him, remembering that he had given up his ambition of running a rice plantation for her. He laughed before becoming serious again.

"I love you so much, Deborah, that there is nothing I wouldn't give up for you. You have made me unbelievably happy."

"Oh, Richard… when are you going to stop talking and show me how much you love me?"

"You are such a hussy. I don't know how I manage to satisfy you."

"By listening to my instructions, so you can start by nibbling on that ticklish spot on my neck." Richard obeyed her, making her giggle and squirm against him.

"What else?" he asked, kissing her shoulder.

"Keep going. You're moving in the right direction." She arched her back to make her point. Richard took the hint and soon Deborah was breathing faster. She ran her fingers through his hair and then pulled his head up for a kiss. Richard needed no further instructions. He knew Deborah's body better than he knew his own; he knew what she liked and how she liked it and he played it like a maestro, making beautiful music, until they reached the familiar crescendo together and the sounds of their mutual pleasure mingled in the air.

"Oh my," Deborah murmured when her heart returned to normal. "That was amazing! Are you going to keep getting better each year, because I don't know if my heart can take it?"

Richard chuckled lazily. "Was it really less than two years ago that we met? I feel as if I've known you forever."

"Well, when I first met you, no-one could have convinced me that we would be civil to each other, far less married."

"I suppose I was rather obnoxious," he admitted.

"Suppose? Do you not remember invading my favourite spot at The Acreage on my day off and interrupting my reading of Romeo and Juliet and then having the audacity to demand that I get you something to eat?"

Richard groaned at the memory. "Don't remind me. You may have been a slave then, but you enslaved me. From the first time I saw you I wanted you."

"That was lust."

"Admittedly, but it soon became love."

"Yes? When did it become love?"

"I don't know the exact time, but when I gave you your manumission papers on your birthday instead of when I was leaving as I had planned to, I knew that I loved you enough to want your happiness more than mine."

"Oh, Richard. I was so overcome that day. I had woken up and it was my eighteenth birthday and I was still a slave. I felt very heavy."

"I know. I could see it in your face. You do not believe in hiding your emotions, do you?" She stuck out her tongue at him. "I had been trying to decide what to give you for your birthday and one day when I was out riding, the answer came to me. Your freedom."

"I could not have asked for a better gift."

"I was afraid that you would take it and leave me, but you agreed to stay."

"I guess I loved you by then as well. When you went back to Carolina, that was a very hard time for me."

"For me too. I felt as if I had left my heart in Barbados."

"I am so glad you came back to me."

Richard started to laugh at a memory. "I remember the look of disapproval on your mother's face when she walked into the shop and saw us kissing."

Deborah started to laugh too. "As soon as you left, she said 'He ain' engaged to a girl in Carolina?' so I told her that you were not getting married anymore but I did not know all of what was happening because we did not have time to talk. And then she said accusingly, 'You ain' had time to talk, but you had time to kiss.'"

Richard laughed. "I can just picture Sarah's face as she said that."

Deborah sobered up. "So much has happened. Some good, some bad."

Richard agreed. "And the visit from my parents would be…"

"Bad!" Deborah finished emphatically. "Do not remind me. Your father was not so bad, but your mother, Richard," she growled. "I tried my best to be polite to her, but it did not help that the first thing she said when she saw me was 'Richard, she's coloured.' and fainted."

"My mother is not known for her tact."

"Indeed? You mean like when she asked me 'How did you snare, I mean, meet Richard?'"

Richard rolled his eyes as he remembered that dinner with his parents. "I thought the two of you would come to blows before the end of dinner."

"We may have, if you didn't intercede with your prayer to bless the meal which was really a warning to behave more like Jesus."

"Well it worked," Richard said, chuckling.

"I think the worst part of our marriage was going to that party at The Acreage."

Richard pulled her close. "I am sorry you had to endure that."

"I chose to go. I did not have to."

Deborah recalled the party that her father had given to introduce Richard's parents to the Barbadian society. He had invited them to come and make it known that they were married. She should never have gone, but she was not one to back down from anything. However, attending a party as a social equal with people she had served as a slave only months before had been a disaster and had served to reinforce her low opinion of the plantocracy in Barbados.

The women had been openly hostile, making comments about her loud enough that she would hear, while the men made no secret of the fact that they still lusted after her, even though she was married. They had even told Richard that while it was permissible to have a coloured woman as a mistress, you did not marry them.

Then she had found that she could not relate to the slaves either, for they had nothing in common. She had felt very lonely that night, knowing that she didn't fit in with the plantocracy and neither with the slaves.

"I am thankful that we have made many new friends among the merchants in town and the few Quakers that are still left," Deborah told him. "But I am concerned for my mother. For both of my parents, to tell the truth."

"I know they are weighing on your mind, but your mother made her decision not to marry Thomas and to teach the girls instead."

"But she still loves him and she is lonely. She pretends that she is fine, but sometimes I see such sadness in her eyes when she does not know that I am watching her. I know that she did not want to marry Jethro, but it makes it worse that even he is married and has a young one on the way."

"Speaking of young ones, "Richard turned so that he could see her face. "Do you want to have a young one on the way?"

"Young one? I do not know, Richard. It will be hard for them to fit in."

"No harder than it is for us. Give it some thought. I will not force you, but I might hide your herbs," he teased, breaking the seriousness of the moment.

Deborah grabbed a pillow and hit him on the head with it, scrambling out of bed before he could retaliate.

"I take it we are not showing our faces at our respective businesses today," Richard said, stretching lazily.

"No. I told my mother not to expect me at the shop."

"Well, come back to bed then," he invited, eying her as she scooped up her chemise and put it on.

"I would advise you to save some stamina for later, Mr. Fairfax and get yourself out of bed to help with the preparations. We are having a dinner party tonight, you know."

"That is why we pay people," Richard grumbled. Deborah ignored him.

"I hope my father comes. I told him he could spend the night here, but he said that if he did come he would stay at a boarding house in town. He is so lonely as well."

"I am sure he will be here. He would never disappoint you."

"But I wonder if my mother will, especially since she knows he will very likely be here. I feel like shaking some sense into her."

"Deborah, I know that you would like your parents to be together, but you cannot force them. You have to accept the decision your mother made," Richard chided her.

"I do?" she asked with an innocent smile. Richard did not like the look of that smile. "I have given her a year to come to her senses and she has not. It is quite evident that she needs a little encouragement. So, I have a plan."

Richard shook his head. He almost felt sorry for Sarah, but he knew that if Deborah's plan worked out, it would result in her happiness. However, if it did not, it could cause everyone involved to get hurt, Deborah included.

❈

Later that evening

Sarah looked at herself in the mirror and was pleased with what she saw. Not that she was dressing to impress anyone. She was wearing a new dress that she had made specially for the party. A bluish-green satin with a square neckline, cut a little lower than she would normally wear and elbow length sleeves trimmed with cream-coloured lace. Some of the same lace trimmed the bottom of the full skirt.

She leaned a little closer to inspect her face to see if there were any lines. However, at thirty-seven her skin was still firm and smooth. She had arranged her hair on her head in a loose knot, and left a few tendrils out to fall against her cheeks.

"Not looking too old," she said aloud. Grabbing her matching lacy shawl, she turned to leave the house. Jacko, one of the slaves Thomas had given her, was waiting to drive her over to Richard and Deborah's house in the new cart she had bought. She had freed him and Mamie, the other slave, a few months before and now she paid them wages.

Thomas. She knew that he would be at the dinner because Deborah would never leave her father out, no matter that she knew it would make her uncomfortable. Deborah was still upset with her for refusing to marry Thomas, but she could not in good conscience marry him. Refusing him was the hardest thing she had ever done, but she could not ask him to give up everything for her. She believed that he would end up resenting her and both of them would eventually be unhappy.

Well, it was over a year now and it had been several months since she had seen him. He had probably started to see someone else, as he was still a very handsome and fit man at fifty-five. She hoped that Deborah would finally realise that they would not get back together and would focus on her own life. She would not mind a grandchild or two, although she was still young enough to have another child herself. Not that it was ever likely to happen.

"Mistress Sarah, you look real nice," Jacko praised her as she reached the bottom of the stairs.

"Thanks, Jacko." Sarah figured that name would stay with her forever. The slaves at The Acreage had started calling her Mistress Sarah from the day that she had saved Jethro from the whipping Thomas had threatened to give him. It was the old house keeper, Ada, who had started it. When Sarah asked why she had called her Mistress Sarah she had said with a cackle, "Well if you got the power to stop Jethro from getting a beating, you must be the mistress of the house." And the name had stuck.

Sarah did not know why she was remembering these things tonight. They were best forgotten, just as the way Thomas used to look at her with love in his eyes was best forgotten. Not to mention the way those eyes would darken with desire. Stop it! She spoke firmly to herself. She was doing fine. She would not remember what it felt like to lie in his arms. Anyway, she no longer lived that kind of life. She was walking the narrow road now, not the broad road, and she would do well to remember that.

It took about half an hour to reach Richard and Deborah's house which was a little way past Carlisle Bay, near to Needham's Point. It was such a beautiful evening that Deborah could not have asked for a better one. The moon was beginning to rise and you could hear and smell the sea. Sarah wondered who else would be there, but Deborah had been very closemouthed. Of course, she knew that Thomas would be and she was bracing herself to encounter him again.

Jacko drove up the driveway and pulled up behind several carriages and carts that were parked with their drivers talking to each other in a corner. Candles enclosed by chimneys on stands lit the driveway and the candle-laden chandelier in the entranceway spilled additional light onto the porch. Richard and Deborah made an extremely handsome couple as they stood together near the front door to greet their guests. On seeing her, Richard walked down the drive way to help her down from the bench.

"Sarah, you look beautiful," he exclaimed.

"Thank you, Richard. You look very handsome yourself."

"Jacko, you can leave. We will make sure that Sarah gets home safely."

"All right, Massa Richard," Jacko replied, making Richard shake his head as he turned to escort Sarah to the door. Old habits were hard to break.

"Deborah," she greeted, hugging her. "You look beautiful. I am so happy for both of you. I hope you enjoy many more years together. Here is a small gift I brought for you."

"Thank you, Ma. I do not think I have ever seen you look so beautiful. Did you dress specially for someone?" she teased in a whisper. Sarah was glad that her light-brown skin kept her response to the teasing a secret. She had dressed to please herself, not Thomas, as Deborah was suggesting. So why did her heart start to beat wildly when a familiar figure joined Richard and Deborah and said, "Hello, Sarah, I agree with Deborah. I have never seen you look so beautiful."

Chapter 20

"Th-thank you, Thomas," she stuttered. "You look good." And indeed he did. He seemed to have lost a little weight and there was a sadness in his eyes that had not been there before. Was it because of her? Nevertheless, he was still as handsome as ever and his suit fit him perfectly, as if he had gotten it made recently.

"You are the last to arrive, Ma, so now we can go inside. I will introduce you to the other guests, although you will know most of them already."

Deborah left Richard and her father to chat while she led her mother around the room to reacquaint her with their guests. There were five couples, two of them were white merchants from the city, there was a free black couple who attended the same Bible study as her and a free coloured couple who ran a boarding house. Two of the ladies were her customers. The last couple she had never seen before.

Deborah introduced them as Archibald Jenkins and Violet Applewhaite. It was then that Sarah learned that they were not a couple as she had assumed, but were brother and sister. The brother had a business in England and he and his sister were on a visit to Barbados to explore the possibility of expanding the business by importing goods from Barbados. That is how they had met Richard and subsequently Deborah.

He was a tall, lean man who looked to be in his forties, with thinning brown hair and a thick moustache. His sister was also quite tall, for a woman, and was very beautiful with smooth creamy skin which contrasted beautifully with her rich brown hair. She had eyes an unusual colour of violet, the likes of which Sarah had never seen before. No doubt they had influenced her parents when they came to select her name. Sarah figured that she looked to be around the same age as her or could possibly be a few years younger. They were both polite, though not overly warm. Sarah could not help but notice that Violet's eyes seemed to be drawn in the direction of Richard and Thomas quite often. She was sure it was not Richard she was looking at.

"Violet and Archibald do not know very many people here, so we were happy to invite them and have them meet some of our friends," Deborah told her mother.

"I was very happy to accept your invitation, Deborah. To tell the truth, I have hardly been out since my husband died a year ago."

"Well, I am glad that you came."

A widow, thought Sarah. Is she sizing up Thomas to be her next husband? Sarah assessed her with new eyes and a sick feeling gripped her stomach. Here was a beautiful woman who could not keep her eyes off Thomas and they were both free. What was to stop them from getting together? If they did who could she blame but herself? What was she thinking? The poor woman was probably still in mourning for her husband.

"How long are you staying in Barbados?" Sarah asked them.

"I believe that we will let the worse of winter pass in England and then we will journey back in March," Archibald answered.

"That is wonderful," Deborah smiled at them. Sarah found it difficult to share her enthusiasm.

Having made the introductions, Deborah and Richard led the way into the dining room which had been transformed into an elegant setting. The dining table, which was set for fourteen people, was a masterpiece with fine china, sparkling glasses, cutlery and white napkins at each place, plus two beautiful flower arrangements down the centre. Sarah wondered if Deborah had gotten Jethro to build a new table or to add on an extension to her old one because it was much longer than before.

Richard stood by his chair at the head of the table while Deborah orchestrated the seating. Archibald was on Richard's left, with his sister next to him, Thomas next to her and the other couples seated with men and women alternating but no-one could sit next to their spouse. Sarah was directed to sit next to Deborah which put her directly across from Violet and next to the husband of the coloured couple. That gave her a good view of Thomas. She had no doubt that her dear daughter had seated them that way purposely. She wondered what Deborah was up to.

After Richard said the grace, a bevy of servants began to serve the first course of potato soup which everyone declared to be delicious. Soon the soup was cleared away and conversation buzzed as everyone waited for the next course to be brought in.

"That was very good, Deborah," Sarah praised her quietly. "Everything looks good."

"Thank you, Ma. At least I learned something from Elizabeth. She certainly knew how to entertain."

The mention of Elizabeth caused Sarah to look across the table at Thomas who was engaged in conversation with Archibald.

"Richard tells me you own a ship as well as a plantation," he began.

"Yes. I am a part owner of a ship that takes sugar, molasses and rum to England."

"I have a merchant business in London so I am here to make contact with people who can ship goods to me from here and bring goods from England. Perhaps we can speak at greater length at a more appropriate time."

"That would be fine. I would like to extend an invitation to you and your sister to come to The Acreage and have a look around. I can show you how we convert the cane into sugar and rum although this is not the harvest season at present. We can have our discussions then."

"That sounds lovely," Violet joined in enthusiastically. "I have never seen a sugar plantation and it would be interesting to see how you make the sugar."

"If you would like to come this weekend I can send a carriage for you. It is quite a long journey so you may want to consider staying for the weekend if it suits you."

"That sounds splendid," Archibald agreed with more enthusiasm than Sarah had seen from him for the whole night. His sister looked very pleased as well. Thomas was inviting them for the weekend? Maybe he was as lonely as she was when the girls had finished sewing and went home to their families.

"As I was telling Deborah earlier, I have not been out very much since my husband died, but I am now over the period of mourning and I am happy to be more sociable."

Sarah almost rolled her eyes at how obvious Violet was being. Now Thomas knew that she was a widow and, apparently, available.

"Well, that is wonderful, Violet," Deborah encouraged from across the table. "Life is too short, so we should grab what happiness we can when it presents itself. It was very good of you to mourn your husband for a year. We do not observe such a long period in Barbados. My father also lost his wife over a year now so you have that in common."

Richard squeezed Deborah's knee warningly under the table. He could see the machinations of her plan unfolding. He did not know how she could manipulate her mother in such a way without conscience. He glanced at Sarah and had to admit that Deborah's comments seemed to be hitting the mark. She looked distinctly uncomfortable with the turn of events. He hoped that this did not go horribly wrong because someone would get hurt.

"I am sorry to hear that," she empathised with Thomas. Then her forehead wrinkled a little as if she was trying to work out a puzzle. It had only then dawned on her that Thomas was Deborah's father, but his wife was not her mother. She recalled that Deborah had introduced the woman, Sarah, as her mother but, truth to tell, she had not been listening very attentively as her focus had been elsewhere.

"Your wife?" she repeated, looking from Thomas to Sarah to Deborah. Her creamy skin turned red as she came face to face with something she had heard about in England.

"Yes, she died in England." Thomas answered hastily to fill the awkward silence at their end of the table. The chatter of the other dinners thankfully continued uninterrupted.

Sarah was very uncomfortable and tried not to appear ruffled under Violet's assessing stare. Thomas looked across and saw her school her face into an unconcerned mask and was angry with himself for putting her in the position to come under the other woman's judgement. He was also not very happy with Deborah for her comment, which left her mother open to judgement. He also blamed Sarah for allowing herself to be found in such a position when they could have been married by now. He even had a priest who had been willing to marry them privately for a nice donation to his church.

Deborah looked helplessly at Richard as she realised that she had unintentionally caused her mother to be cast in a very poor light by the English visitors who were not exposed to the ways of the island. He came to her rescue and smoothly changed the subject.

"Is it your intention to visit any of the other Caribbean islands?" he asked.

"We are considering Jamaica as I have heard that it is likely to catch up with, and possibly exceed, Barbados in terms of sugar production in the next few years. That will mean development and the desire for more imports so it might be a good opportunity for me to get into the country early."

"My son is managing a plantation in Jamaica," Thomas told him, watching Deborah across the table. Her face tensed. "They have just had a bad hurricane there so this may not be the best time to go. His plantation was very badly damaged and they lost some slaves."

"Oh dear," sympathised Violet.

"Besides which, he said that Jamaica is rife with disease, not to mention violence. He caught malaria in the first few days he was there and almost died."

"What is malaria?" Violet asked.

"It is a disease carried by a particular mosquito. I won't describe the symptoms at the dinner table, but rest assured that William said he would not wish it on his worst enemy."

"I did not know that," Deborah said quietly. She was surprised to feel a stirring of compassion for William despite what he had done to her.

"That is not the worst thing to happen to him. I received a letter from him last month telling me that he had been robbed, beaten and left for dead when he was on a journey to buy supplies for the plantation. He would be dead right now if some slaves had not found him and taken him to a neighbouring plantation where he was tended to."

"Oh no! That is terrible!" Violet exclaimed. Deborah had been about to make a similar exclamation. Even Richard was sorry to hear of William's bad fortune.

"He has said that he wants to come back to Barbados." Thomas dropped the comment, although it was really a silent question to Richard and Deborah.

"I would think so," Violet said in agreement, unaware of the undercurrents at their end of the table.

"He said that the whole incident has changed him. I think it is time to get him out of Jamaica." It was an unspoken request for permission. It suddenly dawned on Deborah that The Acreage must be painfully lonely for her father with no-one there but him and the slaves.

Richard looked at Deborah who nodded imperceptibly and gave the permission. "I think that might be best."

"Good. I am planning to visit him in a few months when things settle down there and spend some time with him there or maybe travel a bit and then come back."

Sarah looked across at him in surprise. Thomas was planning to go away and spend time with William? He was moving on with his life too and seemed to be trying to fix the mistakes he had made in the past. Would she get another chance to fix the mistakes she had made, or had she waited too long? Had she left the way open for a woman like Violet?

"It would be lovely if you came to England," Violet said, brightening up. "Then we would have the opportunity to return your hospitality."

"What a splendid idea, Violet," Deborah said enthusiastically, moving her knee away from Richard just in time. "You should do that, Father."

No, he should not! Sarah exclaimed in her head. Everyone turned to look at her, making her wonder for a horrible moment if she had said it aloud.

"Were you saying something, Ma?" Deborah asked innocently. "I thought that you made a noise."

Had she? Sarah wondered. "No. It was nothing," she muttered, turning her attention quickly back to her plate and missing the smile of satisfaction on Deborah's face.

❆

The rest of dinner progressed without any further incidents. Everyone exclaimed over each of the five courses and declared themselves stuffed at the end of the evening. Sarah was very proud of Deborah and all that she had accomplished. She had set a table that was unequalled by the finest plantations and brought together black, white and coloured showing that it was only the plantocracy that stuck to themselves, not even socialising with poorer whites. Sarah wondered if Deborah was trying to tell her something.

Soon the evening drew to a close as it was a week day and, apart from Violet and Archibald who were on holiday, they all had businesses to run.

Richard arranged a ride for the visitors in the carriage of one of the merchants who had a very large and elaborate carriage. Eventually only Richard, Deborah and her parents were left in the living room.

"I have arranged for a carriage to collect me at nine to take me back to the boarding house," Thomas told them, checking his pocket watch, "so I will soon leave you lovebirds to enjoy the rest of your anniversary."

"Would you be able to give Sarah a ride home, Thomas? I told Jacko that I would make sure she got home safely." Deborah tried not to appear too gleeful, but she would make sure she thanked Richard properly later.

"I would be happy to, if that is all right with you, Sarah."

"Thank you, Thomas. As long as I am not putting you out of your way."

"I am staying in Bridge Town tonight and I would be happy to take you, even if it was out of my way."

"Good, then that is settled. I think I hear a carriage coming up the driveway now," Richard said, standing up.

"I can see that you are eager to get rid of us, my boy," Thomas stood, helping Sarah to her feet.

Richard pulled Deborah up to hug her to his side and dropped a kiss on her hair. "I would be lying if I denied it," he laughed. Deborah turned her head up to his and their lips met for a brief kiss.

"I can see that it is time for us to go, Sarah."

They hugged and said their goodbyes at the door. Thomas helped Sarah up into the carriage and they waved again. As the carriage moved off, Sarah looked out and saw Richard and Deborah kissing passionately before Richard pushed the door closed. She felt a pang of loneliness in her heart.

Thomas wished that he was not dropping Sarah to her house, but that they were married and going home together. Could it be that her heart was not aching as his was? All he wanted at that moment was to take her in his arms and kiss her as passionately as Richard had kissed Deborah, but would she welcome it? There was only one way to find out.

Chapter 21

"That was a lovely dinner party, wasn't it?" Thomas broke the silence. "The food was very good."

"Yes," agreed Sarah. There was another silence, but it was not a comfortable one. It was full of unspoken words and unasked questions.

"It was quite unusual for me to sit at a table with white, black and coloured people, but it was not uncomfortable," remarked Thomas.

"No."

"Archibald and Violet were very pleasant and they did not seem uncomfortable with the mixture of guests. I am looking forward to doing business with him."

"Good."

"Are you only going to answer in one-word sentences, Sarah?" Thomas finally asked in exasperation.

"What do you want me to say?"

"I want you to say what you're thinking. Surely we've known each other too long to be talking as if we are mere strangers."

"You are right, Thomas. Did you find Violet attractive?" She had been wanting to know the answer to that question all night.

Thomas tried not to show his surprise. That was the last question he expected from Sarah, but it gave him the opening he needed.

"She is indeed a very beautiful woman. Her eyes are a most unusual and attractive colour."

"Yes, they are," Sarah agreed tonelessly, with far less enthusiasm than Thomas had shown. The next unasked question hovered on her lips, but she would never voice it.

"But to answer your question, while I find her attractive, I am not attracted to her. And while she is beautiful, she does not move me." He paused and gently took her chin and turned her to face him. "Like you do."

His eyes lighted on her lips and he remembered the first time he kissed her. He had hesitated at first wondering, ignorantly, if it would be different than kissing a white woman. Her full brownish pink lips had beckoned him to taste them then and they beckoned him now. Sarah licked her lips nervously, as if she was once again in her room at The Acreage twenty years ago. Thomas' eyes followed the movement of her tongue across her lips and knew that he could not resist tasting them himself.

Sliding nearer to her on the bench, Thomas gave her ample opportunity to stop him from going any further. When she did not move away, he bent his head and kissed her gently, tasting her lips as he had been longing to do. Needing to get closer to her, he curved one arm around her shoulders and cupped her cheek in his other hand, drawing her in so that he could deepen the kiss. He knew that he should probably take things slowly but an urgency to possess her mouth came over him and he began to kiss her as passionately as Richard had been kissing Deborah when they left.

Sarah sank her hands into Thomas' hair and pulled him closer, devouring his mouth as much as he was devouring hers. She felt like she had been dying of thirst and had just found a spring of fresh, cold water. She could not get enough. They parted for breath before continuing to taste and explore each other's mouths when Thomas suddenly pulled back and rested his forehead against Sarah's. The sound of their heavy breathing mingled together was something they had not heard for a long time.

"Sarah, I am fifty-five years old, but you make me feel like a school boy again."

"What do you mean?" she whispered breathlessly.

"Like I cannot control myself. I had to stop kissing you because I started to have thoughts of laying you back on the seat and pleasuring you until you begged me to stop. And we are in a carriage!"

"Thomas…" Sarah began in protest to his bold words.

"Don't worry, Sarah. I respect you too much to do such a thing and I honour the commitment you have made. So as hard as it is, I will bid you goodnight and look forward to my dreams tonight."

Sarah realised with a start that the carriage had stopped moving and it was parked outside her house.

"Oh, I did not realise that we were here. Thank you for the ride home, Thomas. Goodbye." She turned to open the carriage door, but Thomas stilled her hand with his.

"May I come and see you next time I am in town?"

"Yes, I would like that."

"Good," Thomas said with a big smile, reaching around her to open the door so that he could get out and help her down. "I will walk you to your door."

Once upstairs, Sarah took out her key and unlocked the door. Before going inside, she reached up and kissed Thomas on his lips.

"Goodnight, Thomas. See you soon?"

"Most assuredly! Good night, Sarah."

Sarah closed the door and locked it. The smile on her face matched the one that Thomas had on his as he jogged down the stairs like a man half his age.

❦

Richard reluctantly dragged his lips away from Deborah's and locked the door as the sound of the carriage faded.

"Deborah, you have been very naughty tonight," he scolded her.

"Me?" she asked innocently. "In what way?"

Before he could answer one of the maids came to ask if they needed anything else before they started to clean up. Deborah and Richard took the hint that they wanted them out of the way.

"Let us take this discussion to our room," Richard suggested.

"Yes. I want to thank you for arranging for my father to take my mother home." She smiled as she led the way to their room.

"Deborah, I too would like to see your parents together and happy, but you cannot manipulate them and other people in order to do it. Someone might end up getting hurt."

"Who did I manipulate?" she asked testily.

"Did you not invite Archibald and Violet here specifically because she is a beautiful widow and you knew that she might be interested in your father? And did you not hope that your mother might become jealous and start to realise that your father might end up with another woman?

"How is that manipulation? I simply brought them together and left things to take their own course."

"Really? What was 'What a splendid idea, Violet. You should do that, Father.' if not manipulation? Suppose Violet falls in love with your father, do you not think she would get hurt if he and your mother get back together?"

Deborah sighed heavily. "You are right, Richard. I did not think this through very well. I promise not to get involved anymore. In fact, I hope I do not have to. If my father does not use the opportunity of taking my mother home to kiss her like you kissed me at the front door, then he is not the man I think he is."

Richard laughed. "You are incorrigible, my dear wife. How will I deal with you for the next fifty years?"

"If you do what you have been doing for this first year then you should be fine," she said saucily.

"Thank you, my dear. Now let me help you out of that dress so that we can finish the celebration of our marriage the way that we most enjoy."

"Well, I quite enjoyed the dinner party," she teased as he undid the buttons running down the back of her dress. Pushing it off her shoulders, he leaned over to kiss the ticklish spot between her neck and shoulder, making her feet buckle.

"Tell me how it compares after this," he invited, adding the chemise to the pile on the floor before picking her up and carrying her to the bed.

A long time later

"Oh, in all of the rushing around today, I forgot to tell you that I got a letter from my brother. He and Ann would like to come to Barbados for a visit," Richard said lazily, stroking Deborah's hair as she lay on his arm, half asleep.

"Ann, as in your fiancée?" she exclaimed, sleep totally gone from her.

"Well, since we are both married, she is no longer my fiancée," Richard said drily.

"You know what I mean, Richard Fairfax. Will that not be extremely awkward?"

"It will not be awkward for me and I am sure that she has transferred her affections to Charles so it should not be for her either."

"I take it they would stay here," Deborah stated, the reluctance evident in her voice.

"Of course, Deborah. He is my brother. Although he may also want to spend a few days with Uncle Thomas."

"What should I expect? Will they be like your mother?"

"I honestly do not know. Ann probably, but Charles will likely be more like my father. Carolina is very similar to Barbados and has modelled its treatment of slaves based on the

Barbados Slave Code and Ann has grown up on a plantation so she will have similar views to the planters here."

"Like you did," Deborah pointed out.

"Touché," Richard acknowledged her jab as a good come back. "I have not answered the letter yet, so I will let you decide if I should say yes or not."

"He is your brother. I can hardly tell you not to allow him to come."

"You are my wife and your desires far outweigh my brother's. So, I will only extend the invitation if you are in agreement. Alternatively, he can come to Barbados but stay elsewhere."

"I love you, Richard, and you have given up so much for me already, that I could not deny you seeing your brother. Ann I will try to tolerate."

"Thank you, Deborah. To tell the truth, I look forward to seeing Charles. Although he disapproved of my lifestyle he was always a good brother to me."

"Oh yes, your lifestyle," she said drily.

"But you have reformed me," Richard reminded her.

Looking back at his life in Carolina and before he had the encounter with God during the storm on his way back to Barbados, Richard acknowledged that he was without conscience. He had agreed to marry Ann solely to get his hands on her father's plantation and get out from his father's business. It had helped that Ann, who had loved him for many years, was the older of two sisters and her brother had died, so her father had practically offered the plantation as her dowry.

He had readily agreed and had been willing to go through with the marriage, with the full intention of keeping his French mistress, Anise, afterwards. He remembered how upset Deborah had been when she found out that he had a mistress. She had been less concerned about his fiancée since she understood the reason he was marrying her, but she had said that having a mistress was his choice.

He had promised Ann not to fall in love with any of the planters' daughters when he left for Barbados, but he had not counted on losing his heart to Deborah. That she had caused him to desire to end his engagement was one thing, but the fact that she was coloured and was once a slave would no doubt cause Ann to feel completely humiliated. He hoped that she had put that behind her and that she and Charles were as in love as he and Deborah were. However, the quotation "hell hath no fury like a woman scorned" gave him some cause for concern.

❈

Next Day

Richard's hatred of letter writing had not changed and he was ashamed to say how few letters he had sent to Carolina, especially after his parents' visit to Barbados and the dismissive way his mother had treated Deborah. In spite of that he should have made a better attempt to keep in touch with Charles, his sister Charlotte and her husband Albert who was his best friend. It was shameful really, so he was looking forward to seeing Charles, at least. He could not say the same for Ann. He really had no desire to deal with her prejudices and he would not tolerate any disrespect for Deborah. He sighed as he reached for his quill and dipped it in the ink.

January 1st, 1698
Bridge Town, Barbados

> *Dear Charles*
>
> *I was pleased to receive your letter and to hear all the news from Carolina. Please congratulate Caroline and Albert for me on the forthcoming increase in their family. They have certainly not wasted any time. Both Caroline and Mother wrote to tell me the news, but you (especially) know how poor I am at corresponding. You should therefore consider yourself highly regarded for me to take the time and effort to respond to your letter.*
>
> *Deborah and I celebrated the first anniversary of our marriage yesterday and we had a dinner party with twelve of our friends and her family. I am sorry that none of my family was here to celebrate with us, although I am not sure to what extent you would agree that our marriage is worth celebrating. Nevertheless, we are very happy together and I do not for one minute regret what I gave up to come to Barbados.*
>
> *I have discussed with Deborah your desire to visit Barbados and we will be happy to have you and Ann stay with us for the trip. However, let me make*

it clear that if Deborah feels at all uncomfortable, I will drive you to the nearest accommodations or arrange for you to complete your stay at The Acreage with Uncle Thomas. I therefore hope that you can control Ann so that she does not make any disparaging remarks to Deborah.

Having said that, I am looking forward to seeing you, as it has been more than a year since we last saw each other.

Your brother
Richard

Chapter 22

January 18th, 1698
Bridge Town

Thomas was as anxious as a boy on his first outing with a young lady. He had just checked into his favourite boarding house in Bridge Town and he was now eager to go and visit Sarah. He had almost regretted inviting Archibald and Violet to spend a weekend at The Acreage for they had requested permission to come last weekend instead of the one before. So he had had to put off coming into town to see Sarah for two weeks.

They had been very impressed with the plantation and although it was not harvest season time, they were still keen to see the mill and the boiling house and to learn about the process. He had shown them the rum distillery and Archibald got very excited about the possibility of bringing rum into England and distributing it through his business.

Violet seemed more interested in the size of the plantation, the number of slaves he had and the fact that he was a widower. She had said on more than one occasion that he must be lonely with just the slaves for company. He had made it his business not to be alone with her or to in any way suggest that he might be interested in pursuing a relationship, for he knew that his heart still belonged to Sarah and it would be wrong to give her false hope.

He could see through Deborah's scheme clearly and, from what Sarah had asked him in the carriage, it seemed to have had the intended result. At least he hoped so. Sarah had seemed jealous of Violet, but that did not necessarily mean that she was now willing to marry him and he still very much wanted to marry her. Perhaps she had just been reacting to the fact that another woman found him attractive, whereas before she had never had to compete for his attention. He hoped that was not the case.

As he turned the horse onto High Street his heart began to beat faster and he laughed silently at himself. He was opening himself up to possible heartbreak again, but he had not felt so alive in over a year, which was better than the melancholy state that he had been existing in since Sarah refused him. He had to control himself from allowing the horse a full gallop, as people thronged the street as was usual for a Saturday. Slave girls were laden down with parcels, carrying the purchases of their mistresses, while men were heading to the drinking houses to get one or two drinks before they went home to dinner.

He had waited until he was certain that the shop would be closed before he rode over to her house so that he would not have to wait for her to close up. As he approached the house, he was pleased to see that it was still well maintained and the environs neat and clean. Sarah and Deborah had made him very proud of how well their businesses were succeeding. Sarah's business was clearly profitable enough for her to keep the house in good repair and to buy the new cart that Jacko had brought her to the party in. He had even heard from Deborah that she had freed Jacko and Mamie and now paid them to work for her. She had never been comfortable with the idea of owning slaves. Most important to her, according to Deborah, she had paid one of the Quakers to teach her how to read and write and how to speak properly. He had loved her before she had any of those skills so he did not care, but he was happy that she had chosen to improve herself.

While he had appealed to his friends and colleagues for their wives to support her business in the early days and he had used his contacts to get her a contract to make slave clothing, it was her skill and her business acumen that made the business successful. He remembered how reluctant he had been to send Jethro to help build shelves and racks for the clothes when she was first setting up the shop, as he did not want Sarah to be spending time with him. He had been jealous of his own slave.

He was very relieved that Sarah did not choose to marry him for he did not know how he could bear it if she did, even though he had freed Jethro for that purpose. Thankfully, he was now married and had wasted no time in starting a family. Thomas sent business his way, as he genuinely liked Jethro and was happy to help him now that he knew he was no longer available to pursue Sarah.

He wondered if Sarah ever thought about having another child. He knew she would only do so if she were married, but was she now willing to marry him? He hoped that she was not entertaining him because she was lonely, for she had kissed him back with such passion in the carriage that hope had sprung to life in him again. It was said that "hope deferred maketh the heart sick" and his heart had been sick before, so he certainly did not want his hope to be deferred again.

He tied his horse to one of the posts at the bottom of the stairs and eagerly climbed up, patting the pocket of his jacket to make sure that the present he had bought her was still there. It was a small heart-shaped locket on a fine gold chain. It came with a tiny key which unlocked the heart. He hoped she would like it and would not think that he was rushing her into anything again, but he was not getting any younger and neither was she. Mind you, she still looked as youthful as ever at thirty-seven. If anything, he should make way for her to find a man nearer to her own age and have at least one child with him. No. Even the thought of that pained him. Sarah was his and he was determined not to let her get away again.

After knocking three times, and beginning to despair that Sarah was not at home, the door opened a crack. He was glad to see her peep out cautiously and once she saw it was him, she broke into a big smile and opened the door wider to let him in. She was wrapped in a dressing gown that she seemed to have donned hurriedly and her hair was loose around her shoulders. Thomas' body stirred in response.

"Thomas! I didn't expect you today. Come in and sit down while I finish getting dressed. I was just bathing."

Thomas was tempted to tell her not to bother to get dressed, but he held his tongue lest he frighten her off before he could begin to court her again. He remembered the last time they had been intimate and groaned silently. Sarah had told him that she was no longer able to be his mistress because she had made a decision to live her life according to God's ways. It had been hard, but he had respected her decision and still visited her to make sure that she was well. The friendship had been without intimacy until the day that his daughters had left for England.

Putting Mary and Rachel on the boat had made him feel as if he was losing everyone in his life and he went to Sarah's house looking for comfort. Even though he had not been very close to the girls, their leaving within months of Richard's departure for Carolina, Sarah and Deborah being freed and William being sent to Jamaica left a void in his life that Elizabeth could not fill.

When he told Sarah that he was sending the girls to England in hopes of them finding good husbands, he could not help but notice the sadness that flitted across her face as if she too longed for a husband. She did not deny it when he asked her if she did not lie awake aching for him the way he ached for her. She did not resist him when he kissed her until passion exploded between them, overriding her convictions until after it had been spent. It was then that she had cried tears of shame and guilt which tore at his heart. He never wanted Sarah to feel that way again so he would keep to himself.

"Sorry to keep you waiting, Thomas. But I didn't know you were coming today. I thought you would have come last week."

Thomas looked up to see Sarah dressed in a plain brown dress, buttoned right up to her neck. Her hair was also tamed into a plait and hung down her back. If she thought that the plain dress would render her unattractive, she did not know that the power she held over him had nothing to do with the clothes she wore. Even when she wore slave's clothing she had enticed him more than Elizabeth ever could in all her finery, rest her soul.

"I would have, but Archibald and Violet came for the weekend." Sarah grew guarded at the mention of Violet's name.

"Oh. You had a good time?"

"Yes, I was glad to have the company, but I realised that I have to be careful not to lead her on when my heart is not free to love someone else." He had better put an end to her suspicions right away. Deborah's plan may have worked to arouse Sarah's jealousy, but he needed her to know that his feelings had not changed.

"What you mean by that, Thomas?"

He took the heart on its chain out of his pocket and handed it to her. "This represents my heart, Sarah." He found the tiny key on its own chain in his pocket and dangled it before her. "And this is the key that unlocks my heart. Only you hold the key to my heart and when you are ready you can unlock it. Until then I will keep it." He reached into her opened palm for the heart, put it back into his pocket and then fastened the key around her neck.

"Thank you, Thomas," she said quietly, not sure what else to say. He nodded.

"I think I had better go," he told her reluctantly.

"Already? You can't stay for dinner? I have some soup that I made at lunch and some bread. You can share it." Thomas was very tempted and did not put up much resistance after that. He would stay far from her and not make the same mistake as last time. "Come into the kitchen and talk while I get it ready."

Thomas followed her from the room and settled in one of the chairs at the kitchen table while she moved about efficiently getting the food heated up.

"You still planning to go to Jamaica?"

"Yes. I am thinking of going towards the end of March. Richard told me that his brother is coming for about a month some time in February so I would like to be here to meet him."

"Oh yes, I heard so. I wonder how it will be with his brother's wife and Deborah? I hope she won't give Deborah any trouble."

"You should know by now that Deborah is more than capable of taking care of herself. Besides, Richard will not tolerate any disrespect towards her."

"I know, but she is my only child and I want to protect her, even though she is a married woman."

"Would you ever want to have another child, Sarah? You are still young enough to." Sarah stopped stirring the soup and turned to look at him.

"I wouldn't mind. If I was to ever get married."

"I would love to give you another child, Sarah." Thomas immediately chastised himself for rushing things.

"Well, you do make some good-looking children, Thomas," she laughed. Thomas was shocked that she did not reject his words. His heart began to leap with hope. Could Sarah be rethinking her decision not to marry him? He decided to push a little more and see how far he could get.

"Would you consider coming to Jamaica with me?" He held his breath.

"What?" She looked at him in shock. "You know the only way I would go to Jamaica with you is if we were married. Anyway, I thought you were going to spend some time with William so you all could get to know one another better. How will you do that if I am there?"

Thomas took hope from that. At least it was not a no. "Yes, that is true."

"I will miss you when you're gone, though. How long are you planning to be gone for?"

"I don't know. Maybe a month. I may hurry home if there is a good reason to come back quickly," he hinted. Sarah smiled but did not make any comment as she put a bowl of soup and a chunk of bread in front of Thomas.

"It's not going to be as good as the one we had at Deborah the other night," she warned.

"I don't care. Since you made it, I will love it." Like I love you, he added silently.

Sarah smiled contentedly. Having Thomas in her house and sharing a meal made her feel happier than she had in months. What would it be like if they could be together every day? Was there a way for that to be possible? Maybe she should pray and ask the Lord. After all, nothing was impossible for him.

"That was delicious, Sarah," Thomas praised her, cleaning the bowl.

"Thank you, Thomas. It is a pleasure to see you eating so well."

Thomas smiled.

"Please take care in Jamaica," she said anxiously. "After you talked about all the sickness there and how William got beaten until he was nearly dead, I don't want you to go. But I know that you and William need to work out things. So, I will pray for you to get back safely."

"Thank you, Sarah. I had better go now," he said, standing up.

"You leaving already? I thought you were staying in town."

"I am, but if I don't go now I will not want to go at all and I still remember the pain and guilt I caused you that time that we ended up in your bed." He swore that he saw a flush come over her face. "I have not been with another woman since you told me you would not marry me so I don't think I am strong enough to deal with that temptation."

"What? You telling the truth, Thomas?" Sarah was shocked. She was sure that he would have been bedding Hattie or some other slave on the plantation. A feeling of joy burst in her heart.

"If I can't have you, I don't want any other woman, Sarah," he said solemnly.

"And if I can't have you, I don't want any other man," she vowed.

"Just say the word, Sarah."

"But we are not equally yoked, Thomas," she said regretfully.

"That is the only thing standing in your way now?"

She nodded.

Thomas smiled. "Well, we are making progress," he said happily. He bent over and kissed her on the forehead. "Come and see me out and lock the door. I will visit you again soon."

Sarah closed the door after Thomas and heard him wait until he heard the key turn in the lock before he went down the stairs. She felt the key around her neck and remembered him saying that she had the key to his heart. She smiled as the love for him that she had buried pushed its way past her fears to the surface of her heart again. As Deborah had said, life was too short. Perhaps it was time to grab what happiness she could.

Chapter 23

February 15, 1698
Carlisle Bay, Bridge Town

Richard was surprised at the emotion he felt when he laid his eyes on Charles. He had missed him more than he had realised and he was very glad that he had agreed for him to come and visit. Charles had lost his boyish looks and his face was a little firmer. Both he and Ann appeared to be in good health and seemed happy. Ann wore an attractive green dress, trimmed with white and a matching hat. He found it hard to imagine that he had kissed her, had been engaged to her and he had been prepared to spend his life with her. He silently thanked God that he had come to Barbados before he got married.

"Charles, Ann," he greeted, approaching them. He kissed Ann on the cheek and he and Charles embraced.

"Richard, it is so good to see you," Charles said, stepping back to look at him. "You look well. Happy."

"I am," Richard agreed. "Ann, you look very well. In fact, both of you do. Let me get you into the carriage. You must be tired."

"I am indeed. I have never been so glad to see dry land," Ann said with a smile.

Richard looked around at all their trunks and asked, "How long did you say you were staying?"

Charles laughed at the worried look on his face. "Only a month, but my wife wanted to make sure she had everything she would need."

"My dear Ann, Barbados colonised Carolina. The country may be smaller but it is not backwards. You can get anything your heart desires here," Richard informed her.

"Well, I'm happy to hear that."

Richard handed her up into the carriage and stepped back to allow Charles to enter. He arranged for the trunks to be loaded on a cart before getting in and sitting across from them. A feeling of wellbeing came over him to be sitting across from his brother after more than a year and that there was no awkwardness between him and Ann.

"How is everyone?" he asked.

"Everyone is well. Mother and Father are in good health and Father is still very much running the business as before. Charlotte is beginning to increase and Albert is acting as if his wife was the first woman to be with child."

Richard smiled at that.

"What about you and Deborah? You have been married a year now. Are you planning on having children?"

"Not just yet. I want to have her all to myself for a little while longer. I suppose Mother told you all about their visit," Richard said drily.

"Indeed," Charles replied diplomatically.

To say that his mother did not take to Deborah well was an understatement and he had quickly discovered that it was best to keep them far from each other. He hoped that Ann would be of a different ilk. He would soon find out.

"It is quite hot, isn't it?" Ann remarked.

"It is certainly hotter than Carolina, but believe me this is the coolest time of the year," Richard assured her. He hoped that Ann would not be constantly complaining. He had forgotten how spoilt she was. He offered up a quick prayer that the visit would go well.

"The roads are considerably better than I thought they would be and it is quite amazing how similar it looks to Carolina," Charles commented.

Richard nodded but said nothing.

The trip to his house was very short and did not afford much time for conversation. In any event Charles and Ann's gazes were drawn to the azure sea that was so different in the Caribbean from theirs in Carolina.

Ann absently saw the scenery passing by, but her thoughts were of the woman that she would meet soon. While she had grown to love Charles and gotten over her youthful infatuation with Richard, she could not help but feel somewhat unsettled at the thought of coming face to face with the woman who had turned all their lives upside down.

If Richard had not come to Barbados and met her, they would probably be married now. Would they have been happy together? Somehow she doubted it. He would probably have a mistress somewhere and she would be miserable. So it was really all for the best. But to think that he preferred a coloured woman, and a slave at that, to her was unthinkable. It was a closely kept secret in Carolina, only their families knew, but if it was ever discovered among her class, she would be a laughing stock.

"Here we are," Richard announced as they turned down a driveway to a modest-sized, two-storey house painted in a warm yellow with green shutters. They had recently renovated it and Deborah had wanted it painted in the same colours as The Acreage. It was not as big as either The Acreage or the house in Carolina, but it was beautifully decorated and suited their needs. They both also liked that it was close to the beach which gave them the opportunity to walk on the warm sand during the weekends or take moonlight walks at night.

The driver climbed down and opened the door. Richard got out and held his hand to help Ann out, leaving Charles to follow. The front door opened and Deborah appeared looking beautiful to him, but more demure than he was accustomed to. She had changed since he left home that morning and was now wearing a flowered dress of cotton material with a modest neckline and a full skirt. Her hair that was normally wild and curly had been tamed into a knot on top of her head, leaving her long neck bare and stirring in Richard the desire to run his lips along it.

"Charles, Ann, come and meet Deborah." Richard led them to the front door where Deborah waited with a welcoming smile on her face.

"Deborah, this is my little brother, Charles. And this is his wife, Ann."

"Hardly little, Richard. Welcome, Charles. Welcome, Ann. I have heard a lot about you." Deborah saw some resemblance to Richard in Charles but he was a little shorter and certainly not as handsome, in her opinion, or as broad in the shoulders. She remembered that Richard had told her that Charles worked in the office while he had preferred to work on their boats, helping to load and unload goods, something that he still did on occasion to keep fit.

Her eyes were soon drawn to Ann who was much more beautiful than she had expected. For some reason she had thought she would be a plain, mousy-looking woman, not like the one who stood before her with turquoise-coloured eyes and reddish brown hair partly hidden by an elegant hat. Her dress was slightly wrinkled from travelling but she exuded grace and class, making Deborah feel dowdy in comparison.

"Hello, Deborah," Charles greeted her. "Thank you for reminding Richard that I am no longer his little brother, except in age." He smiled at Deborah, earning him some points with Richard.

"Hello, Deborah. Thank you for your hospitality." Ann's greeting was polite and somewhat cautious as if she was not quite sure how she would be received. To say that she was surprised at Deborah's appearance would be a great understatement. When she had heard that she was coloured, she had pictured a brown-skinned woman, not this nearly white one. And since she had apparently turned Richard's head, she had thought that she was a seductress and would be wearing a low-cut dress which flaunted her body, not this modest house dress with her hair up in a neat style.

"Let us go inside," Richard urged, glad that at least Ann had not fainted like his mother did. Granted, she had had a bit more warning about Deborah than her mother who had thought that because she was the daughter of a plantation owner she would be white, not knowing that her mother was a mulatto slave.

"One of the girls will bring drinks to the sitting room so I will let you rest there a bit and have your trunks taken up to your room in the meantime," Deborah told them, leading the way to the sitting room.

Ann grudgingly admired the room which, while not the largest, was decorated in lovely shades of blue and tan with Persian rugs scattered around the room. The blue sofa was very comfortable and stylish with matching armchairs facing it. They were separated by a circular mahogany table with carved legs and decorated with a beautiful vase of fresh flowers. She was surprised that a former slave had such good taste, for she could not imagine that Richard had taken enough interest or had the talent to decorate the room.

Deborah invited the guests to take the sofa while she and Richard took the armchairs. Ann could not believe that she was actually going to be sitting and socialising with a coloured woman and staying as a guest in her house. It was unheard of! What could Richard have been thinking to marry her? From what she had heard, some men took them as mistresses, but no-one was so foolish as to marry one. They certainly would not be able to ever visit Carolina.

Richard wished he could pull Deborah onto his lap and put his arms around her for, although she appeared composed, he knew her well enough to sense that something was troubling her. He did not know what was causing her discomfort and he certainly hoped it was not guilt, for she had nothing to be guilty about. It was he who had pursued her even though he was engaged and she had never given him any encouragement or tried to seduce him in any way. In fact, it had been quite the opposite.

"I cannot believe we are finally here," Charles started. "I have been wanting to visit since Mother and Father came back and had so many good things to say about Barbados. Besides, I missed you, brother."

"I missed you too," Richard admitted, "Although I do not miss the constant badgering about my lifestyle that I used to endure from you," he laughed.

"But then you were a bit of a scoundrel, so it was well deserved, but you have no doubt changed."

"Indeed I have. Deborah has reformed me," he admitted, looking at her lovingly. Deborah smiled back at him before turning her head to see Ann looking intently at her. She blushed guiltily and then chastised herself since she had nothing to be guilty of, apart from falling in love with her fiancé.

"How are your parents, Ann?" Richard asked. Ann's answer was interrupted by the arrival of their drinks of Beveridge, which was the drink he had had with his first dinner at The Acreage. It was made of the juice of oranges, mixed with water and sweetened with sugar. Ann took a sip and expressed her liking of it before answering.

"My mother is well, but my father is not in the best of health. He has had to hire someone to help him manage the plantation and he has converted it to rice as I believe you had wanted to do." Richard was surprised that she had brought that up. It suggested to him that it no longer bothered her, for which he was glad.

"I am sorry to hear that, but I am glad that he has started growing rice. It will be the future of Carolina."

"Richard always was the visionary in the business," Charles told Deborah. "I was content to work on the books and do what I was told, but he always had grand ideas and he and my father would constantly disagree about them. I often played the peacemaker."

Deborah smiled at him.

"My father was rather set in his ways and, like most men his age, does not embrace change easily," Richard told Deborah.

"Richard has not changed," Deborah informed Charles, "for he is always thinking of new ways to improve the business or for new directions to go in." Deborah looked at him proudly.

"And you are the same with yours," Richard praised her.

"You have a business?" Ann asked, as if it was something unheard of and it was among her class. She made the word sound almost dirty.

"Yes, I have my own business," Deborah answered proudly, unconsciously raising her chin. Richard knew that gesture well. Oh dear, he thought, bracing himself. It had been going so well.

"What do you do?" Ann asked and Richard could have sworn he saw her give a small shudder as if work was something shameful. How sheltered she was. How could he even have thought to marry this woman? Once again, he thanked God for putting it in his heart to come to Barbados.

"I grow and import herbs and teas of all sorts. I also make soaps and I have just started making scented candles which are becoming very popular."

"Oh," Ann murmured as if she was unconvinced.

"I remember hearing that your herbs had helped Richard when he got sick as soon as he arrived here," Charles told Deborah.

"I did not know that he had mentioned that."

"Yes, when he finally recovered enough to write home he told our parents that he had been very sick and one of the house slaves had given him some tea that had helped. I assume that was you." There was a deafening silence in response to Charles' words. It was the truth that they had all been trying to avoid. The shameful fact that Richard had not only taken advantage of Deborah when she was a slave, but that he had made her his mistress while he was in Barbados and still engaged to Ann.

Charles wanted to die of mortification. The last thing he had wanted was to bring any shame on Ann and now that he had met Deborah, he had no desire to cause her any either. He had pictured her as a coloured version of Richard's mistress, Anise, but she was nothing like her and now he had embarrassed both her and Ann.

"Uh, sorry," he mumbled, turning red.

"Do not apologise, Charles, for you have done nothing wrong. We cannot pretend that the past did not happen. Let us just be thankful that we are now happy with our respective spouses and let us move on." Richard looked expectantly at Ann, who was the wronged party, and she gave a little nod to indicate her agreement.

"And, in any case, it was a good experience in humility for Richard, for he had to have Jethro, one of the slaves, help him on and off the chamber pot. He confessed to me that pain is the perfect cure for pride." Deborah teased him to lighten the mood.

Charles laughed, glad that Deborah had not taken offence at his faux pas, while Richard feigned a pained expression that his secret had been revealed.

"This is hardly a topic to be discussed in company," Ann said haughtily, looking uncomfortable. There was an awkward silence before Deborah jumped to her feet and said, "Maybe this would be a good time to show you to your room so that you can have a rest before lunch." She called one of the girls to take Charles and Ann up to their room.

As soon as the door closed behind them Deborah turned to Richard and mimicked Ann in a perfect accent, "This is hardly a topic to be discussed in company." Richard laughed in delight at her impersonation.

"This is not funny, Richard! Is that what I will have to look forward to this whole trip?"

"Deborah, bear with Ann a little. She has been very spoiled and very sheltered her whole life. She is not accustomed to things that might seem common place to you."

"You are defending her," Deborah accused him. Richard denied it. "And what is worse, you never told me that she was beautiful. You gave me the impression that she was unattractive."

"I never said that she was unattractive. You obviously drew that conclusion yourself because I told you that I was only marrying her to form an alliance between our families."

"So you find her attractive!"

"I would be lying if I said that she was not attractive but –"

"I can't believe I am hearing this," Deborah interrupted him.

"Deborah, you are over-reacting. You know that I have never looked at, far less touched, another woman since you came to my bed. Do not let the enemy plant thoughts in your head to undermine our marriage."

"You are right. I am sorry for over-reacting."

"Apology accepted. I love you," Richard assured her, enveloping her in a hug.

"I love you too." Deborah hugged him back, fighting off the notion that when he was exposed to Ann's grace and sophistication over the next month he would find her lacking and begin to regret the choice he had made.

Chapter 24

The maid had barely closed the door behind them when Ann turned to Charles with disbelief written on her face.

"Charles, what could I have been thinking to agree to stay at the house of a coloured person, even if it is Richard's house as well? At least she is not as dark as I had thought she would be, but still. I did not think that she would look like that." Charles tried to follow Ann's thoughts which seemed to be a little disjointed.

"Like what?" asked Charles patiently, responding to her last comment.

"I don't know. I thought that somehow she would look like a prostitute or something."

"What would you know about how prostitutes look?" he asked, shocked. Ann rolled her eyes and ignored that.

"I was surprised that she was dressed so modestly. And I suppose she is quite beautiful in an exotic way. Do you find her exotic?"

"I do not know what you mean by exotic, Ann. She is a beautiful woman. I can see why Richard lost his head over her." Even before the words were out of his mouth properly, he knew that he was in trouble.

"What? Charles Fairfax, are you saying that the reason Richard fell in love with her was because she was more beautiful than me? That I was no competition for her?" Ann crossed her arms angrily.

"No, Ann, that is not what I am saying," he pacified her. "I do not know why we are even discussing Deborah. She is married to Richard and I am married to you and everyone is happy." Or were they? He was certainly happy with Ann, but was she regretting marrying him now that she had seen Richard again? Richard had always been more appealing to women with his height and good looks, while he had been the more reserved one. He remembered Richard telling him that women liked incorrigible men when he had called him incorrigible for going to his mistress' house one afternoon before taking Ann to a party that same night.

He had hated the way Richard treated Ann. He had not deserved her and he was very glad when Ann had broken off their engagement on hearing that Richard had fallen in love with another woman. Ann had been the only girl he ever loved and she was the only one he had ever been intimate with. Would she have been better off with someone of Richard's experience who would know how to please her in ways that he was still learning?

Maybe coming to Barbados on holiday had been a mistake. He had wanted to see Richard, but he had not given enough thought to how difficult the visit would be. There were obviously still a lot of issues that they were each dealing with, at least he and Ann. Knowing Richard, he would be oblivious to how uncomfortable everyone else must be feeling.

"And can you imagine her bringing up something so personal and intimate as Richard having to get help to use the chamber pot? How common! But then again, what would you expect from someone who used to be a slave. No doubt emptying chamber pots would have been one of her chores."

Charles hoped that she had finished her tirade now for, to tell the truth, he did not like this side of Ann. He was not ignorant to the fact that she was a trifle spoiled, but she was rarely in a situation where it was evident, for more often than not she got her way.

"Just because Deborah was a slave does not make her less of a human being and so what if she had to empty chamber pots?" Charles was beginning to lose his patience with Ann.

"Charles Fairfax, I do believe you are taking her side against me! I cannot believe what I am hearing. Why, I am shocked that —"

"Ann, not another word! You are acting like a spoiled child. We are guests in Richard and Deborah's house and you will treat her with respect when she is present and speak well of her when she is not. Or if you have nothing good to say, say nothing."

Ann's mouth dropped open in shock. Charles had never spoken so sternly to her or acted so forcefully. She quite liked this side of him. She drew closer and put her hands around his neck, drawing his head down to hers.

"Charles, you have never been so forceful before."

"I'm sorry, Ann…"

"Don't be. I find it quite exciting. In fact, I don't mind us being late for lunch," she smiled suggestively.

Charles' eyes widened in surprise before they darkened with desire and he closed the space between their lips. Richard and Deborah could start lunch without them.

※

Deborah was not sure what had happened after Charles and Ann went up to their room, for not only were they late for lunch, but they were both beaming when they arrived at the table and Ann was very pleasant to her for the rest of the day. Whatever it was she heartily approved as she and Ann were able to have friendly conversations about Barbados and Carolina and anything else that was not personal in nature.

The next day Richard took Charles to his office to show him the Barbados side of the business and to introduce him to the staff. Deborah used the opportunity to give Ann a tour of Bridge Town, taking her to some of the fancier stores that sold perfume, jewellery and clothes imported from England and France. Ann was very impressed and admitted that she was ashamed for thinking that Barbados was backward, when in fact it was very much more advanced than Carolina.

Deborah finally took her to their store so that she could meet her mother and see what they sold. Ann was very polite to Sarah and even ended up buying two of her dresses when she discovered that they were much cooler than the ones she had brought from Carolina. Then she asked about the scented candles that Deborah had mentioned and bought a dozen of them to give as gifts when she went back. Deborah still could not fathom the change that had occurred, but she thanked God for it, acknowledging that the visit would have been a disaster otherwise.

When they got back to the house, the men were still out so they had tea and cakes together in the sitting room and Ann asked Deborah to tell her about her life before she met Richard and how they had come to fall in love. At first she was so stunned that she was unable to utter a word, but then, for the first time, she started to talk about her life to someone else, apart from Richard, and it was as if she could not stop.

She was amazed to find tears streaming down Ann's cheeks as she told her about William and how he had tricked her into coming to his room where he took her innocence. She confessed how she had hated Richard even before he arrived in Barbados and how she had resisted his advances. She stopped abruptly, remembering that Ann was the one in Carolina to whom Richard had been unfaithful, but Ann urged her to continue.

She had Ann laughing when she told her how she had tricked Richard to avoid going to his room after the party. However, Ann soon sobered up when she heard how Elizabeth had ordered a whipping for Deborah for defying her and wearing her own dress to the party. She was horrified when Deborah described the pain of the lashes that Jethro reluctantly gave her before Richard rescued her. Deborah found herself in tears when Ann said that she could understand Deborah's decision to pay the price for her freedom.

Deborah apologised for her relationship with Richard, even knowing that he had a fiancée, and shared the agony of losing him when he returned to Carolina. Ann realised that she

Free at Last

had never loved Richard as deeply as Deborah had and she was grateful that they had not married. She was now very much in love with Charles, especially the Charles that had shown himself for the first time in Barbados.

Deborah told her how she and her mother had gone to a Quaker meeting after they had been freed and had discovered that, although they were free from slavery, they were still slaves to sin and that they had decided that night to change their ways and follow God's ways. So she was especially thankful to discover that Richard had also made that decision during a storm on the way back from Carolina, otherwise she could not have married him. Ann remarked on the change she had noticed in Richard and wanted to know how it had happened, so Deborah promised to tell her more another day.

By the time they finished talking it was evening. Deborah asked Ann's forgiveness for her relationship with Richard while he was in Barbados, which she readily gave, and a new friendship was birthed. With Ann's forgiveness, Deborah felt the last of the guilt and shame that she did not even know she still carried depart from her.

※

"I have invited my parents to dinner tonight so that you can meet my father. He is very lonely since your aunt has died and the children are all away," Deborah told Charles and Ann at breakfast the next day.

"Richard tells me that he wants to bring William back from Jamaica," Charles said.

"Are you in agreement with that?" Ann asked Deborah.

"Yes. I have forgiven him. I cannot expect God and others," she looked pointedly at Ann, "to forgive me if I do not forgive those who have trespassed against me."

"Ann, I, too, would like to ask your forgiveness for the disgusting and disrespectful way I treated you. It shows great character that you can even bring yourself to be civil to me," Richard said humbly.

"I forgive you, Richard. I am thankful for how everything worked out and especially for Charles, who recently showed me the error of my ways." They looked lovingly at each other. Their marriage had gone to another level since they had come to Barbados and looked to grow from strength to strength.

"All I need now is to get my parents married and all will be well," Deborah declared with a smile.

"Deborah, no more scheming. They seem to be making progress on their own. I believe Thomas has been to town on two or three occasions to visit your mother since our anniversary dinner."

"Yes. I believe she has come to realise that life is short and that she should try to be happy while she is still alive and young enough to enjoy love. There is only one thing standing in the way now." Deborah paused.

"What is that?" Ann asked curiously.

"They are unequally yoked. Meaning that my father has no relationship with the Lord and therefore my mother should not marry him. We need to pray for that to change so that there will be no hindrances to their being together."

"Now that I can work with, rather than your schemes," agreed Richard. "And you know what they say about praying in agreement. It will be done for us."

❧

Later that evening

Deborah looked around the dinner table at their intimate gathering and had a feeling of wellbeing. Her father had brought her mother to dinner in his carriage and they now sat next to each other looking happy. She almost forgot that he was eighteen years older than her mother for he looked like a man in his forties and was still very fit.

Sarah had been thrilled to see Ann in one of the dresses that she had bought from her. Thomas was glad that Richard had his brother visiting for a month because he was concerned that he had not been back to Carolina since he and Deborah had married. Having lost his wife and with his children away, he was very much more aware of how important family was.

"Richard, I was telling Deborah that I can see how much you have changed. What caused this change in you?" Ann asked. The table went quiet.

"Well, I assume you mean that I have changed for the better, since I could hardly get any worse," Richard said, making them all laugh. "I take no credit for any good you see in me now, for it was God who did it. I was in the middle of a storm in the Caribbean Sea and I thought I would die and I cried out to God to save me and not only did he save me from the storm, but also from myself. He showed me what a despicable creature I was and he gave me the chance to make it right and I took it. Ever since then he has been helping me to be a better man, a better husband and generally a better person."

Thomas was moved by Richard's testimony, brief as it was. All he had known was that Richard had told him he was caught in a storm that made a believer of him but he had never gone into the details. He knew that he had done even more despicable things than Richard, for he had been married and committed adultery with Sarah and got her with child while living with his wife. He had continued to bed her while neglecting his wife, therefore heaping even more humiliation upon her. He had even caused Sarah to fall away from the life she had been trying to live that one time. He felt dirty and unworthy.

Suddenly he pushed back his chair and stood, startling everyone.

"Richard, can I see you in your office?" he asked quietly.

"Of course, Thomas. Excuse me," he offered to everyone. Deborah and Sarah looked at each other in bewilderment. They had no idea what had come over Thomas.

Richard closed the door behind them and turned to look at Thomas. Curiosity was all over his face.

"Richard, if you thought that you were despicable, you were lily white compared to me. As you spoke about your experience on the ship, I realised how disgusting I was and what a reprobate I still am. I can try to make it seem better than what William did to Deborah, but the truth is I raped Sarah and took her innocence and had an adulterous relationship with her for nearly twenty years. Before that I bedded many slave women all while I was married. I ordered slaves to be whipped and did so many other things that I cannot recount. How can I ever be clean?"

"It is a gift from God. All you have to do is confess that Jesus died for your sins and believe in your heart that God raised him from the dead and you will be saved."

"That seems a little too easy to wipe out all the sins I have done."

"Yet it is all that is required. 'It is by grace that we are saved, through faith, not by works, lest any man should boast.' It is a gift from God. If you want, I can lead you in a prayer of repentance and salvation."

"Please. I need to be free from this sinful nature."

"Thank you, Lord." Richard celebrated even before he led Thomas in prayer, for he knew that before he and Deborah even called, God had answered and now there would be nothing to stop Thomas and Sarah from getting married.

Chapter 25

Thomas and Richard had come back to the table with smiles on their faces. Deborah noticed that her father looked peaceful and content, almost joyful in fact, an expression she had never seen on his face. However, rather than sitting down to finish his meal, he said that he needed to leave and he asked Sarah if she would accompany him or if she wanted to stay. Sarah had no hesitation in taking the hand that he extended to her, muttering her "Good night" quickly before she followed him to the waiting carriage. Deborah had opened her mouth to protest, but one look from Richard and the almost imperceptible shake of his head silenced her. She would find out what had happened later.

Sarah barely settled herself in the carriage before she asked, "What happened with you, Thomas? Are you feeling all right? What was it you wanted to talk to Richard about?"

He took her hand in his and squeezed it gently. "I am feeling more than all right. When Richard began to talk about his experience during the storm and how he realised what a despicable man he was, I looked at myself and I felt so dirty. I have done a lot worse things than Richard and I hoped that if he could be forgiven and his slate wiped clean, I could have that too."

"So you asked him what he did to make things right?" Sarah prompted him.

Thomas nodded. "Yes and he led me in a prayer of repentance. Afterwards I felt clean and light and full of joy. I have never experienced that before."

"Praise the Lord! So why did you want to leave?"

"I did not want to be around other people. I just wanted to go back to my room and be with God."

"But you asked me if I wanted to come with you."

"You are not 'other people', Sarah. You are a part of me. And I wanted to share this with you."

Tears filled Sarah's eyes and ran down her cheeks.

"Thomas, I am so happy for you. I have been praying that this would happen for a long time and God has answered my prayer."

The carriage came to a halt and Thomas looked out the window to see that they were outside Sarah's house. He wanted to stay and spend some more time with Sarah but he would not force himself on her.

"You are home. Let me help you down," he offered, opening the door.

"Thank you, Thomas," Sarah said when she stepped down. "I know you said that you want to be with God, but would you like to come in for a little while?" she asked hesitantly.

"I was hoping you would ask," he confessed with a bright smile. Arranging for the carriage to come back in an hour, he followed Sarah up the stairs.

Sarah unlocked the door and lit the lamp that was kept on the table near the front door.

"Let us go into the kitchen and I will see if I can find something for us to eat."

"Oh dear, I did not let you finish eating your dinner. Sorry. I was just so excited to be alone with you and tell you what had happened."

"That is all right, Thomas. Being with you is a lot more important than dinner." She put the lamp on the table and added one of Deborah's scented candles beside it before setting some cheese, ham and a loaf of bread on the table.

Thomas suddenly realised that he was hungry, but there was something that he had to do before he could even think about eating. In fact, his stomach was beginning to feel tied up with strings of anxiety at what he was about to say. Reaching across the table, he held both of Sarah's hands in his and looked deeply into her eyes.

"This last year has taught me how unimportant things are if you do not have someone to share them with. I have a big plantation, many slaves, money and position in the island, but they all mean nothing and have meant nothing because I did not have you."

"I'm so sorry, Thomas."

"I am not because if you had not rejected me, I would never have understood that. Sarah, I have never loved another woman like I love you. I am prepared to sell The Acreage and move to anywhere in the world that you would feel comfortable for us to be together."

Sarah's eyes filled with tears once again and she waited expectantly as Thomas took both of her hands in his and asked,

"Sarah, will you marry me and spend the rest of our days together, wherever that might be? Will you put aside all of your fears of what might happen or might not happen and take this second chance that has been given to us?"

"Yes, Thomas. I will. You are the only man I have ever loved too and I will go wherever you want me to go and live wherever you want me to live because my life was so lonely without you, I could hardly bear it."

Thomas stood up, pulling Sarah with him and enfolded her in his arms, just holding her as if he would never let her go. Sarah felt him give a slight shudder and his tears began to dampen her hair as hers were dampening his shirt. At last they were free to express their love for each other that for many years had been forbidden.

❈

"Sarah, I cannot believe that you will be my wife after all these years. You have made my joy complete. I already have a priest who I have asked about marrying us. He will be happy to do so for a sizeable contribution to his church."

"Thomas, you were so sure I would say yes this time?"

"I hoped you would and I wanted to make sure I had everything in place if you did."

"When do you want to get married?"

"Tomorrow."

Sarah laughed. "Tomorrow? That is not possible, Thomas."

"Next week then."'

"Next week is better."

"I am almost afraid to believe that this is happening. I have been lonely for so long, Sarah, I cannot wait to be with you again. In all ways." His voice deepened and his eyes darkened in the way that Sarah had been very familiar with.

"I feel the same way, Thomas. I was quite happy to teach the girls how to sew but when they left I was so lonely that some nights I would cry myself to sleep."

"You never have to do that again, Sarah. I will do everything in my power to make you happy and give you everything you desire."

"I desire nothing more than to be your wife and make you happy and do God's will."

Thomas reached into his pocket and took out the heart on the chain that he had shown Sarah before. He added it to the key she wore around her neck saying, "Now you not only have the key to my heart, but you have my heart.

"And you have mine," Sarah replied emotionally.

"I desperately want to kiss you, Sarah," Thomas admitted. "But I am also afraid of what happened that time."

"It does not have to happen again because we now both have the Spirit of God in us to make us strong."

"That sounds like an invitation to me," Thomas whispered, lifting her chin towards him.

"So, are you going to accept it or keep talking all night?" Sarah teased him, causing him to throw his head back and laugh at her uncharacteristic sauciness.

Free at Last

February 25, 1698

Richard and Deborah's house was decorated with fresh flowers, many of which had been brought from the gardens at The Acreage. Deborah and Ann had draped white fabric around the backs of the dining room chairs which they had set up in the sitting room where the ceremony was to take place. They had decided to have a very small gathering with only the family, two couples who Sarah knew and Thomas' attorney.

Deborah was so excited she was flitting from one thing to the next as she could not keep still. Finally, Ann shooed her upstairs to help put the finishing touches on her mother, who was being dressed by her best student who had also made her dress. The dress was made of satin in a beautiful shade of ivory and covered with hundreds of tiny beads. All the girls had helped to sew on the beads and Sarah was touched by the time and effort they had put in to get it ready in such a short time. Instead of a veil, her hair was piled on her head and a jaunty hat made of the same satin was perched on her hair.

Deborah knocked at the door of the spare room and entered when she was invited to do so. She stopped abruptly and looked at her mother in awe.

"Ma, you are more beautiful than I have words to say." Tears pricked her eyes and threatened to spill over. "My happiness is now complete. My parents are finally getting married."

"Thank you, Deborah. Now don't make me cry and spoil the make-up that Molly just put on." She smiled. "I never thought I would see this day and I know that I don't deserve it, but God in his grace has given me the desire of my heart."

"You do deserve it, Ma," Deborah assured her. "I will go down and see if everyone has arrived. Richard said he will walk you to Father."

When Deborah reached the bottom of the stairs Richard and her father were standing together. Both of them looked extremely handsome in their black breeches and jackets. Her father looked very distinguished with a few strands of grey hair at his temples but his eyes were clear and bright and lit up with excitement.

"You both look so handsome," Deborah praised them, kissing both on the cheek. "Is the priest here yet?"

"Yes, he is waiting inside," Thomas told her.

"All right, you go in. I will go and get Ma and Richard can walk her in."

"I never imagined I would see this day," Thomas confessed, "But I thank God for it. I will do my best to make your mother happy and to see that she is comfortable, wherever we live."

"I take it you do not plan to stay here, then?" Richard asked.

"Only long enough to sell my plantation, but that is a few months away. We will spend a week at a special beach house and then we will go to Jamaica and accompany William back."

"I don't like the idea of you going to Jamaica with all that sickness and disease," Deborah fretted. "Not to mention the maroons and all of those rebellious slaves about the place."

"Deborah, God will take care of us," Thomas said with assurance. "Now we will talk more of this later. I am anxious to marry your mother so let us get started."

A few minutes later, Thomas and Sarah stood before the priest. He was a tall, thin man with a few strands of hair clinging stubbornly to his head. He had a kind face which made Sarah think that the generous donation Thomas was giving would find its way to the needy rather than his own pocket.

"Dearly beloved, we are gathered together here in the sight of God, and in the face of this congregation, to join together this Man and this Woman in holy Matrimony; which is an honourable estate, instituted of God in the time of man's innocency, signifying unto us the mystical union that is betwixt Christ and his Church: which holy estate Christ adorned and beautified with his presence, and first miracle that he wrought, in Cana of Galilee; and is commended of Saint Paul to be honourable among all men: and therefore is not by any to be enterprised, nor taken in hand, unadvisedly, lightly, or wantonly, to satisfy men's carnal lusts and appetites, like brute beasts that have no understanding; but reverently, discreetly, advisedly, soberly, and in the fear of God; duly considering the causes for which Matrimony was ordained."

Thomas and Sarah looked at each other with a smile as the priest gave the three reasons for marriage. If they were the only reasons then there would be no need for them to marry for they already had a child, they already knew each other intimately and they had been there for each other in both prosperity and adversity. No mention was made of love, or being unable to live without each other.

They turned back to the minister as he addressed Thomas.

"Wilt thou have this woman to thy wedded wife, to live together after God's ordinance in the holy estate of Matrimony? Wilt thou love her, comfort her, honour, and keep her, in sickness and in health; and, forsaking all other, keep thee only unto her, so long as ye both shall live?"

"I will." Thomas swore solemnly.

"Wilt thou have this man to thy wedded husband, to live together after God's ordinance in the holy estate of Matrimony? Wilt thou obey him, and serve him, love, honour, and keep him, in sickness and in health; and, forsaking all other, keep thee only unto him, so long as ye both shall live?"

"I will." Sarah gave her vow.

"Who giveth this woman to be married to this man?"

"I do," Richard said, after which the priest joined Thomas and Sarah's hands.

"Repeat after me: I, Thomas, take thee Sarah to my wedded wife, to have and to hold, from this day forward, for better for worse, for richer for poorer, in sickness and in health, to love and to cherish, till death us do part, according to God's holy ordinance; and thereto I plight thee my troth."

Sarah then repeated: "I, Sarah, take thee Thomas to my wedded husband, to have and to hold, from this day forward, for better for worse, for richer for poorer, in sickness and in health, to love, cherish and obey, till death us do part, according to God's holy ordinance; and thereto I plight thee my troth."

The minister took the ring and gave it to Thomas to place on Sarah's finger, instructing him to repeat, "With this ring I thee wed, with my body I thee worship, and with all my worldly goods I thee endow: In the Name of the Father, and of the Son, and of the Holy Ghost. Amen."

After prayers had been spoken over them, the priest pronounced them to be man and wife.

"At last," Thomas whispered, kissing Sarah reverently on her lips.

"At last," she agreed.

Chapter 26

"Where are we going, Thomas?" Sarah asked him. After having an early lunch with their guests, Thomas bundled her into his carriage and they started out on the journey, travelling through Bridge Town and keeping to the coast. He had warned Sarah to bring a trunk to Deborah's house with enough clothes to last a week as they would have a short honeymoon before they went to Jamaica.

"It is meant to be a surprise, so do not keep asking me because you know that I cannot deny you anything."

"That is easy to say when I never asked you for anything," Sarah was teasing him, but Thomas fell silent as he thought about it. It was true, Sarah had never asked him for anything, except the one time she had asked if he ever thought about freeing her and Deborah, but even that had not been a true request.

"Sarah, you are right. You have never asked me for anything. I suppose that is also one of the things about you that appealed to me. You did not try to use your position to get money and gifts from me, but I want you to ask me for things. I want to shower you with clothes and jewellery and French perfume."

She laughed. "Thomas, I don't need those things. I have what I need right here." She took his hand and laced their fingers together. Thomas brought their joint hands to his lips and kissed the back of hers.

"I feel the same way, Sarah. Well, if you do not want material possessions, perhaps I can treat you in other ways, like taking you to visit other islands, to Jamaica or to England. Would you live in England, Sarah?"

"I will live anywhere with you, as long as our marriage is not against the law."

"I have been thinking about selling The Acreage and buying an estate in England. Somewhere in the countryside where people do not care too much about class or colour."

"That sounds good, but I have heard that England is cold."

"I will keep you warm," he promised huskily. Sarah laughed as a thrill of excitement went through her in anticipation of the days to come. At last they were married and they could love each other freely and completely, without guilt or shame, for the marriage bed was undefiled.

"You are trying to distract me from asking where we are going again," she complained.

"We are nearly there."

Sarah recognised the road that they would normally take to go to The Acreage by way of the coast.

"Are we going to The Acreage?" She held her breath. She really hoped that Thomas was not planning to take her there, for there were too many memories and besides she did not know how she would deal with the slaves she had left there.

"No, Sarah, I would not be so insensitive to take you to The Acreage for our honeymoon, but I hope that the place I have chosen does not hold bad memories for you."

They soon turned off the main road and travelled down a smaller road towards the sea. Soon a beautiful house came into view which looked familiar, yet different.

"This looks familiar."

"It is the beach house that I brought the family to soon after you came to the plantation. I discovered that it was renovated recently and it was being rented out again. I thought you might enjoy being near the sea."

"It is beautiful, Thomas. I enjoyed the time that I was here with the children because it was the one time that I felt completely free."

"I am glad. I have hired some servants to cook and clean, but they are not from The Acreage."

His thoughtfulness touched Sarah. How well he knew that she would not have been comfortable acting as mistress to any of the slaves from the plantation. The carriage came to a stop and Thomas helped Sarah down. They had changed into clothes to travel in from the wedding, so they walked down to the beach hand in hand.

Sarah took a deep breath of salty air, although the air was not as seasoned as on the other side of the island. Thomas bent down and took off his shoes and then started to do the same for Sarah.

"Thomas, you don't have to do that," Sarah protested.

"Why not? I do not mind serving you. You served me and my family for many years. Most times without thanks."

The sand felt warm and grainy between their toes, becoming damp as they got closer to where the waves were washing the beach.

"I remember when I first came here I looked out at the sea and it seemed to have no end and I felt free. I was as free to enjoy looking at the ocean, to feel the sun on my face and the sand between my toes as you and the mistress were. It almost made me forget that I was a slave."

"I hardly thought of you as a slave. You were the most beautiful girl I had ever set my eyes on. When we were here, it gave me great pleasure to watch you play in the waves with Mary and dig in the sand with her," he said reminiscently. "Your handkerchief had come off and your hair was wild and untamed, the way I liked it."

"I was going to put back on my kerchief and you told me to leave it off. I was so afraid of you that I did not dare put it back on."

"I am sorry I frightened you, Sarah. I knew that you were wary of me but I could not seem to help myself." He pulled her to him for a hug before they walked further down the beach holding hands.

"I wish that we could stay like this forever, just you and me together and not have to deal with the rest of the world," Sarah sighed.

"Do not worry, Sarah. We have waited this long to be together so we will make this work."

※

Later that evening

Thomas and Sarah sat on the patio enjoying the breath-taking sunset. It was as if God had put on an amazing display to celebrate their marriage. The sky had turned from blue to a pink and orange canvas on which grey-blue clouds were scattered. The tide had gone out and the waves no longer crashed to the beach, but trickled gently onto the sand before pulling back to be engulfed in the vastness of the ocean.

They had just eaten a light meal and were enjoying a glass of wine while watching the sun retreat behind the horizon. The chirping of the crickets in the bush near the house was part of the background noise which made the evening perfect.

"Excuse me, Master Thomas," one of the maids interrupted, "We take up the tub and full it with hot water."

"Good. Thank you." Thomas drained his glass before taking Sarah's and finishing her wine as well. "Now, Mrs. Edwards, I have a treat for you on this our wedding night. It will be my pleasure to pamper you as I have never had the opportunity to do."

"Mrs. Edwards," Sarah repeated. "That sounds so strange. Although I have had your surname from being owned by you, it still sounds strange."

"Well, I trust that you will soon get used to it as much as you get used to having me in your bed and by your side every day."

They climbed the stairs side by side and Sarah could not help the memories that rushed back to her. Memories of reluctantly walking down these same stairs as they were preparing to go back to The Acreage. The children had not wanted to leave because they had enjoyed themselves so much on the beach. She had dreaded leaving because she knew that back at the plantation the master would soon visit her room since he had not been able to at the beach house.

Now a completely different emotion consumed her. It was anticipation and excitement to begin her life with Thomas. To be free to enjoy his desire for her and to express hers for him without guilt.

Thomas opened the door to their room where one of the maids had laid out her nightdress and Thomas' dressing gown on the bed. In an adjoining dressing room a huge tub was almost filled with water and a bar of scented soap and towels lay next to it.

"I am to be your lady's maid tonight," Thomas said, undressing Sarah and helping her into the tub. He dipped one of the small towels into the water and rubbed the soap on it until a nice lather formed. "I will start with your back and work my way around and even down to your toes. Not an inch will be left out," he promised her huskily.

❖

Sarah lay on Thomas' chest as he idly played with her curly hair. Contentment filled them as they basked in the afterglow of their physical intimacy. The storm of their passion had taken hold of them, carrying them to hitherto unknown peaks before climaxing in waves of pleasure that left them shaking. The tears of joy that Sarah shed were now drying on her cheeks.

"I have never felt anything like that, Thomas, in all the times we have been together."

"Nor have I. It was a special gift. Your tears tonight freed me of guilt that I have carried for many years."

"Guilt about what?"

"That first time I came to you in your room. I did not intend to hurt you. I knew that you were innocent and I tried to be as gentle as possible, but I lost control because I wanted you so much and you had no pleasure only pain. When I saw you crying afterwards I wanted to apologise, but the words were trapped in my mouth, because one did not say sorry to a slave. At least that is what I saw when I came to Barbados and began to associate with the other planters. So I did not say sorry, but your tears made me feel like the lowest of men. I am very sorry for taking your innocence the way I did."

"Thomas, that is all in the past now. I forgave you a long time ago. Let us no longer speak of the past but look to the future that we have ahead of us. I am looking forward to many years with you."

"Thank you, Sarah. You have always been a loving and generous woman, even when I did not deserve it. Speaking of the future, you forget that I am many years older than you? I hope to have a few good years left in me, but I need to make sure that I amend my will to see that you are included as well as Deborah."

"Thank you, Thomas, but I have my business. I can take care of myself."

"I know you can, but what kind of man does not provide for his wife and children? And there may be other children. Is there any chance that you could get pregnant from tonight? Such thoughts fly from my head when I am with you."

"Very little chance, but I would not mind having another child with you before I get too much older. Maybe a boy this time."

Free at Last

Thomas smiled at the thought. He did not think he could be any happier. He was lying in bed holding Sarah whom he had loved for twenty years and she was his wife. He had done nothing to deserve such a blessing but he thanked God for it.

❖

March 15, 1698
Carlisle Bay, St. Michael

Richard, Deborah, Charles and Ann gathered around Thomas and Sarah and the considerable amount of luggage they were taking to Jamaica for the month. As expected, most of it was Sarah's who told Thomas that she did not know what to expect so she was taking everything she thought she might need. On an impulse, she also packed a bolt of beautiful white satin material and yards of lace that she had in the shop, just in case she was needed to make a wedding dress.

They had spent a wonderful week at the beach house and then moved into Sarah's house temporarily, as she did not want to live at The Acreage. The last ten days had been very busy getting everything in place since they would be away for a month or more. Sarah spent several days finishing off work that she had taken in but she no longer worked at night now that she had Thomas.

She sent messages to her regular customers to let them know that she would be away for a month or so, but they could contact Molly if they needed anything done urgently. She was already thinking that if they did move to England she would give her business to Molly who could continue to share the shop with Deborah and even rent the house if she wanted to.

Thomas knew that this was not the best time to be leaving The Acreage as harvest had started, but it was a testimony of how his priorities had changed that he had no qualms in doing so. He had put his attorney in place to look after the plantation, made sure that there was enough money to meet all the upcoming expenses that were expected and packed his bags and left with a feeling of excitement. For too many years The Acreage had been the most important thing to him, causing him to neglect his family and make hard decisions, but those days were over.

He had found a manager that he recommended to Peter Westhall to replace William. Ned Watson was a servant who had served out his indenture period with one of the other plantations, but found himself unable to afford land in Barbados and was happy to seek his fortune in Jamaica. Thomas had found a letter from Peter Westhall waiting for him at The Acreage when he returned from his honeymoon, accepting his recommendation of Watson and asking him to arrange everything. He would come to Jamaica the following week, once he put his business in order. That meant William could return with them if he cared to.

He wondered how the relationship with the Quaker girl was turning out. What was her name again? Oh yes, Grace. When he had told Sarah about her as they were lying in bed one night, she had started to laugh and said that God had a sense of humour. For William, who had always been a wild young man, gambling, drinking and bedding every woman who took his fancy, to fall in love with a Godly woman was funny. She said that Grace would probably have him converted before he knew what happened. Thomas did not argue, for he knew that stranger things had happened; his own conversion for one.

"I cannot believe you will be gone for a whole month," Deborah moaned, hugging her parents. "I do not even like the idea of you going to Jamaica." She would not say anything to them now, but she had confessed to Richard that she had a strong sense of foreboding. He had tried to put her mind at ease, but it had not gone away.

"We will be fine," Thomas assured her. Deborah had to stop herself from rolling her eyes. Why did men always say that, as if they could control everything? She held her peace for she did not want to cast a pall on the start of their trip. She would pray for them every day.

"I am very glad to have met you and to have been here for your wedding," Charles told them. "I would love to extend an invitation for you to visit us in Carolina, but that may not be possible."

"That is quite all right. I am glad that you came to visit Richard. Family is very important. See that you two stay in contact with each other. It will probably be up to you because we know how it is when it comes to Richard and letter writing. Please give my love to your mother for me," Thomas told him.

After much hugging and kissing, Thomas helped Sarah into a small boat which would take them out to the ship that they would be sailing to Jamaica in. *The Challenge*. He hoped that this trip to Jamaica would not present any major challenges for them. All he wanted at this stage of his life was plain sailing. The shore grew further away as the boat headed into deeper water. As Thomas looked back at the group waving at them, a feeling of unease came over him which he attributed to Deborah's concern. He hoped that he would not have cause to regret making this trip to Jamaica.

Chapter 27

March 25, 1698

Sarah was overjoyed to see the shores of Jamaica come into view as she stood next to Thomas on the deck. She could not say that she found any part of the journey pleasurable, apart from lying in Thomas' arms in their small bunk each night. Thankfully she did not get sea sick like some of the other passengers did, but she did not like the movement of the ship up and down on the waves. She also found that the ocean, which had made her feel so free at the beach house all those years ago, made her feel very small and insignificant when she was on it.

She remembered her mother, who had died several years ago, telling her of the horrors of crossing from Africa to Barbados but she did not have a good appreciation of the hell it must have been until now. If she was sometimes hot in their cabin with its tiny window, what would it have been like in the hold of the ship, packed together with hundreds of other slaves? She shuddered as she thought about those slave ships being tossed about on the waves, the heat, the stench, the humiliation of having to relieve yourself right where you lay. Tears came to her eyes and a pain gripped her heart.

She had never really experienced the true horrors of slavery. At the Holdips she had held a privileged position as the mistress' companion. When Thomas brought her to The Acreage she soon became his mistress and was never exposed to harsh treatment, apart from the few times that the mistress made her displeasure known by increasing her work or with a sharp tongue. But there were other people, other women like her mother, who had experienced the hold of a ship, the lust of an overseer and the sting of the whip.

It was rare times like this that she wondered if being with Thomas all these years was wrong. When he owned her that was one thing, but now she had married him. Some would say that she had married one of the enemy. Granted he did not own slave ships, but he still owned slaves. He bought some of them from ships like the one that had brought her mother to Barbados. Should she not hate him? Yet, how could she judge everyone the same way? They were two people of different colours, but they loved each other. Their love bridged the distance that separated their races and went beyond reason and argument. She would not deny her love for him in order to hold on to hate.

Anyway, Thomas was a new man. God was changing his heart. In fact, she knew that he had been working on Thomas long before now, as she had seen when he had freed Jethro. They had spent time on the trip talking about what he would do with the plantation. His plan was to free the slaves who had been loyal to him, sell the plantation and move to England. He had already sent a letter to his uncle in England to ask him to look around for an estate in the country that he could buy. Sarah was happy to go with him and start a new life. She had proved to herself that she could survive on her own, but now she wanted the companionship that she had with Thomas.

Kingston harbour drew closer and the ship sailed into its protective bay. It was a beautiful day and the sea shimmered in the sunlight. From this distance the town looked like a sea of tents and so far from the well laid out orderliness of Bridge Town that she was glad they were not staying there for any length of time but would buy passages on the next ship sailing to Black River which was the nearest town to Westhall.

"I am surely glad to see land," she told Thomas. He smiled in agreement, but silently wondered how she would survive the six-week trip to England. That was not something he would bring up now, lest she changed her mind.

"I too will be glad to get solid ground under my feet for a short time before we sail to Black River, although that will only take a few hours I am told."

"Praise the Lord."

"I am anxious to see William. He should have gotten my letter by now and knows that we are coming."

"Did you tell him that we married?"

"Yes, of course. I am not ashamed of marrying you and I wanted to prepare him. He said that he has changed and I hope to see that it is true."

"He may have changed, but you think he would have changed so much to welcome the woman who was your mistress when his mother was alive? Or accept that I am now married to you and I am his step-mother?" she asked doubtfully.

"Nothing is impossible with God, Sarah."

Sarah laughed. "You are preaching to me now, Thomas."

❖

Westhall Plantation

The days simply rolled into each other for William. He woke up, got out of bed, worked hard on the plantation and fell asleep exhausted. He had sent letters of apology to both Grace and her father. He did not get a response from Grace, however, George had replied and said he accepted his apology and he forgave him, but he asked him to stay away from Grace and the plantation for a time.

William had honoured his request, but he missed Grace and he even found that he now missed the Sunday services. Susie had asked why they no longer went and he had put her off with a vague excuse. He had no problem with her going but he would not take her because he was not welcome at Friendly Hall. Perhaps he should have told them about his encounter with God in the garden, but now he was not even sure if anything had really happened. Granted, he still felt free and despite the pain of separation from Grace, he felt at peace. He had even begun to read his Bible some evenings and to pray. He prayed that God would make a way for him to get back in the Fullers' good graces. He smiled at the pun and then sighed at his situation.

The sound of a carriage driving into the yard interrupted his thoughts. For a moment his heart leapt in the hope that it was Grace and he hurried from the office to the front door. As he threw it open, the sight that he beheld stopped him in his tracks. His father had just climbed down from the carriage and had turned to help Sarah down.

Various emotions coursed through him rapidly, one after the other – joy to see his father again, disappointment that it was not Grace and hesitation about how to treat Sarah. His father was the first to react.

"William!" he said with his voice cracking slightly. He turned towards him with his arms outstretched. William walked into his arms and they embraced tightly. "I am so glad to see you alive and well."

"Father. I have never been so glad to see you," William told him, stepping back. His voice was also rough with emotion.

Thomas grabbed his shoulders once more and looked closely at him before turning to walk back for Sarah. Her eyes were wet with the emotion of the meeting. Thomas led her to where William was still rooted.

"William, as I told you in my letter, Sarah is now my wife." William thought he detected a hint of a warning in his father's voice, but it was unwarranted. He had no intention of spoiling his father's happiness with any discord. Sarah had not aged a bit in the time that he had left Barbados. She was as elegantly dressed as any planter's wife, but of more importance was the love for his father that shone through the tears in her eyes.

He stepped forward and respectfully kissed her cheek. "Welcome, Sarah. I am happy to see the joy in my father's face that you have brought."

The tears that had been hovering now fell down her cheeks as she received William's acceptance.

"Thank you, William," she said quietly, wiping her cheeks. Indeed, with God all things were possible.

"Let us go inside. I will get two of the slaves to bring in your trunks. I am very happy that you are here at last. There is much to catch up on."

"You will be even happier to hear that I have someone to replace you. He will be arriving in a week, so you will be able to train him to take over your job."

"And not a minute too soon for as I expected the overseer, Marsh, has moved on. He said he was going to find work on a normal plantation."

"From what you said of him, that sounds like a good thing," Thomas said, gesturing for Sarah to precede him as they followed William into the house.

"Well, it is not as grand as The Acreage," William told them, "but at least it has been fixed up and I have had a room ready for you in anticipation of your arrival. How was your trip?"

"It was not too bad," his father told him.

"I don't know about that, Thomas. That was my first time on a boat and I am not too sure that I like it."

"I agree with you, Sarah. I hate to be stuck on a boat for weeks. The only good thing about the next trip I take is that it will take me from Jamaica."

Sarah laughed.

❖

Later, William showed his father around the plantation yard and the closest fields while Sarah stayed at the house and rested as she said that she was feeling a little tired. Thomas was a bit concerned because he had never heard Sarah complaining of feeling tired, but he put it down to the boat trip and then the trip to the plantation.

"I have introduced some of the methods that you use at home now that we have had to replant most of the canes after the hurricane. I expect greater yields per acre than they were getting before. I found the record keeping fairly poor, so I have started recording more information so that better decisions can be made."

Thomas looked at William in amazement. He never thought that he would see this day come, but he thanked God for it.

"I am very proud of you, son. I also want to thank you for making Sarah feel welcome; she was quite worried about whether you would accept her."

"I am glad that you have another chance at happiness so I do not begrudge you that. Perhaps God may grant me another chance too."

Thomas knew that he was staring at William strangely, but he could not help it. Did his son actually mention God? He had changed more than he realised.

"Another chance?" he managed to recover himself enough to ask.

William looked dejected for a moment. "Yes, I made a total mess of my relationship with Grace."

"What happened? It sounded promising."

"It was promising until I did something to treat Grace with disrespect and her father discovered us and has told me to stay away from her," William confessed.

"You treated Grace disrespectfully?" Thomas asked guardedly. He did not want to make any judgements, but he could not prevent his mind from flashing back to the incident with Deborah.

William somehow picked up on his father's thoughts and looked at him in disbelief. "Surely you do not think that I did the same thing to her that I did to Deborah? Which I regret bitterly. I will ask her forgiveness as soon as I set my eyes on her."

"I am sorry that I misjudged you. What happened with Grace?"

"I was treating her with utmost respect, hardly even touching her. I had only kissed her once, which was very out of character for me. I even gave up my dalliances with the slave girls when she asked me to. Then we went to a party over the holidays and we ended up in the garden. I kissed her and got a little carried away and her father caught us.

"He accused me of treating Grace like a common harlot, and he spoke the truth. I felt so disgusted with myself and ashamed of how I had treated Grace. Even when I picture her face now, wet with tears and covered with shame, I cringe to think that I caused her such pain. And George's face! The anger I could deal with, but it was the disappointment that devastated me."

Thomas held back his comments, letting William unburden himself, perhaps for the first time.

"All I could do was cry out to God, right there in that garden and ask him to help me because I felt that I was being controlled by forces outside of myself. And right there, he freed me from my guilt and shame and filled me with his joy."

"William, that is a great testimony. I am delighted that you made such a decision to cry out to God for help. I did the same thing, not too long before we came here. In fact, that was the only thing that was stopping Sarah from marrying me."

"Unequally yoked," William smiled in remembrance.

"Yes, I see you know that expression too. Anyway, I had just heard Richard's testimony for the first time and he said how he felt dirty and unworthy and I looked at myself and the terrible things I had done and he seemed clean in comparison, so I asked the Lord to clean me and take away all my sins."

"That is amazing! Nothing is impossible with God."

"So, does Grace know about the change you have made in your life?"

"No. I have not been to see her because her father has asked me to stay away from her."

"But you are a new person now, you should let them know. I am sure that she will be happy that you have made that change. Maybe now she will be willing to marry you."

"That would make me a very happy man."

"Well, ask your Heavenly Father for what you want. You have not because you ask not."

"I have been asking, but I have had no answer yet. God is taking his time on this."

"I will pray for you. If two or three agree on earth concerning anything it will be done for them."

"How is it that you know the Bible so well already?" William asked, impressed.

"Sarah reads it to me every night so I am learning at a very quick rate. I have a lot of time to make up for."

"So do I, Father, so do I."

Chapter 28

Three days later

The dining room table was laden with a sumptuous dinner that the cook had prepared. William told Sarah and his father that it must be in their honour because he did not usually eat that well, although the food had improved considerably as he changed his treatment of the slaves. The slaves did not seem to know what to make of Sarah for she was coloured like them, but sat at the master's table and was married to his father. However, she was so gracious that they took to her immediately and did all they could to make sure that she was comfortable and had everything that she needed.

During the day, William and Thomas spent time together on the plantation while Sarah sewed handkerchiefs for the slaves from material that she had brought. When they lay in bed at night they talked about William and the changes that had taken place in him. Sarah was very glad to see that Thomas and William were growing closer together, but she could sense some sadness in him which she assumed was because of his break up with Grace which Thomas had told her about.

She appreciated the effort the cook had made to prepare the meal but she had no appetite. In fact, she was not feeling very well, but she did not want to concern Thomas or draw attention to herself. Her head had been hurting for most of the day and her muscles were beginning to ache so she hoped that she was not getting the flu.

"Sarah, you are not eating at all. Is the food not to your liking?" William asked, concerned.

"It is very good, but I don't feel very hungry. In fact, I'm not feeling so well. I think I will go and lie down for a little while."

"What are your symptoms?" he asked, remembering the malaria that attacked him soon after he landed in Jamaica.

"My head is hurting and my muscles feel sore. It may just be the flu."

William hoped so for he would not wish malaria on Sarah.

"My dear, you should have told me. Let me help you to bed." Thomas began to look worried. "William, do you have any kind of tea in the house for pain?"

"I don't believe so because when I asked for willow bark tea when my back was hurting they did not know what I meant."

"Deborah made sure that I brought all kinds of teas," Sarah said with a forced smile. "I am sure she has willow bark or chamomile in the box. If you could send one of the girls to our room I will give them some and tell them how to make it."

"By all means. Father, help her to bed and I will send up Susie or one of the others."

Sarah was glad for Thomas' arm to lean on for she did not know how she would have climbed the staircase. She practically collapsed on the bed from where she told Thomas where to find everything.

"You go back and finish your dinner, Thomas. I will be all right," she assured him.

"Sarah, do you honestly think I can sit and eat knowing that you are not feeling well? I cannot remember a day in your life when you have been ill so this is most troubling."

"Don't worry, Thomas."

"I love you, Sarah, so I can't help but worry about you."

One of the girls knocked at the door and came in to get the tea which Sarah instructed her how to make. As soon as she left Sarah hurriedly asked Thomas to find the chamber pot into which she emptied the meagre contents of her stomach. Thomas held her and helped her to wash out her mouth afterwards before calling for one of the slaves to deal with the chamber pot.

William appeared in the doorway looking as worried as his father. Thomas went outside and closed the door behind him.

"How is she?"

"She just vomited and she feels a little hot to me."

They exchanged glances, not wanting to put into words what was going through their heads.

"Let us hope that it is only the flu," William said.

"What should I look for if it is more than that?"

"Fever and chills," he said gravely. "I will check back on you later. I too have no appetite for the meal."

❈

During the night Sarah took a turn for the worse. Thomas did not know what to do so he frantically rushed to William's room and woke him up. William in turn woke up Betsy who came to tend Sarah, while Thomas paced the room feeling helpless.

"Master Thomas, she was real hot just now, but now she like she starting to get the chills. I hope she ain' ketch malaria," Besty said, pulling the sheet over Sarah.

"Let us pray not," Thomas agreed, even with a sinking feeling in his stomach that she had indeed got the dreaded disease. He wished that it had been him instead for he could not bear to see Sarah so sick. She had barely managed to drink the tea before she brought it back up.

"I will sit with her and I will call you if I need you," he told Betsy.

"Alright, Massa Thomas."

Thomas sat by Sarah's side and picked up her dry limp hand. She did not even seem to know that he was there. He closed his eyes and prayed for her to be delivered from the sickness. He took comfort from the fact that William had recovered so he clung to that hope for Sarah.

Chills shook her body and she moaned in her sleep. Thomas kicked off his shoes and lay down next to her, drawing her against him for warmth. That seemed to work for a while as the shivering soon stopped, but then she grew hot again. He quickly released her and took a towel and dipped it into a bowl of water as he had seen Betsy do, before squeezing it out and wiping her face and arms. He was alarmed at how hot the towel was after wiping her. She restlessly flung the sheet off her as if it was stifling her.

Thomas had never felt so helpless in his life. All he could do was try to keep Sarah as cool as possible when she was feverish and warm her up when the chills shook her body. He badly wanted the sun to rise, as sickness always seemed to be worse at night. He would get William to send for a doctor because, although he had not wanted to admit it, this was no flu.

The next morning before the sun was barely up, William knocked and let himself in. Thomas was dozing in a chair next to the bed, looking as if he had not had more than an hour or two of fitful sleep. William was moved with compassion as he looked at Sarah lying so still on the bed. He remembered how ill he had felt when he had the malaria, and how alone. At least Sarah had his father and Betsy to care for her.

He had come to tell his father that he was going to ride over to the Fullers for medicine for he was sure that Grace would have cinchona bark since her father had periodic bouts of malaria. He had not had any recurrences of it, thankfully, but he should also keep some in the house in case. In fact, since he would not be here that much longer, he should get some to take with him back to Barbados. He would also dearly love to take Grace back with him as well.

"Father," he whispered quietly. William immediately jumped up from his sleep and his eyes went straight to Sarah. She appeared to be resting quietly for now, but William knew from his own experience that it would not last long. "I am going to ride over to the Fullers to ask Grace for some cinchona bark."

"What is that?" his father asked groggily.

"It is a medicine that helps with malaria." He knew that there was no avoiding the word any longer. It appeared as if Sarah had caught malaria.

"Ok. Thank you. Anything that will help her. I can't stand to see her so weak and frail. If anything were to happen…"

"Don't even say that, Father. I recovered from malaria so Sarah can too."

Thomas nodded vaguely.

"You had better try and get a little sleep. I will send Betsy to relieve you. You can lie down in my bed. I will return as fast as I can."

❦

The morning air was quite chilly as the sun had not made its way very high in the sky as yet. As William rode his horse briskly along the same road where he had been ambushed, the dew glistened on the leaves of the trees and on the grass in the sheltered areas where the sun could not reach. He never failed to pass the spot between the two properties where he had been attacked without remembering that day and the pain that had been inflicted on him.

His back had healed but he would forever wear the scars from the beating. The raised flesh revealed where each lash fell. He had taken a brief look at it in the mirror once but it was not a sight that he needed to see again. He wondered if Grace would be put off by the scars, but then remembered that she had seen them at their worst. That was assuming she would ever be in a position to see his back again.

While he was sorry that it was because of Sarah's illness he was now riding to the Fullers he could not contain the anticipation he felt at the thought of seeing Grace again. He wondered if she hated him for causing her to bring shame to her father or whether she was now indifferent to him. He would rather her hatred, for at least that was a strong feeling. However, she would be a hypocrite to pretend that she played no part in their encounter, for it had been her fingers in his hair and her moans that had spurred him on. But he should have known better, for he was the experienced one.

His horse trotted into the yard and he rode up to the front door where he quickly dismounted and tied it to the hand rail. He knocked loudly on the door and only had to wait a few minutes before Liza opened the door. She looked shocked to see him.

"Master William, you all right?"

"Yes, Liza. Is Miss Grace awake yet? I need her help."

"Come in. I will go and get her."

William looked around the familiar foyer as Liza headed for the stairs. He had missed being here, for Friendly Hall had a different feeling about it to Westhall. Once again, he thought about darkness and light. This was light.

"Miss Grace," Liza called, knocking at her door. "You dressed?"

"Yes, what is it Liza?" Grace asked, opening the door. "The last time you came knocking at my door so early, Bella had been found on the front steps."

"This time it was Master William 'pon the front steps."

"What?" Grace's face showed her alarm. "What has happened?" She was already out the door and had passed Liza to hurry down the hallway. Visions of his back and his leg flashed before her again making her feel sick in her stomach.

"He all right. He say that he need your help though." Liza hurried to assure her.

Grace was surprised at the feeling of relief that Liza's words gave her. She had not seen William for about three months and she missed him badly. She knew that what had happened had been equally her fault but she could not bring herself to answer his letter. What could she say? That she had behaved like a wanton? He already knew that. That she forgave him? What was there to forgive, for she had enjoyed every minute in his arms. She blushed as she remembered just what she had permitted him to do. No, encouraged, was the right word. How would she face him now?

William turned to face the stairs as soon as he heard Grace approach. His eyes drank in the sight of her and he realised that her hair was loose and hung down to her waist. Grace seemed to realise at the same time that she had not taken the time to fix her hair in her haste to find out what had happened to William. She self-consciously smoothed it down as she stopped on the last step, as if she needed the additional height to face William.

"Grace, I am so sorry to intrude so early in the morning but I need your help urgently."

William's hair was tousled as if he had not taken the time to comb it that morning, nor had he taken the time to shave. The stubble of his beard made him look very manly and attractive. Grace tore her eyes away from his chin and tried to focus on what he was saying.

"I apologise for my ungroomed state," William said, rubbing his hand over his chin. The rasp of the short hair against his rough palm made Grace wonder how it would feel against hers. A blush stained her cheeks, giving away her shameful thoughts. Why did she constantly have these carnal thoughts around William?

"My father is visiting with his wife Sarah. She seems to have caught malaria and is very ill. I was wondering if you have any cinchona bark that I could have for her?"

Grace took a little while to work out who Sarah was and then it dawned on her that Sarah was his father's mistress that William had told her about. It was her daughter that he had despoiled. Now he was here frantically trying to save her life? What had happened to change him?

"Yes, of course. Sorry that I seem a little dazed."

"I guess it is still rather early in the morning," he smiled slightly, happy to be talking to her again and to be in her presence.

"Liza," she turned to the slave who had been hovering nearby, "Get a package of cinchona bark for Master William, please. I should have about three there."

"Yes, Miss Grace."

"I deeply appreciate this, Grace. Please let me know the cost of it so that I can repay you."

Grace waved away his offer for payment and explained to him how to make the tea. Liza soon came back with the package and gave it to him. William thanked Grace again and found that he was reluctant to leave now that he had seen her again. However, the thought of Sarah lying ill in bed and his father pale with worry overrode his desire to prolong the visit.

"Please come and get me if you need help. You know that I look after my father whenever he gets a bout, so I would be happy to come over if you need me."

"Thank you, Grace. I will bear that in mind." William was overcome with a desire to make some physical contact with Grace so he stepped forward and briefly kissed her cheek before rushing through the door.

Grace absently put her hand on her cheek where William had kissed. None of her feelings for him had gone; she had only put them out of her mind. She wanted to see him again, but not under these circumstances. A thought suddenly occurred to her that the symptoms of yellow fever were very similar to malaria in the first few days. In fact, that is what they thought her mother had contracted at first. She prayed that it was malaria that Sarah had and not yellow fever, for that would surely mean her death.

Chapter 29

Thomas was beyond tired. He had hardly slept in the last three days except when William almost forcibly removed him from the room and let Betsy take over. He was almost out of his mind with grief and despair. They had given Sarah the tea from Grace but it seemed to have no effect. Her fever still raged on only to give way to chills. She could hardly keep anything down and she was wasting away before his eyes.

William felt as helpless as his father. He did not know why the cinchona bark was not working for Sarah for it had helped to bring down his fever every time he drank it. They had sent to Black River for a doctor the day before, as that was the nearest town that might have a proper doctor, but it would take at least two days on horseback. He hoped that the doctor would get there in time, assuming that he could do anything to help Sarah when he got there.

Susie came and put a cup of tea and a sandwich in front of Thomas as he sat slumped on the sofa. He had only come downstairs to rest and eat something after William made him see that he would not do Sarah any good if he collapsed and he certainly felt on the verge of collapsing. He took a few sips of the tea and it made him feel better so he forced himself to start on the sandwich. Before he realised it, he had eaten it all.

"It seems that you were hungrier than you thought," William observed.

"Yes. I feel a little better now, but I am still sick with worry. You said that the tea would work. Why isn't it working?" he asked fretfully.

William knew that he was not accusing him, but that his question was wrought by frustration. He too was frustrated and he had to admit, he was also beginning to suspect that they were dealing with something worse than malaria. He did not even want to contemplate it for there was no cure for it.

"I do not know what I will do if Sarah does not make it," his father whispered brokenly. "Deborah had not wanted us to come to Jamaica at all and I told her that everything would be fine, as if I am God and I can decide that. I should have come by myself as I was planning to at first, but then when she agreed to marry me, I did not want to leave her in Barbados. This is my fault. I should have listened to Deborah," he rambled on.

"Father, do not lose hope. Let us pray for Sarah…"

"I have prayed until I am tired and it seems as if God is not hearing my prayers. Why should he when I am such a sinner?"

William knew better than to get into such a discussion and, in any case, he did not have answers for his father as he too was new to the faith. Maybe he should ask George and Grace to come over and pray. Surely their prayers carried more weight. He was about to suggest it to his father when Betsy burst through the door. Both of them sat up and looked fearfully at her.

"Come and see Mistress Sarah," she urged them.

"What has happened?" Thomas asked, frantically leaping up from the sofa. William sprang up and followed him. Thomas took the stairs like a man twenty years younger and rushed into Sarah's room.

He checked to see that she was still breathing and was about to heave a sigh of relief when he saw what Besty had called them for. Now that the sun had shed light in the room he could see that Sarah's skin had taken on a yellow hue and she was hot again.

"It look like she got yellow fever," Betsy said sadly from behind them, confirming William's worst fears.

Thomas sank into the chair and held his head in his hands. He felt that he could not take one more burden on his shoulders. He did not need either of them to tell him that there was no cure for yellow fever. His shoulders began to shake as the dam that had been holding the torrent at bay broke. He could not believe that he would lose Sarah. Surely God would not be so cruel to give her to him for just over a month and then to take her away. It was too much to bear. The room was silent except for his sobbing.

William could not bear to stand and watch his father's pain. There had to be something he could do.

Is any sick among you? Let him call for the elders of the church; and let them pray over him, anointing him with oil in the name of the Lord: And the pray of faith shall save the sick and the Lord shall raise him up...

He had heard those words before at service one Sunday at the Fullers when George had been talking about faith. Hope leapt into his heart and he laid his hand on his father's shoulder.

"Do not lose hope," he encouraged him. "I am going to get the Fullers to come and pray for Sarah. Let us believe God for a miracle." Thomas nodded absently. He had nothing to lose.

※

Once again William was on his way to Friendly Hall, racing his horse along the road between the two plantations. This time he was not even thinking of Grace, only of Sarah and he prayed each mile of the way. He had never seen a miracle, did not even know if they happened since the days of the Bible, but they needed one now. He remembered Bella's simple prayer for him to be healed and wondered if it was her prayer that helped him or if he would have gotten better even without the prayer. He chided himself for his scepticism, for this was not the time for unbelief but for faith.

This time Grace opened the door as soon as he knocked as if she had seen or heard him coming. She searched his face quickly to discern the problem and whatever she saw reassured her that William still had hope.

"It looks like yellow fever," William said without preamble. The words struck terror in Grace's heart. Her mother had not recovered from her yellow fever.

"Wh-what can I do?" she asked in a panic. "There is no cure for yellow fever."

"You can pray," William insisted.

"Pray? How can I pray? I have no faith to pray for this."

William grabbed her shoulders and gave her a slight shake.

"Find some! My father needs us to believe for a miracle for Sarah. He will be devastated if she dies."

"I-I'll go and get my father," she stammered, turning to rush back into the house.

William paced up and down while he waited impatiently for George to come. Minutes later, which felt like hours, George came rushing out of the house struggling into his jacket and grabbing his hat in his hand.

"I hear that your step-mother needs prayer. I will get one of the boys to saddle a horse for me." He hurried towards the stable.

William was in shock that George had not asked any questions and he had not hesitated to respond despite all William had done. He was humbled and thankful.

"I am coming too," Grace insisted when George returned on horseback.

"We have no time to wait for you to get a horse fitted," insisted William, untying his horse.

"I can ride with you," she said, surprising him. He glanced at George to see his reaction and George nodded his consent. William seated Grace side-saddle and climbed up behind her, reaching around her for the reins.

The softness of Grace in his arms somehow offered him comfort rather than stirred his desire. That alone told him, if he did not know before, that he felt more for her than physical attraction. Without a doubt, he wanted to know her intimately, but he also knew that he loved her completely.

The ride back to Westhall seemed to take a lot less time than getting to Friendly Hall. He dismounted and held his arms up to lift Grace down. George had already dismounted and dropped the reins of his horse on the ground so that it would not wonder off.

"Has Grace told you about my father's wife?" William asked.

"She only mentioned that she was sick and it looked like yellow fever."

"I need you to pray for her. I was wondering what to do when a scripture that you shared one Sunday about the prayer of faith came back to me and I felt that I needed to get you and Grace to pray for her. My father and I will join you and pray in agreement."

Grace looked at William in surprise. He sounded as if he had changed or was he once again only praying because there was a crisis, like the hurricane.

"Grace, do you think you have the faith to believe? If not, it would be best for you to stay down here." Grace was taken aback. Was this William talking?

"Yes, I have the faith to believe…I think."

"'Lord, I believe. Help thou my unbelief.'" William quoted. Now even George looked at him and smiled.

"Son, have my teachings borne fruit?"

"Yes sir, the seed fell on good soil and in time brought forth fruit." He smiled and they could see a new peace on his face.

"Well, praise the Lord. I knew it was only a matter of time," George rejoiced and embraced him. Grace smiled and then lowered her eyes as if they would reveal her thoughts which immediately veered toward the scripture about being unequally yoked, for now that was no hindrance to their relationship. When she looked up, William was smiling at her as if he had read her thoughts.

"We had better get upstairs. My father must be frantic."

William knocked at the door to Sarah's room and Betsy opened it. His father was still sitting where he had left him and was holding Sarah's hand. Although the window was open there was a smell in the room that he was unfamiliar with. He discerned that it was the smell of death.

"Father, I've brought George and Grace Fuller. They are here to pray for Sarah."

Thomas looked up and reluctantly put Sarah's hand back on the bed. Remembering manners that were ingrained in him, he shook George's hand and then Grace's and thanked them for coming.

"The Lord Jesus said that where two or three agree on earth concerning anything it shall be done for them." George quoted. "Let us therefore pray in agreement for your wife to be healed.

"Lord you said that we would do the things that you did, and even greater things because you go to the Father. We call on you to send your word and heal this woman and deliver her from the grave. We declare that by your stripes she is healed so we speak to the spirit of infirmity that is seeking to take her life, and we command it to go in the name of Jesus. We declare that she shall not die but live and declare the works of the Lord. Thank you, Lord, that before we call you will answer and while we are yet speaking, you will hear. Sarah, be healed in Jesus' name."

Everyone opened their eyes and fastened their gaze on Sarah. At first they saw no change, no movement and then her eyes began to flicker and she blinked several times before she opened them fully. She looked around at them in confusion before landing on Thomas. She wondered why tears were streaming down his face as he dropped to his knees by the bed and took her hand to rest it against his wet cheek.

William and Grace stared in amazement, unable to believe their eyes even though they had been praying for the very thing. George was smiling broadly, thankful that God in his sovereignty had healed Sarah.

"We will leave you two alone," he said, patting Thomas on his shoulder.

Thomas managed to look away from Sarah for a moment to murmur his thanks as they filed to the door. By the time he glanced back Sarah was throwing off the sheet so that she could get up.

"I know what I saw, but I can't believe it," William said, shaking his head as he led the way into the sitting room. "That was amazing. I am very happy Sarah was restored to my father. There is only one thing that would make me happier." He paused expectantly.

"What is that?" Grace asked him.

"If you would agree to marry me. You were the light in my darkness, you made me want to be a better man and you extended grace to me." They both smiled at his pun. "Will you marry me, Grace?"

"Yes, William. I will marry you."

William took Grace in his arms and just before his lips met hers, George said, "I think I will wait outside." Making them both laugh.

"You have made me the happiest of men," William whispered against her parted lips.

Chapter 30

William could barely sleep and was up while it was still dark. He had been waiting for this day for three weeks. It was the day that he was leaving Westhall for Black River and then to Barbados. The man his father had recommended to take over had arrived the day after Sarah's healing and had taken to his new role very quickly. Thankfully, he was nothing like Marsh, having been an indentured servant himself. William stayed only long enough for him to settle down before he set the date of his departure.

Sarah looked so healthy that he could not believe she was at death's door only weeks before and his father looked as if he had a new lease on life. He hardly left her side as if he still had a time believing the miracle that had taken place and was afraid that she would disappear if he was not there.

William visited Friendly Hall almost every day and the night before, George had invited them over for dinner. He told William that he had managed to find a minister who would marry him and Grace in Black River so he would come with them there, see them married and set sail for Barbados before he came back and wrapped up things on the plantation and set the remaining slaves free. He had found a man recently arrived from England looking to buy a plantation so he had decided to sell Friendly Hall and return to England.

The sun peeping over the horizon shed soft light on the yard as William gazed through the window. He had mixed feelings about Jamaica. While he had no desire to live here and he had experienced some of the worst days of his life in the country, he had also found joy and freedom in Jamaica, for which he would always be grateful. He realised that sometimes the greatest joy is found in the midst of the greatest struggles.

He looked around the room and his eyes landed on his two trunks which held all that he had brought when he came to Jamaica, but he was leaving with so much more. He could not wait to get to Black River and make Grace his wife. Sailing back to Barbados would not even be a hardship as he would have her to share the trip with him. He was looking forward to being home again and he wanted to see Deborah and ask her forgiveness.

He loved Barbados but there would be nothing there for him when his father sold The Acreage. His father had already asked him if he would accompany him and Sarah to England and help run the estate that he planned to buy. Grace had said she was keen to return to England and he wanted to spend whatever years his father had left with him to make up for lost time. Now that he had been freed of the blinding hatred that had consumed him, he saw that Sarah was a wonderful, compassionate woman who truly loved his father and his relationship with her was growing. She had been more than grateful to him for going for the Fullers to pray for her.

He crossed the room and opened his door, almost bumping into his father.

"What are you doing up so early?" William asked him.

"Same as you, I suspect. I could hardly sleep. The thought that we could be setting sail for Barbados in a few days was enough to get me out of bed before the sun."

"I know what you mean, and you have only been gone about a month. What do you think about me who has not been home in over a year, in fact, close to two?"

"Well, are you not glad I sent you to Jamaica? If you had not come here you would never have met Grace."

"So true. Thank you, Father. Not just for sending me here, but for not giving up on me and writing me off when I gave you so many reasons why you should do so."

"You are my son. I could never write you off. Not only am I getting a second chance with Sarah, but I am also getting a second chance with you and I thank God for second chances."

"Amen to that. I too got a second chance with Grace."

A few hours later, William, Thomas and Sarah piled into the carriage and waved goodbye to Betsy, Susie and the slaves at Westhall for the last time. When they arrived at Friendly Hall, Grace and George were waiting for them, along with Grace's maid, Lucy, whom they had freed and had wanted to accompany Grace. To tell the truth, Grace was happy for the familiar face, for soon she would be leaving her father and all that was familiar to her to be joined with William and become part of his family. She was especially looking forward to the joining with William, she thought wickedly.

❖

Free at Last

The journey to Black River was slow and tiring, with many stops along the way so they were very happy when they finally saw the town in the distance. William and Grace were perhaps the happiest of the group for they knew that they would be married the next day. They found a decent boarding house and managed to get three rooms. Thomas and Sarah had one, Grace and her maid shared another, while William and George shared the third. They barely ate dinner before they all fell into bed in exhaustion.

The following day dawned clear and bright as if the heavens had decided to give William and Grace perfect weather for their wedding day. After a brief breakfast in her room, since the groom was not allowed to see the bride before the wedding, Grace washed and Lucy helped her into the wedding dress that Sarah had spent the last two weeks making from the white satin material that she had brought from Barbados.

"Miss Grace, you look real pretty," Lucy told her in awe as she fastened the hat with the little veil to her head.

"You certainly do," Sarah agreed. "You will turn William's head when he sees you," she laughed.

"I don't know why I feel so nervous," Grace confessed. "I want to marry William but I'm also wondering what I am doing."

"Don't worry. Everything will work out," Sarah assured her. "God brought William all the way from Barbados to find you in Jamaica. He knows what he is doing, even if you don't."

Grace laughed and felt the tension melt from her. "You are so right, Sarah. I should be anxious for nothing. Not even my wedding night." She looked at Sarah uncertainly as if she wanted to say something more.

"Why would you be anxious about your wedding night?" Sarah coaxed her.

"Well, William has had so many women and I have known no men. What if I disappoint him?"

Sarah looked her in the eyes and said, "William knows that he is fortunate to be receiving such a gift as what you will bring to the marriage bed. Far from being disappointed, he will treasure you and your gift, so you have nothing to be anxious about."

There was a knock on the door and Sarah went to peep her head out to see who it was. It was Thomas telling her that he and William were leaving for the church with George to make sure that the priest was there and they could follow shortly.

The ceremony was short but very beautiful. William could not keep his eyes off Grace, who looked more beautiful than ever in the white gown that Sarah had lovingly made for her. He knew that he had a double portion of blessings, not only in finding a good wife, but in having a generous step-mother like Sarah, and above all a forgiving Father in heaven who loved him even when he was unworthy of that love.

They returned to the boarding house to have a celebratory lunch after which George and Thomas went to organise the passages to Barbados on the next ship and Sarah went to her room to give the couple privacy.

"So what shall we do now?" Grace asked her new husband.

"That should not even be a question," William smiled at her wickedly. "I have secured a room under the name of Mr.

and Mrs. William Edwards and I believe we should go and become husband and wife in more than just name."

"But it is the middle of the day," Grace said in a hushed voice, looking around them.

"All the better to see you, my dear," William said with a wolfish smile. Grace remembered their embrace in the garden and scrambled to her feet, now eager to taste more of the pleasure that he had introduced her to.

"Now that is what I like," William commended her, standing up. "An eager wife."

"And you know what kind of husband I like?" she asked cheekily. He raised an eyebrow in expectation. "One who knows how to please his wife," she teased him.

"I will spend all afternoon finding different ways to please you," he promised, making her twinge in anticipation.

As he drew her close for a kiss, one of the other patrons shouted, "Get a room!" They spring apart laughing and took the advice.

※

The sight of Carlisle Bay meant different things to each of them. For Sarah, she was thankful that she was alive to see Barbados again. For Thomas, he was grateful to be home and have his son back and his wife alive and well. For Grace, it was anticipation to see the island that her beloved husband loved so much. For William, it was simply the joy of returning home with a wife at his side and his soul at peace.

"The trip was not even so bad this time, was it, Sarah?" William asked. "I hardly noticed how long it took."

"That is probably because you rarely left your cabin," Thomas said drily, making Grace blush. William laughed as Grace's cheeks turned red and drew her back against him as they sailed further into the bay.

"Look, you can see Richard and Deborah's house," Thomas pointed out. "It's the one on the cliff there at Needham's Point."

"I want to go and see them. I wonder if they are at home." Sarah said.

"We can stop by Richard's office and he can send someone to tell Deborah to come home."

As soon as the small boat that brought them to the shore landed, Thomas and William hailed a carriage and a cart to take their belongings and they went to Richard's office only to hear that he had sent a message that he would not be coming in that day.

Sarah began to worry that something had happened and could hardly wait until the carriage pulled up at their front door. Thomas helped her down, telling her not to worry, that they could not have gone through all that they had in Jamaica only to be greeted with bad news. That eased her anxiety somewhat but she was relieved when a servant greeted them with a smile and said she would get Mr. and Mrs. Fairfax, leading them to the sitting room. That did not sound as if anyone was ill.

William tried not to look nervous, but he did not know how he would be received by Richard and Deborah. Grace sensed his nervousness and gave his hand a reassuring squeeze.

The door to the sitting room burst open and Deborah froze before giving a squeal of delight and hugging her mother and then her father. Richard did the same, while Deborah asked a hundred questions at once.

Then Thomas moved to one side, revealing William who had stood up and Grace with him.

"Hello, Richard, Deborah. Thank you for agreeing for me to come back to Barbados. I hope you will forgive me for the pain and suffering that I caused you, Deborah. I know that I can never change the past, but I hope that we can be family in the future."

Deborah's eyes met William's sincere gaze and she simply nodded, too overcome to speak. Richard stepped forward and extended his hand and said, "Welcome back."

"This is my wife, Grace," William said, bringing her forward. "God sent her into my life to save me," he said, looking down at her with eyes full of love.

"It is a pleasure to meet you. I have heard about all of you," she told them, letting them know that William had told her everything.

"What are you two doing at home?" Sarah asked suddenly.

Deborah laughed in delight. "Well, I am feeling much better now that it is later in the day, but I have been suffering with morning sickness." She and Richard exchanged happy smiles.

"Morning sickness?" exclaimed Sarah. "That means you are —"

"Pregnant," Deborah finished for her.

"We are going to be grandparents," Thomas declared happily.

"How far along are you?" Grace asked.

"Three months."

"Three months? Then you would have known before we left." Sarah said accusingly.

"Yes, but I wanted to make sure that all was well before I said anything and I did not want you worrying about me."

"Wait until you hear your mother's story if you want to know what worrying is."

"What happened?" Deborah asked in alarm. Everyone sat back down as Thomas and Sarah shared their story with William adding in his part.

Deborah was stunned. "I had a great foreboding when you were leaving and I did not want you to go. Now I know why."

"But God was faithful and he brought us all back safely."

"We will stay here for a while until I sell The Acreage and then we are moving to England."

"What, all of you are moving to England?" Deborah demanded. "I have just got my family all together and now you are leaving?"

"Staying in Barbados would be difficult for us, given my connections here, so I believe that England will offer us a fresh start. William and Grace will also be moving there. You and Richard could come too. Richard, you can operate your business from the England side."

"I will have to give that some thought. I certainly don't want to separate Deborah from you, especially now, and when you leave we will have no ties in Barbados. What do you think, Deborah?"

"I think that is a wonderful idea. We can go after I have the baby because there is no way I will travel while I am pregnant."

"I can fully understand that," said Sarah, who still did not like sailing.

Thomas looked around at his family. Sarah his wife, whom he had loved for years before she became truly his, Deborah and Richard who were about to give him his first grandchild and William who had become a man he could respect and Grace, his wonderful wife. God had truly blessed him with prosperity, health, a wonderful family and a new life that was worth living. He could ask for nothing more, for his joy was complete.

THE END

Donna Every Novels

The Merger Mogul

Daniel Tennant, aka The Merger Mogul, is one of Manhattan's top merger consultants. His past has made him vow never to be poor again and so he lives by the philosophy: "Women are great but a profitable company and a healthy stock portfolio are better and definitely harder to come by."

The High Road

In this exciting sequel to The Merger Mogul, Daniel Tennant, formerly known as The Merger Mogul, has landed the project of a lifetime – to help transform the nation of Barbados. However, he doesn't bargain for the opposition he will receive, or the lengths to which the conspirators will go to discredit him in an attempt to bring an end to the project.

The Price of Freedom

He owned her and was prepared to give her freedom, but was she prepared to pay the price? An exciting, page turning historical novel set in Barbados and Carolina in 1696.

What Now?

Rock star Nick Badley has no bucket list; he's living it. He's been there and done that, yet a part of him is still unfulfilled and he's beginning to ask himself the question: What now?

Free in the City

Free in the City is a compelling story of forbidden love between Thomas Edwards and his mulatto slave mistress, Sarah, set in Barbados in the late 1600s. This is the prequel/sequel to The Price of Freedom.

Printed in Great Britain
by Amazon